CW00815995

ALREADY FALLING

ALREADY FALLING

AUBURN HILLS
BOOK 1

ANJELICA ROSE

PAPER THORN PRESS

Published by Paper Thorn Press

www.paperthornpress.com

Cover Design and Illustrations by Anjelica Rose

Copyright © 2023 by Anjelica Rose

All Rights Reserved. No part of this book may be reproduced in any form or by any electronic or mechanical means, including information storage and retrieval systems— except in the case of brief quotations embodied in critical articles or reviews-without permission in writing from its publisher, Paper Thorn Press.

All brand names and product names used in this book are trademarks, registered trademarks, or trade names of their respective holders. Paper Thorn Press and/or Anjelica Rose is not associated with any product or vendor in this book.

Paperback ISBN # 979-8-9884722-1-6

ebook ISBN # 979-8-9884722-0-9

This is a work of fiction. Names, characters, places, and incidents either are the product of the author's imagination or are used fictitiously, and any resemblance to actual persons, living or dead, business establishments, events, or locales is entirely coincidental.

❀ Created with Vellum

To the daydreamers, looking for a sign to try something new.

This one is for you.

AUTHOR'S NOTE & CONTENT WARNINGS

Dear Reader,

I wasn't too sure how things would pan out as I started writing this story. I never thought that I'd discover a new life long passion in writing and how deeply fulfilled I'd feel afterwards. This story is a love letter to my twenties. To growing up, falling in love, getting heartbroken and discovering one's self.

I am releasing this just before I enter my thirties and what a way to wrap up the decade. By telling a story that I can relate to immensely and I hope as you read, you can relate to it too. I think about these characters everyday. They've helped me heal my over-thinking and self-doubting self. I hope they can help you heal in your own way too. Thank you for reading and enjoy Annika & Reid's story.

xoxo,
Anjelica

Content Warnings

Explicit Language
Sexual Abuse
Parental Abandonment
Explicit Sexual Content
Infidelity (committed by a side character)

Visit anjelicarosebooks.com for further details and page locations.

PLAYLIST

listed in recommended listening order

1. hate to be lame - Lizzy McAlpine, FINNEAS
2. Daydream - The Aces
3. Coast - Hailee Steinfeld, Anderson .Paak
4. San Diego - Hinds
5. Difficult - Gracie Abrams
6. I Think I Like You - The Band CAMINO
7. In Too Deep - Sum 41
8. Love - Lana Del Rey
9. sunburn - almost monday
10. What If I Love You - Gatlin
11. Life Was Easier When I Only Cared About Me - Bad Suns
12. Memories - Conan Gray
13. Little Freak - Harry Styles
14. The State of Dreaming - MARINA
15. All I Wanted - Paramore
16. Already Over - Sabrina Carpenter
17. Flight Risk - Tommy Lefroy
18. Anti-Hero - Taylor Swift, Bleachers
19. Want Want - Maggie Rogers
20. Better Than I Know Myself - Del Water Gap
21. Satellite - Harry Styles
22. Scars - Papa Roach
23. Bruise - BETWEEN FRIENDS
24. Labyrinth - Taylor Swift
25. Parachute - Neck Deep
26. SUGAR (Remix) - BROCKHAMPTON, Dua Lipa
27. Nobody Gets Me - SZA
28. Sweet Creature - Harry Styles
29. Peppers - Lana Del Rey, Tommy Genesis
30. golden hour - JVKE

Scan for full playlist on
Spotify

PART 1

CHILDHOOD

Greeting from OJAI california

POSTCARD

Dear Chloe,

OMG, I miss you SO
MUCH!!!
Summer is so boring
without you. (p.s. me
& my mom saw Reid &
his dad at the store. I
almost fainted!)
I Miss you!!!
Love, Anni

Chloe Marshall

64 Begonia Street

Nashville, TN 37143

ONE

ANNIKA

AS SOON AS I push myself through the heavy double doors to the cafeteria, I know today won't be like any other day. The smell of floor cleaner and two-day-old pizza hits my nose first. It is a typical smell for this place on a Monday. As soon as I walk in, I see the new boy for the first time. The girls in my class were whispering about him this morning before our teacher did roll call. They mentioned there was a new kid in the other fourth-grade class across the hall. They were saying how cute he was and who was going to kiss him first.

Gross.

I don't understand why the girls in my class are so obsessed with boys. They smell like dirt and are always burping.

But here he is, the new kid, standing at the salad bar. Looking at him gives me a weird tingling feeling in my tummy. I grab a peanut butter and jelly sandwich after scanning my lunch card and make my way to the salad bar, standing across from him with only sliced tomatoes and celery sticks separating us. He is about my height, which isn't out of the ordinary since I stand in the back row of the class pictures. He has messy brown hair with little blond streaks that look like the sun brushed its fingers through his hair.

I grab an apple, so it doesn't look weird that I'm staring at him. His arms are tan, and there are freckles along his hands and cheeks like he spent all summer outside. I wonder why he moved to Ojai. It's so boring here. Especially since we are already a few months into the school year.

I wonder where he's going to eat his lunch? I think as he fills his plate with orange slices and wanders over to the table with the rest of his class. The lunch room is divided by classes, with each getting their own long lunch table. But everyone sits in clumps along the table, huddled around their friends. The kickball boys, as I like to call them, sit at the far end of the table, while me and my friends sit on the other end. The boys are usually too rowdy and throw food at each other. As the new boy approaches his class's table, I see my friend Isaac wave at him to sit near them. I look down at his outfit. He's wearing baggy jeans and a sweater without a hood. He has skateboard shoes on. Those big chunky ones.

I join my friends at my lunch table and try to be smooth about glancing over Chloe's giant head of curls to look at the new boy. He is laughing and chatting with the other boys in his class as if he's been here since kindergarten. Chloe keeps waving her hands around the air as she tells a story about her parents arguing last weekend. She said she locked herself in her room, and they promised to buy her a new toy if she unlocked the door. So that's how she ended up with a new paint set.

Chloe is my best friend for life. "BFFL," like our friendship bracelets say. She knows me better than my own mother! I can have a look on my face, and she just knows I ate too much bread and my tummy is hurting. She's been my friend for as long as I can remember. Which isn't that long since I'm only nine. We do everything together. We are always in the same class and hang out almost every weekend. Last spring, we both played soccer, and after the first practice, we both decided we hated playing soccer.

∾

I MOVED to Ojai in first grade. I don't remember too much before we moved, but my parents said we used to live in Santa Barbara, which is a few towns away. But I remember the first day at my new school like it was yesterday. I was so nervous to be in a new school and didn't know anyone. The school looked so big back then.

My mom, Mia (or Mamma Mia as my dad calls her), walked with me to my classroom and introduced me to my teacher, Mr. Kelly. He looked younger than my parents, was tall, and wore a brown suit jacket like my dad wears when he goes to work. My dad, Eddie, sells people their dream houses for work. Sometimes he takes me with him when he gets it all nice to show people. I like pretending which room would be mine if I lived there.

Mr. Kelly had a seating chart and led me to my seat. The classroom was decorated for the fall season, and Mr. Kelly had made a big paper-mâché tree in the corner with orange and red leaves on it.

Everyone else in the class filed in, and a girl with wild curly hair plopped down next to me. She looked to be a whole head shorter than I was and had those cool light-up shoes I always see commercials for on TV. All the desks were paired up in rows in the room. She pulled out a purple notebook with "Chloe" written in big letters with a heart around it on the front.

"Welcome to first grade, everyone! I'm Mr. Kelly, and I can't wait to learn new things with you this year."

"Hi, Mr. Kelly," we all responded in a sing-song way that made him laugh.

"First, I'd like you all to grab a leaf from this big tree over here, write your name and birthdays on it, and stick it back on the tree. Go ahead!"

He made a big jump back as kids started rushing over to the tree.

I grabbed a pretty orange leaf and started shuffling through my backpack, looking for my pencil. I felt my stomach drop when I realized I forgot my pencil case in my room. I made a big deal at the store with my mom that we needed to get pens and pencils for school, and I couldn't believe I had left the case on my desk at home. I felt tears start to form in my eyes. I kept holding my breath, hoping the rush of feelings would stop.

"Hey, are you okay?" The girl next to me poked my arm.

I sniffled and looked over at her. She had a really pretty pink ruffle shirt on and heart earrings that sparkled like her blue eyes. Her nose was turned up a little bit like a button, and her cheeks were pink like my mom's roses.

"I forgot my pencil case, and now they're going to put me back in kindergarten," I responded to her, sniffling again.

She knocked her head back, laughing.

"Shhhh, I don't want Mr. Kelly to find out." I looked over at our teacher, who roamed the class helping the other kids write their names.

"You are so silly. Mr. Kelly is *so* nice, don't worry." She tried to pat my shoulder to calm me down, but I was still worried. "Hey, I have some extra pencils. You can have one of mine."

She reached into her bag and handed me a green pencil with hearts on it.

"You really like hearts," I said to her while taking her pencil. "Thank you, I'm Annika. I'll give you back the pencil tomorrow when I bring my pencil case with me."

"I'm Chloe, and keep the pencil, my gift to you as my new friend." She gave me a big smile, and I saw she was missing one of her front teeth.

Chloe sat next to me during lunch that first day, and we've been sitting next to each other ever since. She introduced me to her other friend, Desiree, who always wore her brown hair in a ponytail. The three of us played on the monkey bars at recess.

Chloe is like the sister I don't have, braiding my hair while we have slumber parties. I help her with her long division, and she helps me pronounce big words during our reading. I know she'll be my best friend for my entire life.

IT'S BEEN A WHOLE MONTH, and I've only seen the new boy a couple of other times since first sighting him in the cafeteria. Every time I see him, I feel these swirls of bees in my stomach. One time, his class passed by mine in a single file line on their way to the safety assembly. I tried to pretend like I was tying my shoe, and when I stood up, he was inches from my face as he passed by. I didn't have the salad bar blocking my view that time and, unfortunately, discovered that he was the most gorgeous boy on planet Earth.

None of the other boys in my class, heck in my grade, even compare to him. His hair flops when he walks, and every time he smiles, his twinkly green eyes curl up at the corners. He smells like a typical boy. But in a good way, not that sweaty smell like my little brothers. He smells like my dad's cologne mixed with freshly cut grass. It was a matter of time before Chloe was going to start catching on to my peeks.

There is another assembly today, and we are waiting in a single file line for the multi-Purpose Room. Our class is always ready first, but Miss Barone's class across the hall goes first because her last name is before my teacher Miss Hazel. I know the new boy is going to come out, so I keep looking toward their door. Chloe is talking her head off to me, and I try to nod to look like I know what she's saying.

"So I begged my mom to rent that new movie, *The Notebook,* but she said it is for grown-ups. Even though I already have a boyfriend and read teenage fashion magazines—hey, Anni, are you listening?"

She turns her head around her shoulder to see where my eyes keep darting.

Chloe is absolutely obsessed with love and romance and anything with a heart on it. Anything the color pink and red. She will not stop talking about the movie *Love, Actually* ever since she saw it at her aunt's house over Christmas. When we got back from holiday break, she asked Isaac Mercado to be her boyfriend. Isaac tells fart jokes and wears ripped jeans. The way his curly, black hair would fall into his eyes was pretty cute, but he always interrupted class during assemblies, and the principal made our grade leave last to recess. Isaac was so excited to be her boyfriend that he told almost everyone he saw right away. He even told my mom when she gave him a ride home one time since he lives across the street from me.

Chloe's eyes bug out big when she turns back to me. "You're looking for the new boy, aren't you?"

"*Shhhhhhhhhhh*, keep your voice down!" I whisper as I grab her shoulders to look back at me.

"Oh my gosh, you love him." She giggles as her eyes move to my cheeks, which are warming up by the minute. I feel like I'm going to barf.

"I do not! His eyes just look like green marbles, and I like his band T-shirts." He passes us, and we see him wearing a dark green shirt that says "Sum 41" on the front.

"Psh, like you even know what band that is, whatever, you love him." She rolls her eyes and resumes her thought. "Anyway, my mom let me rent *Mean Girls* instead. Desi said it was hilarious. And I was thinking of getting cheese pizza."

I'm relieved she stopped talking about the new boy. I might've fainted if she kept saying I love him. I do not love him. I barely know him. And, no, I don't know any of the bands on his shirts, but I think they are still cool.

All I know about him is he is tallish, smells like nature, has a laugh that makes you laugh and knows how to do a wheelie on his bike. I noticed one day after school he went to Isaac's house, and I saw them through my bedroom window, riding around on bikes. I so badly wanted to work up the courage to join them.

"Can I get mushrooms on my half?" I say as Chloe scrunches up her nose.

"Ugh, I guess so, but don't have them creep over to my half!" She is the pickiest eater ever and never wants to try anything new. My mom buys basic white bread just for Chloe when she comes to my house.

THE SCHOOL YEAR is almost over, so the last recess feels like a taste of summer vacation. We finished our testing the week before, and I got all A's. As a reward, my dad is taking me and my brothers to the minor league baseball game after school. The Ojai Owls! It is one of my favorite things to do, especially with my two younger brothers, Joey and Wes. It's one of the few times we aren't arguing with each other. I love getting sunflower seeds and cheering when our team makes a big hit.

Only one more recess and one more reading hour of school left before my dad picks me and my brothers up. They are in first grade, so I usually walk over to their classroom after school so we can wait for Dad together. My little twin brothers are so annoying sometimes, but it is my job as big sis to protect them. Even though they are twins, they look completely different. Joey and I look like our mom, Mamma Mia! Who said she took after her mom, who immigrated to California from Ireland. We each have black hair, fair skin, and dark eyes that practically look black. But he and I both have full lips like our dad. Joey likes to dress like a tough guy. Our dad helps him spike his hair into a faux-hawk.

Wes looks like a mini version of our dad, Eddie. They have Brazilian olive skin, fluffy light brown hair, and hazel eyes. He's obsessed with dinosaurs and wears shirts that have T-Rexes on them. I love my little brothers so much, but they drive me nuts. Whenever I try to focus on my reading, they always come into my room and bounce on my bed, wanting me to play baseball with them in the backyard. I act like I don't want to, but I secretly have fun playing with them.

THIS LAST RECESS before summer break, I will use every second to beat my other friend Desiree's record in the monkey bar race. We are meeting at the park by my house next weekend to compete, so I'm using this recess to practice.

Desiree always wins, which bugs me.

I grab the hot metal bars and fling myself across. I am one bar away from beating her record, counting the seconds in my head. One bar away, and then Caleb Marconey jumps up and pushes me off the bars from the other side. I land hard on my hands and knees. The playground has wood chips to break your fall, but I always just end up with splinters and a piece of bark in my shoe.

I growl and am about to pummel Caleb's face, but I see a freckled hand reach down to me. I look up and see those sweet, sparkly green eyes. I grab his hand and immediately feel tingles through my fingers.

"Are you okay? I saw you fall on my way to the kickball field."

This is the first time I've heard him talk up close. He has a deeper, scratchier voice than I expected him to have, but I want him to keep talking so I can hear more of it.

"I got *pushed*, actually." I stick my tongue out at Caleb, who ignores me and runs away to the swing set.

He giggles and reaches up to my hair. "Hey, you have some wood chips in your hair."

He gently brushes the chips out of my hair, and I lose focus staring at his face. He has light freckles across his nose. I want to connect the dots and see what picture comes out. He also has dark eyebrows that look like caterpillars. When he touches my hair, I feel my knees turn into jelly.

He turns to run to the kickball field, but before he takes off, I yell after him, "Hey! What's your name!"

He whips back around and gives me the most beautiful smile I've ever seen in the entire world, those little corners of his eyes curling up with his smile. "Reid Parker. What's yours?" he asks, slowly walking back to me.

"Annika Gomes!" I shout back a little too loudly. I realize this when the kids on the jungle gym look over.

"Nice to meet you, Annika Gomes."

I want the way he says my name to be permanently tattooed on my memory. He says it the way you're supposed to say it. *Ann-ika Go-mess*. People always smoosh it together. I watch as he runs over to the kickball field to meet up with Isaac and some other boys from their class. *Reid Parker.*

Chloe rushes over to me from the drinking fountain. "*Oh my gosh*, he loves you, Anni! And you love him!" She jumps around me like a little bug. "I saw the whole thing. It was the most romantic thing I've ever seen. We have to plan your wedding!"

"You are obsessed with love. It's a little scary." She laughs and grabs my arm as we head over to our other friends by the playground. I've never been in love before and don't know what it's like, but ever since he touched my hand, that fuzzy feeling never went away.

TWO

ANNIKA

Three years later

"IT'S the first day of the rest of our lives," Chloe says as I slide into the back of her dad's car.

I am a bundle of nerves. I changed my outfit four times and begged my mom to put on some of her lip gloss. Chloe's dad is taking us to school before he goes to work since we go to middle school now. I'm sure my little brothers are going to miss me. I won't miss them bothering me, but I told them they need to tell me if anyone is mean to them now that I can't keep an eye on them.

Chloe's dad pulls up to the front of the campus, and we shuffle out. We make our way to the middle of the school, which is a huge amphitheater. It feels so much bigger than it did on our orientation day now that all the students are here. It has two stories of classrooms, not like elementary school. Plus, there is even a track and an entire soccer field to the side. We even have to change into gym uniforms for PE class. Chloe is right. This feels different from everything we've been used to doing.

Chloe is on her tiptoes, scanning the crowd. I'm sure she's

looking for our other friends so we can secure our meeting spot for lunch.

"Hey, I'm going to head to the music room and see if Desiree is there. Save me a seat next to you in first period!" Chloe skips off, and I'm left to wander and try to find our first class. We only have three together, and one is the first class of the day.

I make my way over to the second floor, where the seventh graders have their classes. I enjoy being early and picking the best seat. I turn the corner to head up the stairs. At the same time, someone comes barreling down and knocks into my shoulder, nearly toppling me over, but not before they grab my arm to keep me steady on my feet.

"Whoa, whoa, my bad, didn't see you there." My heart skips a beat as I recognize that soothing scratchy voice. I look up, and a pair of twinkly green eyes meet mine, and the corners turn up as a smile hits his face. "Oh hey, Annika, aren't I always there to catch you when you fall."

"Only because you're the one to knock me over."

I try to regain my balance and pull away from him, still not comfortable with the tingling feeling he gives me. He's grown at least two inches over the summer, and his face looks more grown up somehow. I was hoping I'd run into him but didn't think it would be the first day, heck, within the first minutes of stepping onto campus.

"That is so not true, and you know it!" he says, giving me a soft pat on my shoulder and then flipping the end of my hair. "Hey, did you get a haircut? It's really straight along the bottom."

I'm speechless as he drags his finger along the bottom of my shoulder-length hair. My mom took me to her hairstylist last week to get a fresh trim.

He scrunches his eyebrows up and chuckles at my inability to speak. "You're so silly. I'll see you around."

He walks off but pivots back around me to give me a fist bump.

I return his fist bump and stand there in awe, still mute, nodding my head, a goofy smile on my face, and my fist hovering in the air. He runs his fingers through his hair, flings his backpack around one shoulder, and bounces off to class. I replay the incident about five times in my head as I walk up to my classroom. Gosh, Chloe is right. I might be in love with that boy.

BY THE TIME the fourth period comes around, I find out Reid has gym class at the same time as I do. I see him across the gym, stretching with his class. There are four different classes in the gym. His class is across from mine, and we are facing each other. He looks so cute in his gym outfit, even though it is the same one I am wearing. He just makes it look so sporty. When he lifts his arms during shoulder stretches, the sleeves of his shirt fall, and I notice some arm muscles on his tan arms. Reid is turning into a man. Who am I kidding? I have such a crush on him. I should work up the courage to just ask him out already. I don't know where we will go, but that's what everyone says when they get a boyfriend or girlfriend.

LAST PERIOD of the day is History class, and luckily for me, my best friend is in it. Chloe and I try to make a mad dash for the back row, but our teacher clears his throat, and we look over to the whiteboard, where a seating chart is displayed. We grunt and wander over to see where we sit. We are still in the back row but not sitting next to one another. No, instead, Reid sits in between us.

Chloe turns to me, wiggling her eyebrows.

"Will you stop it!" I say in a shouting whisper.

She sticks out her tongue and finds her seat. I find my own seat and turn to Chloe, putting my hands on either side of my head with my tongue sticking out to her. She returns the gesture by crossing her eyes and puffing her cheeks out.

The classroom door opens and interrupts our display of silly faces as I see Reid strolling in and heading to the whiteboard. He turns and scans the room to look for his seat and walks down the row. As he slides onto his chair, he looks over at me and gives me a big smile.

"Heyyy, Anni, I had a feeling I'd see you again today." He reaches over to give me a fist bump. The sound of my nickname out of his mouth sends a wave of tingles down my back.

"Are you psychic or something?" I return his fist bump.

"Dang, I might be! I also predicted it would be sunny today."

"You sure are in a good mood for the first day of school." I look up at our teacher, who is still waiting for a few more kids to file in.

"History is my favorite subject, so I've been looking forward to this class all day." He pulls out his binder and pencils.

"You're kidding. History is so boring. What do you like about it?" I glance over Reid's shoulder and see Chloe blowing kisses in my direction, which makes me blush immediately.

Reid flips his head around, and Chloe almost falls out of her chair.

He turns back to me, laughing. "Oh man, it is going to be a trip to be in the middle of you two, isn't it?"

Our teacher starts talking, introducing himself as Mr. Francisco, and I realize that I still don't know why Reid likes history class so much.

A MONTH into the school year and we start learning about European history, more specifically, the Vikings. Reid makes a fist-pump gesture as he walks into class, reading the whiteboard. It says, "Viking's Unit" with a picture of a mean-looking Viking next to it.

"Wow, I've never seen anyone so pumped about Vikings before," I say to Reid as he takes his seat.

"This is why history class is so cool. We get to learn about different time periods. I think it's fun to learn how people used to live their everyday lives. Imagine living in Sweden or Norway, sailing around in fancy boats and making your own bowls out of rocks."

"I thought the Vikings weren't very nice."

"Yeah, they were big jerks, but still, it's interesting to learn things were so different from they are now."

His eyes light up when he talks about the subject. I could listen to him talk all day about anything, really. I rest my head on my hand as I continue to listen to him talk about different time periods in history he thinks are cool. He likes the Renaissance era because of all the new things that were discovered. Ancient Greece had cool buildings, but his favorite time period was the Roaring Twenties for the way people dressed and when women could vote.

Our teacher starts playing a movie, and I see Chloe scribbling something on a small piece of paper in the corner of my eye. I try to ignore her and keep my eyes pointed toward the projector playing a documentary about the history of Sweden.

"Psst, Anni." Butterflies start swirling around my stomach as I hear Reid whispering to get my attention.

I look over, and he has a folded piece of paper in his hands.

"From Chloe," he whispers.

I take the paper making sure the teacher isn't looking, and open it up.

Do you want to marry Reid?
0 - Yes 0 - No

I bug my eyes out, crumpling the paper on my chest, and look over to Chloe, who has her head lying on her desk tucked in her arms. I can see her chest bouncing up and down, holding in her laughter.

Reid looks over at me and Chloe with an eyebrow raised before shaking his head and turning his attention back to the movie.

I scribble a note back to Chloe.

~~Do you want to marry Reid?~~
~~O - Yes~~ X - No

I do NOT like him like that!

I nudge my foot against Reid's to get his attention. I slide him the note, and he starts to open it, filling me with panic.

"No!" I say loudly.

Reid stops opening it and turns to me, as well as everyone else in the class. Chloe clasps her hands to her mouth, trying to hold in her laughter again. My teacher looks up from the movie with their head angled to the side and pauses the movie.

"Everything Okay Annika?" The teacher stands. *I hope they didn't notice us passing notes.*

I swallow and look at the movie that I haven't been watching. It's frozen on a herd of Vikings with swords that look like they are invading a little town. "I'm just so upset that the Vikings hurt villages like that." *Please believe me.*

Our teacher lets out a sigh and nods. "It really is upsetting. This part should be over soon." They sit down and resume the movie. *Phew*

I look over to Reid, and he passes the note to Chloe and then turns to me, giving me a little smirk. *Did he read my note? Did he see his name?* I try to focus on the movie for the remainder of class, pushing down the embarrassment bubbling up through me.

THREE

ANNIKA

IT'S a tradition for Chloe and me to see the premiere of the new vampire movie *Darkfall*. Well, this is only the second year we've done it, but after seeing the first, we swore to each other that it would be a tradition, just the two of us. This year is extra special because we are seventh graders, which means we can go to the mall alone. Usually, my mom tags along with us, but I begged her this time. I had to promise to text her every half hour, but it was worth it.

My mom drops us off at the entrance of the theater about an hour before the movie, so Chloe and I can walk around the mall and sneak some snacks in the giant tote bag she brought with her.

"Remember, Anni, every half hour! If you forget, I'm going to call you," my mom yells from her Jeep.

"Stop yelling. Everyone can hear you." I swear my mom lives to embarrass me.

"I'm not yelling. I'm raising my voice. Have fun! Text me!" my mom yells again and waits until we walk inside to drive off.

She's so protective of me it feels overwhelming sometimes. However, I push those feelings away because I think of Chloe and her parents.

As we step into the mall, Chloe reaches into her bag and pulls out a small stack of papers and her strawberry lip balm.

"Anni, my grandma Alice gave me a box of random crafts and paper. I found some old postcards inside that have these stamps with the letter 'A' on them. I thought they were cool, and you could add them to your scrapbook."

She applies her lip balm and hands me three postcards that I flip over and look at each as we start walking around the mall.

One has "Nashville" in big letters on one side, which is where her grandma lives. The back has some cursive scribbles that are hard to read, but Chloe is right. There's a pink stamp in the corner with a fancy "A." The others are pictures of cats, with the same hard-to-read scribbles on the back and the same stamps but in blue and the other in green.

"These are so cool. I love them so much! I wonder what the note says," I say, trying to squint and read.

"I'm not sure. I was trying to figure it out too, but my grandma writes so sloppy, I can never read the birthday cards she sends me. There were a lot of cool papers in the box, too, that I'm excited to paint on."

I look at the postcards again, remembering the first postcard I ever received. It was from Chloe in fourth grade. She was visiting her aunt in Florida during Christmas break. We missed each other so much and tried to talk on the phone, but when I tried to call, she was already asleep. So one day, I got a postcard in the mail, and it was from Chloe. It had a picture of a beach with palm trees on one side. Chloe wrote, "Hi!! I miss you!! Love, Chloe!!" on the other side. There was a daisy stamp in the corner. I got a scrapbook so I could keep the postcard safe, a little memory tucked in the pages.

I sent her a postcard back, and we always send one to each other when one of us travels far away from home. I think I've filled up half of the scrapbook with her postcards so far. Chloe's the only one to send me postcards, but it's cool to see these old ones that her

ANJELICA ROSE

grandma got. It's kinda like reading a mini-story about someone's life. I wonder if my mom has any old postcards I can add to the scrapbook as I take another look at the fancy "A" stamp.

"I'm definitely going to put these in my scrapbook. Thanks again," she responds with a little wink and grabs my hand, skipping in the direction of the candy store.

I fill up a bag of peanut butter cups, and Chloe gets a mixture of gummy bears and sour straws. We are so different sometimes it makes me wonder why we are friends. But maybe us being different is why it works so well. We are never competing for the same things.

"Do you think I can fit a lemonade in my bag?" She walks over, slurping a sour straw in her mouth.

"Maybe if you don't put the straw in and if you keep it really still."

Before heading back to the theater, we load up her bag with two pink lemonades, a giant pretzel, and two corn dogs. I can already feel the stomach ache I'll probably get later today, but this is our traditional movie food.

We buy tickets and make our way to the theaters, trying to act sly and hide Chloe's bag from the theater attendant so they aren't suspicious. We make it through easily and quickly slide over to Theater Five, where the movie is playing. Technically it premiered last night, but there was no way my mom was going to let us see it at midnight. Which reminds me I need to text her.

We find our seats at the very back center, unload her purse, then lay out all our snacks.

"So, is Reid your boyfriend yet or what?" Chloe gives me a sly look while sipping her lemonade.

My mouth drops open. "You can't just say things like that out in public! What if someone from school hears you?" I quickly scan the theater. We arrived so early that we were the only ones in the theater. The previews haven't even started yet.

22

"Oh, *puh-lease*, everyone knows you two like each other." My face heats up at the topic of my crush. I can't help it. I get all nervous but also excited to talk about Reid.

"Puh-lease back, not everyone knows. And besides, I don't know if he likes me the way I like him." I sip my lemonade, trying to remember any hints he's given me.

"The way he looks at you in history class is so sweet. They could have an entire aisle dedicated to it at the candy store."

"What kind of looks?"

"Like." Chloe makes an exaggerated, happy puppy-dog look and then a silly smile. "Like that."

"You look like you have the flu."

She rolls her eyes. "Fine, maybe you don't see it, but I do, and I think you should do something about it."

I shrug and decide to eat my corn dog first while it's hot. Chloe shoves a handful of gummy bears in her mouth. I notice that she has a sparkly bracelet on her right wrist that I haven't seen before.

"Hey, when did you get that?" I ask, pointing to it and flicking one of the charms dangling from it. It looks like a dolphin.

"Oh, my dad got it for me." She says quickly and then shoves another handful of candy in her mouth.

I squint at her because it's not her birthday. I know the reason why her parents usually get her a present when it is a random day. It's because they argued with each other in front of Chloe. Chloe hates when they argue. I've never seen them argue, but I don't really see them often. When we hang out, I never go to her place. My mom always takes us to places, or we have sleepovers at my house. Chloe's dad drives us to school, but that's just because it's on his way to work.

I think her parents don't get along very well. My parents argue sometimes, but they always end their arguments laughing or talking normally. One time last year, my mom got a phone call, and my dad went to Chloe's house to pick her up. Chloe stayed at our house for two days that summer. It was so fun to have her basically living with us, but I did think it was weird. I asked my mom about it after, and she said Chloe's parents weren't getting along and needed to work things out. I still don't know why my dad went and got Chloe, though.

"Chloe?" I try to make my voice a bit more serious, so she stops inhaling candy. She freezes and looks at me. "Why did your dad get you a bracelet?"

Her eyes start to get watery, and she blinks the tears away. "Oh, he left for a couple of days. My mom was upset at him about something, and he left. But he's back now, and he brought me back this bracelet," she says, holding up her wrist and dangling the charms side to side.

I want to ask her more, but it makes me uncomfortable. I just want Chloe to be happy, and whenever we talk about her family, she gets sad. Besides, the movie is about to start.

THE MOVIE IS JUST as awful as we both thought it would be, but we sit at the bench outside the theater, waiting for my mom to pick us up while debating who is the hottest character.

"Definitely, Jake the Mermaid is the best one," Chloe says.

I wince back. "Jake? The fish? Ew, no way, my favorite is Lucian."

"Lucian was the bad vampire! He kept trying to kill Freddie and his vampire family."

"I like the villains. I feel like nobody roots for them."

"That's because they are the bad guys."

I shrug and see a light shine on my face. I realize the sun reflected off a charm on Chloe's bracelet, which reminds me of what we talked about earlier.

"If you need to stay at my house, I'm pretty sure my parents would be cool with it," I say to her.

She scrunches her eyebrows. "Why would I need to stay at your house?"

"If… you know." I point to her bracelet. "If your parents argue, you can stay at my house."

Her eyebrows knit together, and she looks down at her bracelet. She covers it with her other hand pressing it hard into her wrist. I don't know why she's doing that, but it looks like it hurts.

"Hey, Chloe, stop! That looks like it hurts you." She pulls her hand away from her wrist, and I notice the charms left indents on her skin. Her eyes are glassy again.

"My dad didn't come back home," she says quietly to me. "I lied."

I don't say anything. I don't really know what to say, so I just stay quiet.

"My mom got me this bracelet because she said my dad probably won't come back for a while."

My only thought is, who is going to drive us to school? But I don't think that's the right thing to say. Instead, I reach my arm around her shoulders and bring her close to me.

"I-I don't-that really sucks," I finally say, which makes Chloe laugh and lean into my shoulder. I don't know why she's laughing, but I start laughing too.

"It sucks a lot. I miss my dad." She sniffles. I think she's crying. "Can I sleep over at your house tonight?"

"Always," I say as she pulls away, wiping her tears.

"Promise you won't leave me," she says to me with the saddest look on her face. As if she actually thinks I'll ever leave her. She's my best friend for life, I'll never leave her, and she better not leave me.

"I promise. You promise you won't leave me," I say back.

"I promise." She smiles and pulls me in for a hug, nearly choking me with the force of her love.

My mom pulls up a few minutes later, and I ask if Chloe can stay the night, which she easily agrees to as if she knew I would ask, anyway. I feel bad that Chloe's parents aren't like mine, but I'm happy they treat her like she's part of the family.

FOUR

ANNIKA

FOUR MONTHS GO BY, and my courage to ask Reid out still has not been found. During gym class, the different classes rotate doing different sports so nothing is too crowded, but every Wednesday, all the classes run the mile together.

Chloe says I'm in denial about my love for Reid. I don't like him like that, *I swear*. Yes, he is the cutest boy in the school, and he always makes my stomach flurry when I see him. But I'm not *in love* with him like Chloe always says. It's just a little crush. Tiny, teeny, little crush.

Last week I tripped on a rock while running the mile, falling on my hands and knees. The gravel track dug into my knees and palms as I fell, making me wince in pain. I turned around to sit and brush off the gravel when I saw Reid running over to help me up.

"How come you are always around whenever I embarrass myself?" I said to him as he helped me up. I swear I saw his cheeks blush a little when our hands touched.

His eyes brightened as he said, "Just trying to help you out. It looked like that trip hurt a lot."

I rolled my shoulders back, trying to brush it off. "Well, thanks, but you don't have to help me."

"It's okay. I like helping you when you fall. Your cheeks turn pink whenever I do."

Oh my god. If I wasn't embarrassed before, I definitely was then. He totally knows I have a crush on him.

"Hey, what's that?" I said, pointing behind him. When he turned, I ran down the track.

He turned back and saw me running, laughing, and tried to catch up to me. He nudged my side as he met up with me, and we finished running the mile together, side by side.

OUR NEXT GYM unit is the dance unit. Our teacher tells us all the classes this period are doing the unit at the same time and that the girls have to pick partners, but we can ask anyone in any other class. I get so nervous at the thought of having to ask someone to dance. I wish Chloe was in this class with me or, at the very least, Isaac. Chloe and Isaac broke up in forth grade after dating for a month.

She said she liked him better as a friend rather than a boyfriend, whatever that means. But Isaac is my neighbor, and we give him a ride to school sometimes, so he's really the only boy I'm closest friends with and would be an easy, safe choice to dance with. But neither of them are in this period of gym class, so I scan the room, looking around to see who I can partner up with. I look at the other boys in my class, and some look at me and then look away.

I'm going to have to dance with the teacher if no one wants to be my partner. I decide to walk over to the boy I sit next to in my math class because he seems nice until I feel a tap on my shoulder.

I turn around and see Reid standing across from me. My stomach starts flipping around in cartwheels.

"Hey Anni, do you have a dance partner yet?"

I breathe in a shaky breath. "No, not yet. I was trying to figure out who to ask."

He looks down at his feet and then looks back up at me. "Well, you can ask me."

"Ask you what?" I freeze, wondering what he's talking about.

He giggles, and I can see his face turning red like a strawberry. "You can ask me to be your dance partner."

My mouth forms an "O," and I think I might faint in the middle of the gym.

"I mean, if you want to, no pressure." He starts to fidget and look around.

I take a deep breath. "Do you want to be my dance partner, Reid?" He looks up at me with a huge smile on his face, the corners of his eyes turning up.

"I thought you'd never ask," he says, reaching his hand out to take it and swirling me around in a circle.

Our dance unit lasted exactly a month. Reid and I learned how to waltz, square dance, and salsa. I could barely breathe the entire time while our hands touched and shoulders brushed as we do-si-doed. He kept tripping over his feet during the salsa, making us stop and start over every minute or so.

"You are a terrible dancer," I'd say, laughing each time he tripped.

"I'm nervous, okay. Dancing is hard." Reid huffed out a breath as we took the starting spot to begin the salsa dance again.

SPRING BREAK IS COMING UP, which means the spring dance is coming up. Our school has been talking about it all week. Whenever the announcer says, "Go with some friends or bring a date," I get flooded with nervous feelings because I know who exactly I want to go to the dance with. The school is having it on the Saturday right before Spring Break, which is in two weeks.

I hope Reid asks me to the dance. Whenever he walks into

history class, his eyes find mine first. I can't help but smile and hide my blushing cheeks each time. Chloe is tired of my crush by now. Instead, she just rolls her eyes.

"Just ask him to the dance!" She tells me at lunch, leaning over the table and reaching for a cheese puff in my lunch box.

"I can't do that. I think I'd die on the spot."

"You asked him to dance in gym class. What's the difference?"

"The difference is the girls were forced to ask for partners. And he came up to me. I was about to ask Trevor from my math class."

Chloe scrunches her head back. "Trevor? Still, it's so obvious you both like each other. Just ask him."

"It isn't obvious, and I'm still not one hundred percent sure if he likes me. Besides, who are you asking?" I say, trying to divert the attention away from me.

"I'm going solo," she says, waving her finger around in the air. "Me, Desi, and Kate are all going as single girlies, less pressure, and we are going to form a circle so no boys try to dance with us."

I roll my eyes because I know Chloe is going to end up finding a boy to slow dance with. I know about three guys who all have a crush on Chloe. She's already turned down one of them.

THE FRIDAY before the dance arrives, and I'm still without a date for the dance. I decided on Monday that I'd ask Reid to go with me, but I've only seen him once all week. He wasn't in gym class, and he showed up right as the bell rang for history class, which was the day we had our midterm, so I didn't have the chance to ask him. I hope he didn't catch a cold. Then I really will miss my chance to ask him. I guess I can go with the rest of the girlies and Chloe. A part of me hopes he still goes to the dance. I sit through my last class period of the day, drifting off in a daydream.

I walk into the gym that's been transformed to look like a whimsical garden, lights are dim, and there are bubbles floating around in the air. I'm wearing a new pink and green dress that I got over the weekend. I see Reid across the room, and he's wearing a matching green shirt. It's perfect. He's perfect. We walk to each other and dance. He's the best dancer ever, spinning me and laughing. A slow song comes on, and we get closer to each other. He leans and gives me a little kiss. I smile.

"Excuse me, Miss Gomes. Please hand in your test." I'm jolted out of my fantasy and pass my test to the front of the class, glaring at the kid next to me who is looking at me funny.

I hope my daydream comes true.

SATURDAY AFTERNOON, Chloe and I walk into the gym, and it's nothing like my daydream. All the lights are on, and only a few paper flowers decorate the space. Whoever was in charge did a terrible job. We find our other friends huddled by the refreshments area and join them.

I try to have fun all night, but I keep looking at the door and around the gym. Looking to see if Reid shows up. Chloe keeps saying I should've asked him earlier. But he's clearly sick or busy. I hope he's okay. It pains me when I realize it will be a full two weeks before I see him again. Okay, maybe my crush is a big one after all.

SPRING BREAK WAS SO much fun. My family took a road trip to Yosemite. We saw the biggest trees of my life. My brothers and I took a picture holding hands, trying to hug a tree at the same time, and our arms still weren't long enough to wrap around it. It was extra fun because Chloe got to come with us. We got matching Yosemite stickers at the gift shop that we put on our diaries, and I got three new postcards. Chloe gave me the best idea to use one to give to Reid when we get back to school.

I pick one that has a bunch of redwood trees and a little path winding through. A couple is holding hands, walking on the path. I think it's perfect to ask him to go out with me. On the other side, I write a note to him.

To Reid,

Do you like me too?
0-Yes 0-Yes

Love, Anni

I almost wrote the "No" option, but I didn't want him to say no, so I didn't give him an option. I know my dad keeps stamps in the top drawer of his desk. I fly downstairs, clutching the postcard close to my chest just in case my little brothers are running around. They might rip it out of my hands if they see.

I quietly open the drawer and flip through the stacks of envelopes and papers until I see the stack of stamps paper clipped together. I look through them and find the perfect one. "L-O-V-E," it says with red, green, and yellow flowers.

I tuck the postcard in my binder to keep it safe just as I hear Chloe's mom honking from outside. My dad tried to tell Chloe's mom that he could go to work later to take us to school, but she insisted that she wanted to take us.

We get to school just as the bell for class rings, and Chloe and I run to our classrooms to not be late for the first day back from spring break.

The day goes by so slowly, and I'm counting the minutes until history class. In gym class, the classes were separate, so I haven't seen Reid yet. Which is probably for the best because I think I'd throw up from nerves.

Finally, the fourth period rolls around, and I arrive early, placing the postcard, picture side up, on Reid's desk. I contemplate going to the bathroom as class starts to avoid seeing him look at it.

Chloe comes in and walks to her desk, noticing the postcard on Reid's desk, giving me a giant smile with two thumbs up. I give her a wobbly smile and thumbs up back.

The final bell rings, and Reid still hasn't come to class. He is never late. I notice our teacher starting to walk in between the seats, and I swipe the postcard back, shoving it in the back pocket of my binder.

Just as he passes my seat, I tap him on the shoulder. "Hey, Mr. Francisco, is Reid sick or something?" I try to ask casually.

"Reid Parker? Oh, yes, he moved. Friday before spring break was his last day." He must see my pained expression and continues. "However, that doesn't mean you can take his seat just so you're closer to Chloe. Stick to the seating chart Miss Gomes."

I hate how he says my name, *Go-mez*. It's almost right that it bugs me even more than when it's pronounced terribly wrong. *Wait, did he just say Reid moved?*

"Chloe!" I whisper to her, leaning over Reid's former desk. "Did you just hear that? He moved!"

"Who moved?" she asks, looking confused.

"Reid, Reid moved!"

A kid who sits in front of Chloe, I think his name is Steven, turns around to us, clearly listening to our entire conversation.

"I heard he moved to Colorado," he says. "His dad got a job, and they moved, lucky. He didn't have to take all the midterms."

Chloe gives Steven an evil squint and fans her hand at him, which makes him turn away from us.

My heart falls out of my butt. *Reid moved.* I'm devastated.

. . .

AS SOON AS I get home, I run up to my room and launch myself into my bed, crying into my pillow. I think I hear one of my brothers coming in after me.

"Get out!" I say, muffling into my pillow.

I feel a small hand caressing my head. "Why are you crying?" It's Joey. He might dress in all black, but he's a big softie on the inside and hates whenever I'm sad.

"Just leave me alone." I don't feel like explaining what heart-break is to my nine-year-old brother.

He stays for a few minutes, not saying anything, just brushing my hair with his fingers. I feel him give me a little kiss on the head, and my bedroom door closes.

I wish I had asked Reid out earlier. But I was scared. I didn't want to find out he didn't like me back. I don't know what is worse, being rejected by Reid or him moving and never getting the chance to find out. I roll off my bed and sit at my desk. I unlock my secret drawer in my desk and find my diary. "A+R," I wrote on the cover with my favorite gel pens. I run my fingers over the letters and open the diary.

Fourth Grade - December

Dear Diary,

There's a new boy in our school. He just moved here and doesn't know anyone but has a ton of friends. He's kind of cute, but I don't like boys like that. They stink.

Love, Anni

Fifth Grade - September

Dear Diary,

You'll never guess who is in my class this year. Well, yeah, Chloe, she's always in my class. I'm pretty sure my mom is behind her, and I am always in the same classes. Anyway, it's Reid. I think I have a crush on him. I didn't know what it meant to have a crush, so I looked it up when we did computer lab. It said something about flutters and feeling excited to see someone. I have both of those things whenever I see him.

Love, Anni

Fifth Grade - March

Dear Diary,

Reid said my shirt looked cool today.

Love, Anni

Sixth Grade - July

Dear Diary,

Chloe is staying with us tonight. I think my mom said she's staying tomorrow too. Chloe is brushing her teeth while I write here. I wish she could stay at our house all the time. I wish she was my real sister, not just my best friend. She makes me want to be brave like her. I never see her sad when her parents argue. I would be sad if mine argued like hers. Although I wouldn't be sad if I got to sleep over at my best friend's house.

I told Chloe about my crush on Reid tonight, and she said, "DUH!" I hope not everyone knows about my crush! Only you and my mom know. Well, now Chloe knows she better not spill the beans. Oh, I think she's done brushing her teeth. Bye diary

Love, Anni

Seventh Grade - February

I <3 Reid Parker I <3 Reid Parker I <3 Reid Parker I <3 Reid ParkerI <3 Reid Parker I <3 Reid ParkerI <3 Reid Parker I <3 Reid ParkerI <3 Reid Parker I <3 Reid ParkerI <3 Reid Parker I <3 Reid ParkerI <3 Reid Parker I <3 Reid Parker

I have probably twenty entries about all the times Reid made my heart skip a beat. I grab a pen from my drawer and start writing a new entry.

Seventh Grade - May

Dear Diary,

My heart broke today. I didn't know if I was in love, but the way my chest aches now is proof enough. I loved a boy and never told him. I wish I could go back in time. He's gone. He didn't even say goodbye. He could've told me. How did Steven find out!? Colorado? That's not even in the same time zone. I don't know if I'll be able to recover. I just want to cry for the rest of my life.

Unloved,

Annika

I never want to be reminded of this heartbreak ever again. I slam the diary shut and shove the postcard I was supposed to give him inside. I tuck it under my arm and run to the side yard and throw it right in the big trash can. Garbage day is tomorrow, and it will collect all the pieces of my heart with it. I'm clearly not meant to fall in love.

I head back to my room and close the door, sulking for about another hour until Chloe storms into my room with an arm full of DVDs and a giant bag of kettle corn. We sit on my bed in my room, binge-watching cheesy rom-coms and eating popcorn while she listens to me complain about all the love scenes. She doesn't even mention the boy I once loved at all, which I'm happy about. I don't want to think about him. During the third movie, I'm sitting on the floor, and she's braiding my hair while I cry at the part where the couple lives happily ever after.

I watch as the couple runs to each other, kissing in the rain. It makes me sick. As the credits roll up the screen, I vow to never fall in love. Ever. Again

PART 2

COLLEGE

Dear Mom,

   Thanks for the care package.
Chloe was so happy with the snacks
and art markers. We are all moved
into our dorm. It's nice, but boring.
   Classes are going good so far. I
miss you all so much! Tell Dad, Joey
& Wes I miss them. See you soon.

♡ Anni

Mia Gomes
399 Green Valley Blvd.
Ojai, CA 93023

FIVE

ANNIKA

I GLARE at a piece of hair that refuses to brush down with the rest of my shoulder-length black hair. Of course, my hair chooses eight a.m. on a Monday to be temperamental. Thankfully our suite mates don't have class until later in the day, so I can take my time getting ready. Mine and Chloe's dorm room share a bathroom with two other girls. They are nice, but I rarely ever see them. To be fair I don't really make an effort either. Probably because I wake up earlier than everyone else just so I can have our small bathroom all to myself. It's a process to look this cool and confident so no one realizes I'm second-guessing every decision I make.

I decide water is going to be the only thing that can tame this beast of a head of hair. So I gracefully shove my hair under the faucet and fish out Chloe's blow dryer from under the sink that her mom gave her as a graduation gift. She rarely uses it because she says it changes her "natural wave." The other suite mates and I use it more often than Chloe thinks about it.

Working meticulously, I tame the strand of hair that is trying to make me look like Alfalfa from The Little Rascals and flip the ends of my hair out so they land on my shoulders. Satisfied with the result, I move on to makeup, which these days is pretty simple. I cannot be bothered to go all out with blending eyeshadow and contour as I did in high school when all I do is sit through day-long lectures. I dab a bit of concealer under my eyes, a few swipes of my eyebrow pencil to define the ends, and a swoosh of mascara, which I stab the wand in my eyeball at least once a week. Before I duck out of the bathroom, I snap a few mirror selfies that I tell myself to post on my socials but probably won't.

Tip-toeing out of the bathroom, I see Chloe is still in her bed, curled up with her comforter swirled around her like a nest. When we learned we could dorm together at UC San Diego, we squealed so loud I'm pretty sure my mom's hearing hasn't been the same since. I cannot imagine going through college, let alone life, with anyone else by my side. Chloe and I have always been there for each other.

We are both marketing majors, even though neither of us is certain what we want to do with our lives. I mean, does anyone even know what they want to do? Even if I did know what I wanted to do, how do I know I'm going to want to stick with that forever? It's too much pressure.

If Chloe had her way, she'd probably ditch all pleasantries and become a beach bum, reading books all day, painting strangers' portraits for cash, and couch-surfing her way through life. Yet here we are, both pretending to live a life we think we are supposed to live.

I don't dislike marketing, per se. I think it is all helpful information to learn, and if anything, I can use what I learn to be an influencer or publicist. It's just each time I have to get ready for class, this cloud of dread looms over me. Like my subconscious is telling me it's not really what I'm meant to do.

My intrusive thoughts tell me to drop out, but that will never happen. It means too much to my parents and my family that I see this through. I graduated high school with honors. It only makes sense that I go to college and continue the good streak. I'd be the first of my family to graduate college with a degree. I picture the future with my parents at my graduation as I walk across the stage with my diploma. That thought alone makes each day I climb out of bed to sit through a lecture on "Quantitative Methods of Business" worth it.

Moving on from my existential dread.

My outfit, or as I like to call it, my uniform, consists of high-waisted "boyfriend" jeans, a slouchy graphic tee, and a crew neck sweater that I tie around my shoulders. San Diego is seemingly always above seventy-five degrees, but the professors insist on keeping their classrooms at a bone-chilling sixty-two degrees, so a sweater is a necessity. I learned the hard way my first week of freshman year when I was giving the entire lecture hall a peep show through my tank top. My graphic tee today is a faded dark gray *NSYNC T-shirt. I slip on my dirty white Converse high-tops and grab my bag, chucking in a few books.

I smooch Chloe on the forehead before she pulls the covers over her face. "Bye, Chlo, don't miss class at eleven!" I yell at her before leaving our room.

I walk past a few other students studying on the plush bean bags in the lounge as I head through the halls of our dorm. Zura Hall isn't anything special with its gray carpets and gray walls except for the "pop" color wall here and there. The lounge has a tangerine orange wall with a cork board where people tack flyers and notes. At least it's a little more updated than the other dorm buildings, and lucky for me, it's only three buildings down from my first class of the day.

The sun burns my eyes immediately as I walk outside, and I scramble to fish my sunglasses out of my giant tote bag. I will never get used to how the sun in Southern California can somehow see into my soul with its brightness. Even though I grew up a few hours from San Diego, it feels like I'm in the Mojave desert down here.

Even in the morning, the sun is out at the crack of dawn as if saying, "Good Morning Anni! It's time to face the rest of your life!"

As I strut along one of the winding paths toward my lecture hall, I spot Isaac in the corner of my eye, walking in the same direction. Before I get the chance to swivel away so he doesn't see me, he immediately spots me and jogs over, yelling my name and waving his hands around in the air. *Crap.*

Isaac's been my neighbor growing up through childhood, so we've stayed friendly enough to each other. It is nice to know someone else from our hometown here. I can tolerate him most of the time, but he is always trying to get me to come to one of his parties. I went to one at the start of freshman year, and it was something I'd never like to relive. His fraternity, Delta Psi, is no doubt the party, wild boy frat. They throw parties almost every weekend and it usually consists of music that is too loud, beer that is watered down, and frat guys trying to feel you up whenever you walk past. His frat brothers, especially the upperclassman, are a little too eager to get their hands on all the new pretty girls that show up for their parties, and unfortunately, I was one of those at that first party I attended.

Isaac is nearly out of breath after his thirty-second jog over to me. "Hey, Anni! How's it hanging? We missed you at last weekend's rager."

I roll my eyes, and my gaze goes down to inspect his outfit today. He is wearing dark blue cargo shorts and a brick red shirt that reads "Don't Worry, I Pull Out!" with a winking cartoon loveseat below it. *Sick.*

"Yeah, you know I haven't shown up to one of your parties ever since Trey grabbed my ass within the first minute of walking in," I say as I try to keep walking toward my class, hoping Isaac gets the hint that I don't want to have a morning chit-chat.

"Well, I hope you change your mind. This weekend is my birthday, and hopefully, you can make an exception for me."

He strokes my arm and gives me the worst display of puppy-dog eyes I've ever seen.

"Yeah, yeah, I'll see about that. I have a lot of studying to do, and exams are next week."

Which isn't a complete lie? I do have a quiz in my photography elective class. And it's not so much of a quiz and more so we have to submit all the pictures we've taken in the past month. Still, I'd rather get a root canal than go to another Delta Psi party.

"If it makes you feel any better, it's not hosted by my frat. Well, I guess, yes, it is technically *at* the frat house, but I'm hosting it and only inviting my closest compadres." He finishes with a wink and finger guns.

I roll my eyes, pondering over the possibility of maybe going to another college party. It does help the smallest bit that Isaac is in charge of the guess list. Isaac's friends are mostly guys in his major, a few other people from our high school, and Chloe and I.

"Chances are still slim, but I'll let you know. Gotta get to class, see ya."

He does a double-air punch as if he's made a touchdown and waves goodbye as he saunters to the building next to my lecture hall. The invitation lingers in my mind a bit longer as I consider actually going. I'm not sure why, but a part of me is drawn to go to this party. Not because it's Isaac's birthday. I really couldn't care less about that. I feel like I should be going to more parties and outings as a college student. It's only been a few months, but I am in the same routine of waking up, going to class, getting lunch with Chloe, doing homework, rinse, and repeat.

Occasionally Chloe and I venture out to the beach or thrift shops. Even though I'm away at college, it feels like I'm not getting the *college experience*. I haven't even made any actual new friends since being here. I can't even remember the names of my suite mates I share a bathroom with. Is it Charlotte and Abby? No, no, I think it's Carly and Aimee. *Shit, I'm the worst roommate.*

All I know about Carly and Aimee is what they look like and that they are always trying to get Chloe and me to go partying with them. Carly is the louder of the two. She is always singing out loud with her headphones in, and we can clearly hear her through the shared wall. She's almost six feet tall and has envious long silky brown hair. I think she's here on a volleyball scholarship. Aimee is the polar opposite, standing at just under five feet tall with a short blond pixie cut. She's studying archeology or anthropology. Or was it architecture? I really should get to know them better.

With Chloe being my roommate and studying the same major as me, we see each other all the time. It's effortless for us to stick to each other like glue. Even a handful of people from my hometown go to UCSD, like Isaac, but what's the point of hanging out with anyone else when I can hang out with my favorite person? The guilt of feeling like I should do more and not doing enough sticks to me, and I try to brush it off as I walk into the lecture hall. I need to focus on class and pretend like this is what I'm supposed to be doing.

"CLASS WAS BRUTAL. Mr. Tahoma lectured for two hours straight. I was starting to hear him like a Peanuts teacher by the end of it." Chloe slides into the picnic table seat with her lunch tray. She is vegan this week, so her lunch consists of iceberg lettuce, an array of fruit slices, and a cup of baked beans.

I cannot help but notice how her outfit today is so sweet and effortless. She can do the smallest amount and still look like a goddess. Her long, ashy blond hair has two braids on either side of her face while the rest cascades down her back in a mass of tangled curls. She is wearing her trusty paint-splattered overalls with a white tank top underneath and Rainbow-brand flip-flops. Her fair skin has freckled quite a bit in the San Diego sun. She pulls out a tube of strawberry lip balm and reapplies. I cannot believe she still uses those, but she swears the scents are better than any other brand. I think it tastes like candle wax.

"Can you bring me dinner tonight when you come to the show? I won't have time to pick up anything because I need to set up my stall," Chloe says, scooping a portion of beans in her mouth.

"Sure, you want a bean and cheese burrito?"

Chloe winces and looks at me like I said something dumb. "Cheese is not vegan."

"Well, then, what, beans only?"

"Yes, actually, that's perfect." She nods and smiles.

I'm looking forward to when she starts incorporating more foods in her diet, or at least less beans.

"What time should I come by, and do you need help setting up?" Chloe has her second art show tonight.

She's been taking an art elective that I'm pretty sure she spends more of her energy on than her actual major. She's an amazing artist. I thought she should've majored in fine art, but she said she could never do that. I get it. What kind of jobs can you get with a degree like that? Even though she'd probably enjoy studying it more than Marketing.

I have a painting Chloe gave me when we graduated high school hung above my desk in our dorm. It's a painting of two girls sitting on the beach, looking out at the water. It makes me so happy and relaxed whenever I look at it. Chloe is her best self whenever she's painting. She zones out as soon as a paintbrush enters her grasp, and she'll paint for hours like it's meditation.

"Can you come by around five? It starts at six pm. You can help me hang the canvases."

"Sounds good," I say, adding a reminder on my phone. "Oh hey, I ran into Isaac. He invited us to his birthday party this weekend." I reluctantly bring up my interaction as I push around my mac and cheese on my plate, hoping that Chloe will say she planned something else for us to do this weekend instead.

"Oh yea! He texted me about it. We should totally go! I know you never want to go but come *onnnnn*, Anni, how are you supposed to enjoy all the hot dudes who go to school here if you don't get out there."

Dammit.

Chloe has been so hung up on me finding "the one" ever since she started flirting with the barista at the campus coffee shop nearest to our dorm. She dreams of having double dates with our significant others. But then she also reminds me to play the field. It's all so confusing. I don't know what I even want, let alone if I want to date anyone right now. Besides, it's not like I haven't tried. I went out with a boy from my Intro to Marketing class a couple of months ago. We went to get ice cream at the boardwalk by the beach, and twenty minutes into the date, he said I would look prettier with a boob job, so suffice it to say, he wasn't the one for me.

"I don't know if I want to date any of the 'hot dudes' at a frat party. I'd rather be flipping through the vintage rack at one of my favorite thrift stores. I look up and catch a cute boy's eyes. We buy matching T-shirts, and the rest is history." I look up, and Chloe's mouth is agape.

"Wow, you've put some thought into this."

"Not really, just random fantasies. Honestly, I wouldn't mind dating someone tolerable, but I haven't had much luck."

"Well, keep an open mind this weekend. You never know who might steal your heart." She clutches her chest like she's been shot by Cupid's arrow.

I may regret this later.

"Fine, fine, we can go to his party, but you need to promise not to leave my side. We need to keep the buddy system. I don't trust any of those frat guys."

Chloe shimmies in her seat. "Yay! I'm so excited. I'm bringing Dane."

She bats her eyelashes at the mention of her current fling. The barista boy. She flirted with him endlessly since we started the second semester, hoping he'd get the hint. He didn't, so Chloe just gave him her phone number one day because she was sick of waiting. So far, he seems nice. I haven't talked to him much, but I can tell Chloe is having fun.

Who knows, this party could be amusing. I am already feeling stressed from school, so it will be a nice break from constantly thinking about all the assignments that are due soon. Maybe we'll go shopping for new outfits beforehand.

Shopping is one of those moments for me where I'm completely in bliss. I love bopping around Gaslamp and seeing what new items arrive at the vintage shops each week. The thrill of putting an outfit together or stumbling upon a vintage band T-shirt gets me eager to run out of this cafeteria just thinking about it. I'd never admit it to Chloe, but a part of me is a little excited to go. It feels like this party might be different from others.

SIX

ANNIKA

I ARRIVE PROMPTLY at five p.m., bean burrito and a dairy-free yogurt in hand, to Chloe's art show. The art department set it up in the courtyard of the fine art buildings toward the back right corner of campus. I only come over to this side for my photography class, but I always enjoy it. They have funky sculptures set up around the walkways. The weather is perfect today to graze and admire art. Sunny without a cloud in the sky and a slight breeze to keep things cool. Once the sun sets, the soft glow of the lights strung from tree to tree will illuminate the art in all its glory.

I spot Chloe buzzing around carrying paper-wrapped canvases to her station. She is wearing a short denim overall dress and an airy pink top underneath. Her long, curly blond hair is tied up in a half-up look that she secured with two paint brushes. Very on theme for today. She sets down the canvas and then pops over to other people's stations, helping them set up. There are faux walls on wheels, with pegs scattered on them, propped around the area where the students can hang their art. Some students brought extra easels to display their dominant pieces. There are about twenty different showcases. Chloe said they had to submit their art, and the professors picked who gets to showcase their art. This is the second time this year Chloe's been selected.

I set down the bag of food and start unwrapping Chloe's art while she's still helping other students. Her theme for the show is called "A Study on Love." Wherever we went, she'd carry a little sketchbook with her, and as soon as she saw any inkling of romance, she'd start sketching the interaction so she could paint a larger scene later. I find her obsession with love fascinating. It's something I never look twice at, but Chloe is always one to absorb those sweet moments a beat longer. A look of longing washes over her face as the interaction passes.

"Anni! Did you bring me a burrito? I'm starving." Chloe bounces over.

I hand her the bag, and she tears into it, inhaling half of the burrito, slowly chewing and sighing as if she's never eaten a burrito before in her life.

"Mmmmm, this hits the spot. Okay, so I want the eight-by-eights hung up evenly on the panel and then the two big pieces on easels. Someone in my class brought extras they are letting me borrow for tonight."

"Everyone in your class is so nice. And I got it. You had these lined up on the dorm floor for three days. I practically have the layout memorized."

"You know me so well," she says, giving me a smile and tearing off the foil on top of the yogurt.

She has nine small square canvases, and each has a couple in a different pose. My favorite one is with a couple leaning into each other. They look like they are dancing. It's a soft moment of love I can appreciate. Nothing too dramatic but one where you can feel the love they have for each other.

We finish setting up her stall as Aimee and Carly approach. "Hey!" they say in unison.

"Oh, hey guys, I didn't know you'd be here." I greet them each with a half-hug.

"Chloe invited us! We wouldn't miss the chance to support our suite mate," Aimee says with a bright smile.

I instantly feel bad I didn't invite them to a similar show my photography class put on. Chloe is the kind of person who wants everyone to be included, no one to be left behind or forgotten about.

Since her dad left, I noticed a mask forming over Chloe's bright and personable exterior. Anyone in passing wouldn't be able to tell, but I caught the few brief moments of Chloe lingering on a thought or the empty gaze before snapping into conversation. I'd pick her up from her house, and it's like her face would morph from one of darkness to one of light as she walked out her front door. I think she stayed at my house more often than her own through the last couple of years of high school. I can't imagine what it feels like to have one parent leave you and one never try to bring you back home.

College has lessened her mask, and she is trying new things and leaning into her passions. I haven't seen the joy in her eyes like this since we were kids. She is truly in her element when she gets to create art.

Chloe tells Aimee, Carly, and me to go and roam around the show. She has to stay at her stall in case people ask questions or want to buy anything. I remind her that I want that dancing painting and to not sell it to anyone else.

"So, how do you two know each other?" I say to Aimee and Carly as we start wandering through the different booths.

I feel a wince of embarrassment that we've lived next to each other for six months, and I barely know a thing about them.

"We went to high school together in Irvine," Aimee responds, stopping to look at a student's abstract collection featuring giant splotches of royal blue and black.

"Aimee and I were in the same English class freshman year and had to do a project on Romeo and Juliet. We've been besties ever since." Carly finishes and grabs Aimee in a headlock, kissing the top of her head dramatically.

We continue on, swerving around the other stalls. I admire a collection of landscape watercolor paintings that provide a familiar ease.

As I've been chatting with Aimee and Carly, I didn't realize that they were best friends too. I'm also struck with the realization that their names also start with "A" and "C." If I believed in coincidences, I'd say this was a pretty funny one. They are like the Irvine version of Chloe and me.

"What are your majors?"

"Graphic design," they answer in unison, which makes me smile. I actually love that they are in the same major too.

"I'm starving. Is there food here?" Carly dramatically grabs her stomach, wincing in pain.

"Yeah, they are selling hotdogs over there." I point to one side of the courtyard, where the art department has a snack bar set up.

Aimee and Carly wander over to get some food, and I head back to Chloe's booth.

Chloe is talking to some other students and showing them her art. By the looks of the "SOLD!" sticky notes on half the art, she's had a successful night so far. I'm not surprised. She's an insanely talented artist.

The crowd disperses, and I meet up with Chloe again.

"Wow, what a successful night! What are you going to do with any that don't get sold?"

Chloe does a spin and smiles at me. "I think I might hang them in the dorm lounge. The RA said it was cool as long as I used removable hooks."

"Definitely will spice up the fifty shades of gray. Oh hey, is Dane coming?"

She scrunches her face, and I see her quickly scan the crowd. "He said he was going to try to make it after his shift, but I haven't seen him. I dunno, I don't think he's coming."

I try to remain with a neutral expression while my brain is spinning in circles. He couldn't stop by his girlfriend's art show? What is with this guy? I am trying not to judge him, but this simple gesture would make Chloe so happy.

"That's lame of him. I'm sorry." I give her a hug to console her. "I'm sure he got busy with studying or something. Maybe you can give him one of the small paintings since he didn't get to see the show." She seems to lighten up at this.

"Good idea, and you're right. He probably got hung up with something. I'll text him later." She lets out a sigh. "You always know the thing to say to calm me down from starting to freak out. I really like him, Anni. I want it to work out."

"I know, it's still early. Take it easy, and don't force anything. Everything happens for a reason."

"Just like your mom always says. By the way, she texted me that she wants the big one on the easel. She wants to hang it up in her office." A sense of pride fills me that my mom is supporting my best friend.

The show is starting to wrap up, so I help Chloe take down all her art. Aimee and Carly must've ditched because they never came back. I'm sure we'll see them again. I might even accept their invite to hang out sometime.

Canvases under arms, we make the trek back to our dorm. Chloe's phone starts buzzing, and she juggles the art in her arms to quickly grab it, reading the message and halting in her tracks.

"It's a text from Dane. He had to work late and feels terrible for missing my show."

"See, I told you it wasn't on purpose." A feeling of relief envelopes me. She seems to relax more now, knowing her new boyfriend texted her. Chloe always puts her whole heart into every relationship and always falls in love so fast.

I hope this Dane guy doesn't break her heart. I'm not sure if she can handle another man in her life letting her down.

SEVEN

ANNIKA

THIS WEEK FLEW by because I am not sure how it's already Saturday and how I'm already approaching the frat house. We arrive an hour after Isaac says to show up to the party. There is no way in hell that I am going to be the first one there. Almost immediately after walking in, Chloe pulls her boyfriend, Dane, off to the side, leaving me looking like an abandoned puppy in the middle of the foyer. Up until this moment, I was having a great time.

We spent Friday morning picking up iced chai lattes, elbows linked as we frolicked through the streets of Gaslamp, hopping between stores and gathering different clothes and accessories for our outfits. We then spent four glorious hours today getting ready, which might seem like a lot to the average person, but this is why Chloe and I are best friends. We both love the process of getting ready, even if it means different things to each of us.

For me, it includes two face masks, one detoxing and one hydrating, showering, and blow-drying my shoulder-length straight hair so it's sleek and shiny. For Chloe, it's dancing and singing to her favorite songs and changing her outfit ten times. Then Chloe and I sit on the floor as we do each other's makeup.

Now, usually, I don't approve of this. However, she begged me and said it would be fun to get out of our comfort zone. I figured I was already stretching my comfort zone by attending this party, so why not let Chloe draw on my face? Chloe gave me cobalt blue eyeliner to match the holographic halter top I picked up from Crossroads. Then she drew little white daisies on either cheek.

I have to admit, I look rather cute, and it makes me want to exude the same carefreeness that Chloe wears naturally. I drew my signature black wing on Chloe's eyelid, then added an emerald glitter to the end of the wing. When she opened her eyes, the glitter made the light green flecks in her blue eyes sparkle. She pulled on a strappy black and green floral jumpsuit and slid her feet into her trusty Birkenstocks.

Shoes are always my hardest choice because I don't have a lot of options. We live in a small dorm room with limited space. So I decide to follow Chloe's suit and settle on my ol' faithful: a pair of high-top white Converse. It gives my blue halter top and high-waisted jean shorts a casual look. I feel a little exposed with most of my back on display, but I layer with a lace bralette just in case anything tries to slip out. Chloe reassures me and says I look hot, so I'm taking her word for it. I want to look hot but also be comfortable.

MY COMFORT LEFT my body with Chloe as she left my side once we stepped inside the frat.

She yells to me, "I'll meet up with you in a second!" and drags Dane with her to the study off to the left.

They are clearly on better terms after him not attending her art show.

It looks like a cozy spot to curl up with someone and suck their face, which about three other couples are already doing. May his lips rest in peace after she's done with him. I thought it would just be Chloe and me, the dynamic duo, Thing One and Thing Two, dumb and dumber, the two cool rats. But no, she brought Dane along, of course. He gave her a million compliments when he slid into our ride-share that stopped at his apartment before coming here. Something just seems off about him. I can't place it.

The house looks exactly the same since the last time I was here at the beginning of the year. A pain in my chest starts to rise as I glance up the foyer at the iron staircase. It swirls up each of the four levels to the bedrooms and *executive* bedrooms, which, regrettably, I know all too well. Before the flashbacks hit me, I swerve to the room on the left to look for Isaac. If I make myself known within the first five minutes, then I don't feel as bad if I ditch the party shortly after. The living room is packed with people. College students are draped over the three large sofas surrounding a massive flat-screen, some are chatting, and others are engrossed in the soccer game on the TV. I spot Isaac sitting at the edge of the sofa closest to the wall and head over to him.

"Well, well, well, if it isn't lil' Ojai Anni! Jed, you owe me twenty dollars!"

Gosh, I hate that nickname he gives me. Isaac springs up from the sofa, arms open wide as if he thinks I'm going to greet him with a hug. *In his dreams.* And then I remember it's his birthday, and it's probably the least I can do.

I meet his hug, pat his back twice, and quickly separate my torso from his.

"Wow, you have got to be the world's worst hugger," he says with a belly laugh.

"Happy Birthday!" I say, grinning, and pull out a card from my crossbody purse. Before I can hand it to him, he snatches it from me. "So you bet on me showing up even though the chances weren't in your favor?"

"Well, it is because, selfishly, I was hoping you would." He glances up from the card in his hand to meet my eyes.

The softness in his expression lasts a moment before his eyes shoot back down to the card. *What the fuck was that?*

I promptly change the subject. "So, anyway, the gift card is from Chloe and I. She's, uh, preoccupied at the moment but wishes you a happy birthday."

I glance through the hall and see her straddling Dane's lap in the study near the fireplace. Her face is engulfing him, and he has his hands running through her hair. Seeing their PDA gives me a strange pang in my chest. *Is it disgust or envy?* I hope the former.

Isaac tears open the envelope and pulls out a green mermaid gift card. "Oh, coffee shop gift card, sweet, ya know I can always use those."

Isaac tries his best to force a genuine smile, but he knows it's a lame gift. He starts to lean in for another hug, but I pull back before he can.

"Hey, drinks in the kitchen?" I slowly step backward, motioning towards the double doors I'm hoping lead to the kitchen.

I think I catch a look of disappointment on Isaac's face that washes away in a split second.

"Yea, just through there, down the hall and through the dining room, we have like every kind of beer, some tequila, and mixers. Help yourself." He motions with his arm and bows like I'm a royal. "*Mi casa es su casa.*"

Unfortunately, the double doors do not lead to the kitchen. It opens to what looks to be an endless hallway going in both directions. I try to remember where Isaac said the kitchen was. *Was it the left or right?*

I decide to go right since I see more people sprawled along the walls in that direction. There are photos of the frat bros through the years along the wall and pairs of college students scattered throughout the hallway.

Word definitely got out that there was a party here. This is not a small gathering like Isaac suggested it would be. Each room I pass has students milling about. Some have already had way too much to drink. Others are hooking up or sitting in groups, talking. I can't say I recognize anyone here. I'd like to find the kitchen as quickly as possible, so I can have a drink to distract me from the lonely dread that is bubbling to the surface.

Finally, at the end of the hall is the giant kitchen. There seem to be twice as many people in the kitchen as in the living room, if that is even possible. I doubt Isaac invited all these people, let alone knows all these people here.

Two girls dressed in matching pink mini dresses sit on the kitchen island, flirting with two frat brothers. One guy stocks one of the two industrial fridges with Coke, White Claw, and various La Croix flavors, while two others argue about where to put all the beverages. In fact, this entire kitchen is a professional chef's dream.

Marble countertops blanket an island the size of a full-size bed. Two sinks, two fridges, two stoves, two microwaves, and two instant coffee machines are at the disposal of these forty frat dudes. I try to wiggle my way through the crowd to grab a watermelon La Croix before it gets shelved in the massive fridge, but a glacier of a guy steps in front of me, and I run into him like the *Titanic*. The familiar stench of men's body spray stings my nose.

Trey Roberts.

He towers over me uncomfortably. My gaze follows the buttons on his pastel floral shirt up to his slimy smirk. His icy blond hair flips over his forehead as he looks down at me. I'm considered taller than the average girl at five foot nine, but Trey, standing at six foot five, towers like a yeti in front of me. Suddenly all the memories I've tried to push toward the back of my head come rushing forward all at once.

My vision blurs as I think back to the first week of college. Isaac invited us to his first frat party. He was so excited, and we were happy to support him. The haze washes over me. I recall stepping foot in this exact house as Trey opens the door for me.

I'm dressed in my favorite blue metallic skater skirt and a twist-front crop top. He scans my body as I walked in, looking at my curvy figure like it's a sandwich board and he's about to choose which cheese he wants. Chloe gets pulled off to the side, and before I can follow her, Trey grabs my hand and whispers in my ear if I want a tour. Naively, I nod all doe-eyed and excited that I caught the attention of an upperclassman. Except it's not a tour. Except he doesn't explain what's on the glass display shelves. Except he doesn't tell me the history of the building. Except he doesn't show me the theater or gaming room.

Instead, he leads me directly into one of the executive rooms. His room. His private room is two floors above the party and away from the crowds of people. I'm caught a little off guard, but I don't want to come off as rude. He motions for me to sit on his bed with him.

So I do.

As I sit down, he grabs me by either side of my hips and brings me to his lap, where I immediately feel his hardness through his pants.

The horror must have blanketed my face as he laughs and says, "Oh, you must be a virgin."

I am.

I realize that I didn't put any boy shorts under my skirt, so the only thing separating me from him are a couple of thin layers of fabric. I try to squirm from his hold, but he starts to rock me against himself, moaning along, trying to coax me to relax. But I don't relax. I keep squirming and trying to push myself off of him. He doesn't relent and instead flips me around so my back is on his bed, and he's hovering over me. His wide chest puts me in a panic as I'm caged in. Thoughts race through my head.

Any girl would kill for his attention.

Shouldn't I love this?

Isn't this what I want?

A hot guy to find me attractive and make a move on me?

Except I don't feel that way. I feel gross and violated and desperate to be anywhere but this bedroom. In one panicked move, I scrunch my knees up and kick my feet against his chest, separating him from me. He cursed several profanities as he stumbled back to the other side of the bed. But I'm able to roll away and run to the door. I reach the hallway, and it's the most beautiful hallway I've ever seen. I never thought I'd get to see a hallway ever again.

I thought I'd be in that room, trapped under him forever. I sprint down the stairs and hear the door close behind me. He's following behind me fast. I quickly try to find Chloe and spot her drinking beer with Isaac and a few of his frat brothers. She sees my pleading eyes and rushes to my side. I'm about to tell her what happened when Trey appears behind me, reaching his arm across my waist. I immediately jolt away and push him off.

"Ahahaha, you crazy girl," he says as he smacks my ass.

I grab Chloe and leave the house immediately. Ten minutes, that's as long as we were in there. In the Uber, I broke down in tears, telling her everything.

A hand on my shoulder transports me back to reality, and I realize I'm breathing irregularly.

Once I see the hand on my shoulder belongs to Trey, I step back a foot and give him a glare. It's only been a few months since that incident so I've attended the self-defense classes the college offers, and I've developed a sharp tongue. But still, the hurt and the anxiety of his presence make me tense in place. I didn't report it because nothing happened. Or I guess something did happen, but I've convinced myself that no one would care. I was wearing a short skirt, and people would say I was asking for it. I was asking for a twenty-year-old guy to take advantage of a seventeen-year-old girl.

"Hey, sweetheart, it's been too long since I've seen your rosy cheeks around here. We should really rekindle our spark. You can make it up to me," he says while moving a strand of hair away from my face.

Stupid hair that never stays in place. I suddenly feel the need to shower away his touch.

"We never had a spark, Trey. You just forced yourself on me."

He finds my statement amusing because his smile rises, and a breathy chuckle comes out of his mouth. He steps forward, reaching for my arm, but I step back and knock into someone behind me. I realize I made him spill his drink on his shirt. I'm about to apologize profusely until I realize who I bumped into.

I'd never forget those green multicolored eyes swirled around like marbles. Shining and twinkling with each blink. The tan skin spreads across his nose because he spends too much time outside and doesn't wear a strong enough SPF. His pine tree and musk smell comforts me and transports me to a safe place. I could never forget Reid Parker. And right now, even though he's the reason I swore off love at age 12, he might also be the thing to save me from the wrath of Trey.

Reid turns around with his bushy eyebrows scrunched like he's annoyed by my presence. He meets my eyes, and his irritated expression seems to wash away.

"*Honey,*" I say dramatically. "There you are. Oops, I didn't mean to spill your drink. Let's get you another."

I sense Reid is picking up on the way my eyes are boring into him, trying to tell him to play long.

He seems to get it because he responds with a soft shrug, "Oh, hun, it's all right. This beer sucks anyway. Do you think there's any watermelon La Croix left?" I nearly swoon that he would pick the same flavor. *What is going on with me right now?* I must be off my game because of Trey.

Reid looks over at Trey, extending his hand, and says, "Hey man, I'm Reid, this cutie's boyfriend. If she's not causing you trouble, we'll be heading to the fridge."

Trey shakes his hand, narrowing his gaze between me and Reid, not completely believing us, but I can tell he's losing interest.

"See ya, sweetheart. I'm sure our paths will cross again." And he turns away, but not before giving my ass a squeeze.

Scum of the earth. Great, now I have to burn my shorts.

I grin at Reid, trying not to look into his eyes in fear I'll be hypnotized. "Hey, sorry, and thank you and sorry."

I can feel his gaze across my face, scanning my features. He tilts his head as he looks at me like he's trying to solve a riddle about my eyes and lips. "I know you, don't I?"

"Ya, I'm your girlfriend, duh," I joke terribly and nudge his side with my elbow.

He smiles back at me, the corners of his eyes curling up with the corners of his mouth just like they did when we were kids. *Oh god, I'm weak.*

"Hahaha, no, no, we went to school together, wait, it will come to me....Anni? Right? It's me, Reid. Reid Parker."

Oh, I know who you are.

I nearly melt into a puddle at the fact that he not only remembers my name but my nickname. I shake an embarrassing grin across my face and nod.

"Yeah, it's me, Anni...or Annika. I go by either, really," I say, avoiding looking him in the eyes.

"Wow, you look so different but also the same. You have the same haircut," he says as he takes a finger and runs it along the bottom of my hair, flipping it out when he gets to the end.

He gazes down. I fidget as I'm very aware of Reid quickly scanning my outfit and stopping at my feet. "Hey, I'm wearing the same pair."

I meet his gaze at our feet and see he is wearing the exact same white high-top Converse. His are more scuffed than mine, and he has little doodles on the toe caps. I smile at the thought of him scribbling on them as he's bored in class or just because he wants them to be different. As I look up, I take the time to examine the rest of his outfit. He wears dark wash jeans cuffed at the hem just above the top of the Converse. On top, he has a blue and gray striped T-shirt that has a shallow V-neck at the collar. It's not tight, but it's fitted so his shoulders and pecs are slightly defined through the fabric.

I try not to hold my gaze too long at his shoulders, but my mouth betrays me, and I say, "You've gotten bigger."

Are you kidding me right now?

I immediately fly my hand up to my mouth, fearing what might come out of it next. I can feel my face getting hot. Reid's eyes sparkle at this comment, and he laughs in response.

"Yahhh, I grew a few inches since eighth grade. Thank goodness, too. I always wanted to be taller than you."

Which he is now, but only by a few inches. I don't have to strain my neck to look up at him. He's the perfect height. Not that I'd ever admit that to anyone.

"Hey, do you wanna get out of this kitchen and play ping-pong in the other room?" He throws his thumb behind him to an open room with fewer people.

"I would love nothing more," I say, following him to the great room.

He grabs my hand as we swerve through the crowd, and it feels like my hand might burst into flames. I feel tingles from the tips of my fingers through my arm. I'm so confused right now. On the one hand, I want to follow Chloe's advice and date around, but on the other hand, I don't know if I'm ready for all of that. Freshman year is kicking my butt. It's so much harder than high school was, and I feel like I'm barely treading water to stay afloat. We snake around the crowd, Reid's hand grasped firmly around mine. As soon as we make it past the herd of people, he releases my hand, and I miss the warmth.

We play three rounds of ping-pong, talking the entire time, catching up on memories from elementary and middle school. I also discover that Reid is alarmingly good at ping-pong. He beats me in almost every game, but I'm in the lead this time. Although he might be easing up a bit.

He tells me all the places he went after he left Ojai. From Ojai, he and his dad moved to Colorado, to Florida, and then to Northern

California. I can't help but imagine how exhausting that all sounds to move so many times before graduating high school.

When he was a senior in high school, he reconnected with Isaac online and found out they both got accepted to UCSD. He studies biology and wants to work as a physical therapist one day. He tells me how that's what his uncle does and will intern during summers at the wellness center he runs, so it was a no-brainer. It sounds like he's pursuing a degree in something he actually wants to do in life. I wonder what that feels like.

I feel brave enough to admit something to him after making him lose a point because a guy knocked into the table, making Reid miss the shot, which means I finally win a game. I pump up my fists in victory.

I pause before starting a new game, looking at him. "Promise you won't laugh."

"I can never promise you that," he says with a devilish grin.

I squint my eyes and proceed reluctantly, not sure what has gotten into me to admit this. "It's just funny to run into you because I never thought I'd ever see you again, and I had a little crush on you in middle school."

I try to say it casually, intentionally leaving out the fact that the crush actually started in fourth grade, resulting in a three-year-long infatuation.

His whole face curls up in a smile, and he says something that would make my seventh-grade self collapse on the floor.

"Well, maybe the feeling was mutual."

I finally look him in the eyes and feel sick to my stomach from the constant flutters.

I look away and feel my cheeks get hot, preparing to serve to start the next game until Reid interrupts.

"Let's make this next round a bit more interesting," he says with a wicked smile. "If I win, you go on a date with me."

My legs almost give out, but I pretend I'm cool as a cucumber and ponder his request as I put my finger on my chin like I'm thinking hard about his question.

"And what do I get if I win?"

"Whatever you want." *All I've ever wanted is you. Did I really just say that in my head? Or did I say that out loud? Oh god, he's staring at me.*

"Okay, if I win, you give me your sunglasses." I noticed his pair of high-end aviators in his pocket earlier when I was scanning his body.

He gives me that wicked smirk again and says, "Deal."

EIGHT

REID

I DIDN'T EVEN WANT to come to this party. I told Isaac it wasn't my thing, frat parties. People stacked on top of each other, drinking too much, music too loud, and not enough food. I know I sound like a forty-five-year-old dad, but it just isn't something I look forward to, which is why I didn't join a fraternity in the first place. I am happy with my quiet freshman dorm room, with my quiet roommate, who is hardly ever there, and a big window overlooking a courtyard with a dolphin fountain in the center. I could have been in my room, studying for an exam on Monday, ordering a pepperoni and mushroom pizza, and having reruns of *That 70's Show* playing in the background. Thank god I decided to go to this party.

If I stayed in my room all night, I would have missed the opportunity to run into a girl I went to middle school with and who I had a massive crush on. My eyes always seemed to find her around school and loved the feisty comments she'd reply with. I moved to Ojai during my fifth-grade year, which was a tough year to adjust because it was in the middle of elementary school. Everyone already had their best friends and inside jokes. They knew where the bathrooms were and how to get to the cafeteria for assemblies.

I was used to it at that point. My dad was a salesman and was always moving us around wherever he landed a new gig. My dad, Sean Parker, my twin if I was thirty years older, has the same light brown hair and tan skin as I do, except he wears his hair clean and short. He's my best friend. It's always been the two of us. My mom passed away giving birth to me, so I never had a mom figure in my life. Just my dad, and he did everything to support and love me as much as two parents could. Even though he transferred jobs often, he tried his best to help me adjust. We were never in the same spot for longer than a few years at a time. To this day, I struggle with the fact that no place feels like home.

It was annoying, but just part of the life of living with a single father trying to pay the bills. He worked hard and always taught me to keep hustling, keep going after my goal, and never stop going after what I truly want. All I wanted as a kid was to find a place to call home and live there for more than three years at a time. It wasn't until I was about to leave for college that we finally found that place.

In my senior year of high school, we moved to Northern California, and he seemed to finally settle down there. He started dating a woman at the company he worked for, and she moved in with us, Pam Westfield. Pam is a shy woman, no taller than five feet, and makes the best desserts I've had in my entire life. She dresses in soft colors and smells like hyacinths. She makes my dad the happiest I've ever seen, and I am happy he has her since I left for San Diego.

This past holiday break, I took a quick plane ride up there to see them. Pam started an herb garden in the backyard, and my dad is taking up yoga. It's the best feeling to see them thrive. My dad mentioned to me that he is ready to pop the question to Pam, and I couldn't be happier for him. I believe that's all he truly wanted in life since my mom passed, to find *the one* and have a home.

San Diego is a dream so far. The sun is bright and warm, which makes people smile more. I give a big grin and wave to people as they pass, even if I have no clue who they are. I was stoked to learn

Isaac also got accepted here. Though it had been a while since we went to school together, we were great friends. He was the first kid to talk to me when I moved to Ojai. I was sitting alone at the edge of the playground, and he walked over to say he wanted me to be on his team for kickball. We played every recess that entire year. We'd go to movie premieres together, build ramps for our bikes outside his house, and my dad even took us fishing one weekend. When we started at UCSD, we picked up our friendship like no time passed. It's the great thing about friendship. You can go years without seeing someone and just naturally drift apart. Then one day, reconnect and pick up where you left off.

That same nostalgic feeling hits me as I play ping-pong with Annika. Seeing this old friend's face brings me so much comfort. Like when you rediscover a blanket you had as a kid or drinking out of your favorite mug. Chipped and faded but no other mug can compare to the familiarity it brings.

She always brought a smile to my face when we were young. She didn't even have to look at me, just seeing her would make me blush and stare a bit too long at times. I reminisced about the first time I saw her when I moved to Ojai. I was playing kickball with Isaac when the ball rolled off to the jungle gym. I ran over and retrieved the ball and saw her climbing the monkey bars. She flew across like she'd done it a million times. Her short hair braided into two French braids on either side and patchwork overalls gave her the cutest tomboy look. She jumped off as a first grader waved down at her. She gave him a hug and helped tie his shoes. I thought that was so sweet and something you never saw, older kids interacting with the younger ones. I later learned that was her little brother, but I still found the action tugging at my heart.

A week later, I saw her flying across the same monkey bars when a Caleb, a mean kid from my class pushed her off as he jumped on the other side. She flew down to her knees and put her hands on the bark chips. Without thinking, I ran over and helped her up. She stared at me without saying a word, and I got a good look at her dark eyes and the watercolor of freckles that danced along her nose and cheeks. I grabbed her hand and helped her up. She had bark chips in her hair, so I reached over and brushed them out. As I turned to leave, she yelled after me.

"Hey! What's your name?"

I turned to hear that raspy little bark call after me and responded, "Reid Parker. What's yours?"

"Annika Gomes," she said as she stood up confidently, brushing the rest of the chips off her clothes.

"Nice to meet you, Annika Gomes," I said to her, and before I turned away, I made a mental bookmark of the way she looked at me.

Her eyes narrowed, and a sideways smirk appeared on her lips. Her braids flipping out at her shoulders, and the knees on her overalls scuffed up. She was cute as a button without even trying, and she probably would kick me in the shins if she knew I called her cute.

In middle school, we had gym during the same period, and it was my favorite hobby to say *hi* to Annika whenever I saw her. I loved seeing her flush and light up when she said hi to me back. Occasionally I'd pass her in the hall and wave to her, ask her how she was doing, complement the outfit she was wearing, or just give her a smile. I intentionally would try to sit near her during assemblies or talk to her whenever I could because I had the fattest crush but was too chicken to do anything about it. Until they announced the spring dance at the end of April before Spring Break.

I decided I would work up the courage to ask her to the dance with me. I started making her a card and planned to pick flowers from my neighbor's garden to give her. Things were lining up, and I was starting to settle in, which is usually when my Dad uproots us to start over again. I never got to ask her to the dance, and I left without saying anything to her, not even goodbye. I figured I'd never see her again.

I keep shaking my head, thinking I'm dreaming. It seems surreal that she ran into me at this frat party and is playing ping-pong across from me now. She still wears that mischievous smirk across those rosy lips, but that is about the only thing the same as she was when she was twelve. She's sprouted at least five more inches and has curves that my eyes are drawn to. Her hips fill out around her jeans, and a soft stomach meets her full chest. The halter top she's wearing dips low on her back, which I am fighting for my life from running my fingers along. She's got a couple of little daisies drawn on either side of her cheeks.

Her hair is no longer in braided pigtails but chopped to a blunt black chin-length bob that she's been threading her fingers through the entire time we've been playing. Each time she lifts her hand to flip her hair, I have to will myself from collapsing to the floor. I am baffled at how stunning she is. Her dark eyes ooze with confidence. Eyes that she squints as she is focused on the ping-pong as I casually tap it over the net. There is no way she is winning this game. I played tennis all through high school and ping-pong might as well be an arcade game for me. Besides, according to history, I've been waiting to ask her out for six years now.

Game point, and I ace her with my serve. I can't help but have the biggest, goofiest smile wash over my face as I look over at her in victory.

"Well, well. Looks like we're going out. I'm thinking…picnic? At a park…no! At the beach. Or perhaps we get coffee first." I casually saunter over to her, tapping on my chin as I picture the perfect first date.

She is glaring at me, but I think I see her trying hard to hide her grin. "All right, fine, Parker, you win fair and square."

"Parker? We've got to get back on a first-name basis." I reach out to flip the end of her hair again. I can't help it, I am obsessed with her flippy hair style. And her.

Just as I'm about to ask her what her favorite food is, an uproar emerges from the kitchen as I see Isaac being carried on the shoulders of his frat brothers. I have no interest in figuring out what the hell is going on and lean down to Annika's ear. Goosebumps rise on my neck at my proximity to her.

"Hey, let's head to the backyard." Pointing toward the screen door, she nods, looking equally as uncomfortable with the commotion.

I get the chance to gently place my hand at her back, guiding her through the crowd that stormed in through the great room, heading toward the kitchen. Her skin is warm, and goosebumps surface on her back as my fingers touch her. *Hmm, interesting.* I'm holding back from running my hand around her waist and instead hold the back door open as she steps through.

Unlike the house, the backyard is quiet and serene. The house is close enough to the beach that you can hear the waves crash against the sand in the distance. We make our way to a bench at the corner of the yard under a big oak tree. The backyard has party lights strung along the fences providing soft ambient light. I take my place beside Annika, leaving about an inch between us. I saw the way that creepy frat dude tried to make a move on her and how uncomfortable she was that she used me to avoid him. I don't want to scare her away like he did. I need to remember to ask her about that whole situation later.

"So." I gaze over at her, smiling and taking in her perfume. She smells like woodsy roses. "What should we get for our picnic on the beach lunch?"

She side-eyes me. "Hmm, not sure. Although I'm expecting our food to be covered in sand."

"You need to have more faith in my beach picnic abilities." I scoot a half-inch closer. "I'll bring an extra-large blanket, a basket to keep the food safe, lots of napkins, and wet wipes. I'll even bring your favorite drink, which is…" Raising my eyebrows, I close the last half inch until our knees are touching.

I see her glance down at the spot and wonder if it's tingling for her like it is for me.

"I like water," she delivers in all seriousness, and I almost roll off the bench laughing. *"What?* My mom didn't let me drink soda, so I actually love a nice cup of ice water!"

"You are a mystery to me, Annika Gomes." I don't restrain my hand as I reach up to tuck a strand of hair that is falling forward behind her ear.

She holds my gaze, and I notice those goosebumps trailing up her shoulders. If I wasn't mistaken, I think the warmth I feel being near her is mutual.

Still holding my gaze, she says softly, "Well then, surprise me, food, drinks, everything."

I lean in and say, "I can't wait to surprise you."

She keeps her eyes locked on mine, but as I lean in closer, they venture down to my lips. I lick my bottom lip, and I can nearly feel her breath as she tips her head up to me just before we hear a blood-curdling scream.

Annika clearly knows the person connected to the scream because she shoots up and darts toward the house and leaves me, comically falling on the bench where she was just sitting. She turns back at me, her eyes in a panic, and without words, I jog over beside her as we make our way back inside the house.

Once inside, Annika grabs my wrist and pulls me with her through the crowd until we reach the other end of the scream. It's been a while, but just as I recognize Annika, I recognize her best friend Chloe kneeling on the floor, holding a pair of Birkenstocks covered in some green liquid. Maybe I wouldn't recognize her separately, but Annika and Chloe were always a pair and looked like they couldn't leave each other's sides. She looks absolutely distraught, and to my surprise, Annika kneels down on the floor with her.

I'm half expecting her to tell Chloe she's overreacting, but instead, Annika grabs a napkin on the counter and helps her wipe the goo off, peeling the sandals out of Chloe's grip. She tells her something that softens Chloe's face immediately. I'm entranced by Annika's ability to quickly grasp and relax the situation. Chloe stands up and goes over to a guy with a dark tan and bleach blond hair who cradles Chloe in his arms. Annika tosses the napkins, gives a glare to the crowd staring at the commotion, and turns back to me, looking apologetic.

"Hey, I'm sorry, but I gotta head out. Chloe is a wreck."

"It's all good, but hey, you owe me a date." I smile, pulling out my phone and handing it to her.

I see her eyes light up ever so slightly as she punches in her number. She gives it back and stands there for a moment. I debate giving her a hug, but before I can choose, she gives me a quick wave and dashes off to meet up with Chloe and the tan guy. I make a silent prayer that years won't go by before I see her again.

NINE

ANNIKA

I GLANCE over at the clock on my nightstand.

12:34 am

Chloe is sleeping on her twin bed, tangled in the full-size comforter. She spent the rest of the night scrubbing her Birkenstocks, trying to get out the liquified Jell-O that spilled on them before knocking out from all the emotional distress. A part of me is upset that she ruined the moment I was having with Reid in the backyard, and another part of me is mad at myself for being mad that the moment was ruined. *What was I thinking?* I didn't want to fall in love with a boy. And I'm clearly falling for him already. We only started college five months ago. I have years to have fun, flirt and have flings.

I can hear Chloe's voice reverberating inside my head, *"Have fun, date around."* I'm not supposed to be engulfed by a herd of butterflies when a boy tucks a piece of my hair behind my ear. I lay in my bed wide awake, replaying the events in my head and comparing Reid now to the Reid I was so love-struck with as a kid. He is still the goofy, bright Reid I've always had the pleasure of interacting with. Except now, he's a man. A man with muscles and a hot haircut. A smile that whisks me off into a delusional fantasy. I yearn to be closer to him.

In fact, I know more about him now in the time we played ping-pong than in the entire years in school together. I think it's the longest conversation we've ever had. I have this creeping doubt about all of this. I hope it was all a mirage and he doesn't text me. I don't know if this is the right thing to do.

As if I gave the universe a sign, my phone buzzes. I hesitate, staring at it on my nightstand. I should be asleep. I force my eyes closed, ignoring the notification that pops up on my screen. I know it's a text because of the type of buzz. I have specific alerts set for texts and calls, such as, when my mom calls, it's the same sound as a car alarm because if I don't answer, my mom gives me a hard time about it for a week. I am doing a terrible job of ignoring the buzz. I feel the vibration in my head *Buzzz bzz*, and imagine what the text says. Maybe it isn't from Reid. Maybe it's Aimee checking in on Chloe. Or maybe it's my hair salon sending a reminder. I can't stand it anymore and reach over to my phone and yank the charger cord out, tucking myself under my comforter so the brightness doesn't wake Chloe.

UNKNOWN

Hi :)

Oh, it's Reid by the way

U know? Ping Pong champ?

I catch the smile that floods my face after scanning the messages. *Relax Anni.*

I add his contact to my phone, and before I start typing back, another message comes in.

REID

Shoot, I just realized how late it is. I'm totally not thinking about you and can't sleep because of it. Nope.

The feeling is mutual.

ANNIKA

Good thing I'm awake trying to plot my ping-pong revenge

REID

Revenge? I won fair and square. Don't try to back out now. I have the perfect beach planned for our date :]

Stupid butterflies, you are not welcome here.

ANNIKA

Which beach? Please tell me it's PB, I love the chill tides

REID

Chill tides? Lmao, are you a hot surfer too?

Omg did he call me hot?

ANNIKA

Haha, no. I just like walking out to the water. I do my best thinking when my legs are at least six inches submerged in ocean water

REID

Well, ur in luck because I've picked the best spot on PB to split a veggie sandwich while sippin' on ice teas.

I have to admit, that sounds like an awesome time. Eh, what's the harm in going on one date with him? I'm probably just feeling shortness of breath and chills because I caught some bug at the party. I peek out from the comforter to check on Chloe. She's still zonked out. *Buzzz bzz*

> **REID**
> let me know if i'm too much, i'm just...

> **ANNIKA**
> ur wut?

> **REID**
> Promise you won't laugh at me?

> **ANNIKA**
> I can never promise you that >:)

> **REID**
> ahah touche
>
> Do you remember before I moved away? Seventh grade before spring break?

I contemplate whether I admit knowing the exact moment I found out. After spring break, going to school and seeing his chair in history class empty. It matched the hole that was left in my heart.

> **ANNIKA**
> yeahhh, I think so

> **REID**
> Well, i was going to ask u to the spring dance. I made a card and everything.

And with that text, I melt into my bed. That's it. I'm here forever now. How could I go on existing after learning the boy I had a massive crush on was about to ask me to the dance? I can't help but picture my twelve-year-old self and how elated I would have been. I might have peed my pants from equal parts excitement and nerves. And now here I am, eighteen and curled up in my dorm bed texting the same boy, except now he's a tall man that smells like evergreen trees and has eyes that undress me with one look.

REID

don't block my number lmao

i'm embarrassed, forget what I said, just delete my number, forget i exist, k bye

ANNIKA

No no! It's okay, i'm just processing

REID

...

ANNIKA

Do u still have the card?

REID

:[no, i think it got lost in one of the many moves

ANNIKA

for what it's worth, I would have said yes

Who am I right now? Where did all this charm come from? Reid just brings something out of me. I don't feel weird admitting to him something that is so vulnerable. Although, I am tempted to throw my phone across the room so I don't see his reply. *Buzzz bzz*

REID

I'm glad you said yes again.

THE SUN WAKES me up as it creeps through the cracks in our window shades. Chloe is already up and in the bathroom. I can hear her humming a song to herself. Then I remember what happened yesterday, and I immediately lunge for my phone and read the last texts again, noticing another came in after I fell asleep.

REID

I'm glad you said yes again.

Do you want to get some coffee tomorrow morning?

It was real. It actually happened. Reid admitted that he had a crush on me in middle school too, and now we are going to have a romantic beach date on Saturday and a coffee date tomorrow. Tomorrow? Did I really agree to *two* dates already? Panic fills my brain as I try to figure out what to wear and how to do my makeup. Despite having a full week until our date, it's all I think about now. I fling myself out of bed and pace over to the bathroom, where Chloe is braiding her waist-length hair.

"Reid Parker asked me out." I don't have time for good mornings.

Her eyes bug out, and she drops her hair tie to the floor, letting the braid loosen. "What? Who? When? How? When? Who?" she says, swinging her head from side to side.

"Okay, you're broken. Let me explain."

I tell Chloe every detail from last night. How he saved me from Trey and beat me in ping-pong. How he was centimeters away from my face before I heard her screaming, which she profusely apologized for. I told her everything and even reluctantly told her how I'm excited but not sure I should be.

"You were there, Chloe. I was heartbroken when he moved. I vowed to never love again."

"Yah, but you were twelve and overly dramatic. Give it a chance. It's one date. You'll at least get a free meal out of it."

"You're right, but also, what if I fall in *love*? I mean, I practically loved him once already. I don't know if I have time for that! I'm already behind in two of my classes. Besides, you told me to play the field. I'm freaking out!" I dramatically fall on my bed.

Chloe lets out a little laugh. "Hey, crazy lady, it's one date. Cool it. Plus, you are having a coffee first. You can always back out after. Besides, you are doing what you wanted, going out on dates. Go out with Reid, then move along," Chloe says as she sits next to me, petting my head.

"Something tells me it's not going to be that easy with Reid." I take a pillow and squish it against my face.

"You are the most dramatic person I know. Have I mentioned that before?" she says.

"At least once a week," I say, tossing the pillow up at her.

MY MONDAY MORNING class ends at nine-thirty, so I'm going to be terribly early for my coffee date with Reid. Is it even a date? It sounded more like a coordinated run-in. I kept my outfit casual today, flared ripped jeans with a loose band T-shirt. My hair is braided into pigtails on either side. I can't be bothered to try on Mondays, even if I'm about to see my childhood crush again. Except for my eyeliner, I always have time to do a winged eyeliner look.

The coffee shop is one of the three the campus has spread around. One is by my dorm, where Dane works, another is by the sciences buildings, and the third is near the main entrance and student bookstore. The inside is a simple scheme of dark wood with green accents, just like the other campus cafes. A few students are sitting at the tables, working on their laptops. There are some armchairs by the windows where a couple is chatting. I stand in line, looking at the menu, despite knowing exactly what I'm going to order.

"Fancy seeing you here," a deep, raspy voice says to me, coating me in warmth.

I turn and see Reid standing in front of me in the flesh and not a figment of my imagination. He's wearing dark wash jeans and a faded red *Nirvana* band T-Shirt. It's as if we coordinated on outfits.

"Are you following me, Parker?" I tease him and nudge his side.

He laughs and scans my face, so I quickly do the same now that we are in the daylight. Even as years passed, he didn't cease to make my nerves tickle, my center ache, and my breathing uneasy. It's probably just my crush resurfacing, that's all. Nothing more than that.

"What are you ordering?" He breaks my gaze and looks at the menu.

"An oat chai latte with a shot of espresso and one pump of caramel syrup," I list off with no hesitation. It's my favorite drink, so why change something I already like?

"Wow, you know exactly what you want," says Reid. I wish I could treat my life like my coffee order.

"What about you Reid?"

"Back on a first-name basis already?" He pumps his arm in victory, which I shake my head at. "I get a cold brew with whipped cream on top."

"Whipped cream?"

"Don't knock it 'till you try it."

WE QUIETLY WAIT for our drinks and then wander over to a table at the corner of the coffee shop. As much as I'd like to say our banter picked up where we left off as kids, we've always been a bit awkward and shy around each other. At least I was, always in fear my crush would be discovered.

Reid breaks the silence. "Can I ask you something? If you don't feel comfortable answering, that's cool."

"Sure, go ahead, ask away."

"Why did you use me as a human shield against that frat bro? I mean, it's not like I didn't enjoy seeing the defeat on his face, but I've just been curious about that."

I take a deep breath.

"Wow, that bad, huh?" Reid jokes.

I smile. "I had a bad experience the first time I went to a frat party there. Trey Roberts, or the yeti as I call him, took me to his room and tried to hook up with me, but I pushed him away. I was in there for like five minutes," I say, trying to brush off the subject.

Reid's face scrunches up. "That's really shitty."

"It was nothing, really."

"It doesn't really sound like *nothing*. Plus, you used a strange guy to save you from interacting with him."

"You're not a stranger."

"Well, not anymore, I guess. If he ever tries to come on to you again, you call me." Chills trail down my back as Reid's tone turns protective.

"Are you going to be my knight in dirty Converse again?" I try to flash my most damsel-in-distress look his way.

He laughs and says, "I never realized how much I've missed you. How do you like San Diego so far?" *Did he say he missed me?*

"It's too hot here. I feel like I'm melting as soon as I step outside. But I do love the proximity to the ocean."

"Right, right, it's where you do some of your best thinking." I blush at him, remembering our late-night text exchange.

"Yeah, I'd say the ocean is my equivalent to a confessional. I go when I just need a breather, some time to think."

"You're only eighteen. What are you carrying that's so heavy?"

I let out another sigh because he points out something I keep trying to remind myself. I'm so young, so why does it feel like I'm putting pressure on my life to be perfect? I never know which is the right path to go, and I'm waiting for the day it will suddenly click.

Instead, I say, "School is stressing me out right now. I just hope I made the right decision with my major."

"You can always switch. What other majors are you thinking of?"

"That's just it. I have no clue. Nothing really is making me excited. I feel like this is all just something I have to do." Well, I've officially killed the mood. Reid's eyes scan the table then he grabs his coffee, lifting it to his mouth and meeting my eyes before taking a sip. I swallow my breath.

"If you could travel anywhere, where would you go?" Reid asks, changing the topic and saving me from downward spiraling.

"I think it would be cool to backpack through Europe, try different foods, and hear all the different languages. It would be a fun adventure, and I feel like I wouldn't be tied to anything. I could just roam."

"I was thinking of actually signing up to study abroad next year. I'd love to explore other countries."

For some reason, my stomach drops at the thought of Reid leaving again. We barely just reconnected, yet I want to hold him down so he doesn't drift away.

The rest of the coffee date is simple and peaceful, which is just what I need. If every date was like this, maybe I would date more. No pressure, just a simple chit-chat. It's different with Reid. I keep flipping through our memories like reruns in my head as we talk. My class at 11:30 cuts our discussion short, but we confirm beach plans for Saturday at noon. Walking to my class, I notice the soft flutters in my gut that haven't left since I ran into Reid at that party.

THE REST of the week couldn't have gone any slower. As each day passed, I changed my outfit idea for the date. Chloe keeps telling me I am overthinking it all and to let it be *casual*. She does the motion with her arms and shoulders, replicating a wave every time she says it. I think of all the scenarios of how the date can go and have three text drafts canceling it completely.

Reid texted me throughout the week, saying things like "Good Morning" and "Have a great day!" and even sent me a photo of his view from his dorm room. I was tempted to wander around campus until I found that dolphin fountain. A part of me wants this to be a casual date like Chloe suggested, but a bigger part of me has wanted this since I was twelve years old; to go on another date with Reid Parker. A beach date even!

My alarm on my phone blares as I reach to turn it off.

7:00 a.m.

Today is the day. I feel like I'm going to hurl. Our dorm room is still dark, and I could sleep in. The date isn't until midday. I can't sleep in anticipation of it all. I could barely fall asleep last night. I'm about to go on a date with my middle school crush. How often does that even happen? That doesn't happen to normal people like me, and yet here I am, lying in bed, already reconsidering what I should wear today.

It's early February, so not the postcard beach weather that you see in magazines, but it's also San Diego, so it rarely dips below sixty-five degrees. I check my weather app: seventy-two degrees and sunny. I stare into my closet for five minutes before settling on a pair of loose pants and a fitted T-shirt with my oversized denim jacket on top. Knowing me, I'll probably end up changing two more times before the date. But before I can function, I need caffeine.

THE NEAREST CAMPUS coffee shop is unusually quiet this morning, and then I remember it's seven a.m. on a Saturday. Only three baristas are working today, one of them being Chloe's fling she's seeing, Dane. Unfortunately, we are not that close yet, so I do not get the advantage of the free drinks that he always treats her to.

Dane holds up a cup, and I can sense it belongs to me. "Ah-nick-a?" A pause. "Ann-eeka?"

"Hi-yah, thanks, that's me, also hi, Dane, you know me, you are dating my roommate. And you know how to pronounce my name,"

I say a little too sassy, but it gets annoying quickly when people have a hard time saying my name.

"Uh, do I? Sorry if you're hitting on me. I already got a lady."

Is this guy for real? Did he even hear what I said? I don't know which to feel, disgusted that he thinks of me correcting him as flirtation or pride that he already is exclusively dating Chloe.

"Yeah, your *lady* is my best friend. I'm her *roommate,* Annika." I try to make myself clear, but he's barely paying attention.

"Ohhh, right, sure. Anyway, enjoy your chai latte with oat milk, extra hot with a shot of espresso and one pump of caramel syrup."

I force a grin out and try not to flush at my embarrassingly long order, but all of that shame melts away at the first sip. *Goddamn,* that's good stuff.

CHLOE IS awake by the time I come back to the room. Before I left the coffee shop, Dane waved me over to give Chloe a hazelnut latte, which she nearly rips out of my hand upon entry into our room.

"Isn't he the absolute sweetest!" Chloe says, cozying up in her blankets. Only her head and one arm is poking out so she can sip her latte.

"Actually, he's not that bad, although he didn't even recognize me. I've met him like five times already."

"Anni, you know he's a surfer, so he's always falling into the ocean. I'm sure his brain gets scrambled around, so what does it matter if he forgets he meets people once in a while?"

I shrug it off and head to the bathroom to get ready. I don't have to leave for another three hours, but I can't wait to get ready anymore. I've reread my text conversations with Reid probably four times now and made myself sufficiently nervous for this date. This is my first date in college that feels special and wildly important. Like it will set the tone for how the rest of my college dating experience will go.

Since I have so much time, I decide to do my ten-step skincare routine in hopes it will relax me. There's just something about rubbing serums and creams on my face that alleviates any problem I may be having just a teensy bit. I finish off my morning routine by running a flatiron through my hair and dotting some lip gloss on. Except…what if he tries to kiss me and then sees I'm wearing lip gloss and changes his mind? No lip gloss. Let's go with a strawberry-flavored lip balm that Chloe got me for my birthday last year. She says it isn't the same as her lip balm, but I think it still smells good.

I step out of the bathroom and check my phone. I've been in there for two hours, *whoops*. Hopefully, no one else needed to use the mirror.

"How do I look?" I ask, striking a pose for Chloe, who is lying upside down on her bed reading a fashion magazine.

She sits up and gives me a quick one-over. "You look stunning, as always, and frankly, it's annoying."

I roll my eyes because I can say the same for her. "It's about a fifteen-minute drive to the beach, plus trying to find parking, so I'm heading out now. Please tell me it will go great."

"It will be better than you expect. And remember, be *casual*." She says the last line while moving her hand like a wave.

I don't think I'll ever be capable of being casual.

TRAFFIC WASN'T LONG ENOUGH. I was hoping it would be backed up so badly that I would miss this date. I'm so nervous, and I hate to say it but maybe excited? What if he tries to kiss me again? I'm too weak in his presence. I'm just going to melt upon the smallest touch. I'm in deep shit. I park my car and start walking out to the pier.

I can see Reid standing at the pier. His arms are at the edge as he is leaning over, looking down at the water. He looks deep in thought, and I almost don't want to disturb him. I want to take his picture, but that's probably weird, right? Eh, I'm going to do it, anyway. I try to be discreet and take a quick picture. It's weird to put it as my phone wallpaper, right? Yeah, definitely weird.

Is it too late to turn around and leave? Right when I think that, he stands up and looks over at me. *Damn, I've been spotted.* I somehow manage to get my legs to move and walk over to meet him, ready to live the date my childhood self has always fantasized about.

TEN

REID

I AM no expert in date planning but this date is going great so far, and Annika hasn't even shown up yet. I slept great last night and woke up just after eight and walked to the coffee shop a few dorms down from me. I saw that guy who Annika's friend, Chloe, is dating there. I gave him a big wave that was met with a blank stare. I picked up veggie sandwiches from this great walk-up sandwich spot near the beach and laid out the spread of goodies over a couple of blankets.

Even though it's a little cooler today, the sun is out, and the beach isn't too crowded. I decide to walk up to the pier to wait for Annika so she can see me when she arrives. Nothing is worse than meeting up with someone and having to look frantically for where they are. I was too excited and might have got here an hour early. But apparently, Annika was too because I see her walking towards me a half hour before noon.

She's quite possibly the coolest person I've ever met. She's wearing an oversized denim jacket and big sunglasses. She saunters over to me and pushes her sunglasses up on her head, pushing her hair back. She has little black flicks on her eyes and rosy cheeks.

She is taking her sweet time walking to me. "Hurry up before

90

the seagulls eat our food!" I shout over to her and then decide to just jog toward her.

"I thought you said you were a professional beach picnic goer? You should know how to wrangle a seagull."

"I never said such a thing. But don't fret. The food should be safe in the picnic basket." We stand about a foot apart, just looking at each other for a full minute. "I'm glad you actually showed up." I interrupt the silence. "I was worried you'd cancel on me."

"I may have drafted a few cancellation texts, but I couldn't pass up a veggie sandwich on the beach." She rewards me with a little half-smirk.

Motioning over to the stairs to the sand, I say, "Shall we?" And kick off my sandals.

I jog over to the spot I picked to make sure the blankets haven't shifted since I laid them out. It's the perfect distance from the water so we could dip our toes in, but not too far, so we can keep an eye on our things. I plop down next to the picnic basket, enjoying the view of Annika walking over. Her breezy cotton pants make her look like a goddess floating over to me. I can tell she is examining my setup as she picks a spot on the other blanket.

If I'm being honest with myself, the date is starting off a bit slowly. We eat the sandwiches and exchange a little chit-chat. She's studying marketing, and I get the idea it's probably not her favorite thing. I wonder if I've just hyped up this moment in my head too much. I wanted it to be perfect, and maybe that is ruining the vibe.

"Can I ask you a random question?" Annika says to me as she's finishing up her lunch, interrupting my intrusive thoughts.

"Of course," I say, clapping my hands to dust off sandwich crumbs. "Ask me all the random questions."

"If the zoo was giving away an animal, what animal would you take? All supplies included." She leans in, squinting a little. I can tell there's a wrong answer to this question.

"Penguin," I say with zero hesitation.

"Ahh, that's a good answer, small, cute. Probably cuddly." I can't help but smile at her analyzing my answer in depth.

"What about you? What would you take?" I'm guessing she's going to say some cat.

"A baby giraffe." She's clearly answered this question before because she doesn't miss a beat.

I can't help but laugh at her response. "An interesting choice. Definitely not small, but cute and maybe cuddly. Why a baby one?"

"They are clumsy and silly. Plus, I could raise it, and maybe it would think we are family." My heart can't take these sweet lines she keeps delivering and probably doesn't realize it. She's still so cute and I'd never admit that to her in fear of being met by her eye daggers.

"Okay, my turn to ask a random question."

"Is that how this works? Otherwise, I don't think I would have started." But she seems on board with the back and forth because she starts rifling through the basket I brought and pulls out a bag of barbecue chips.

"What's your weirdest hobby?" I ask, leaning back and digging my hands into the warm sand.

"Great question, but I don't have one. I'm completely normal and not strange. Next question." She flips her hair and pops another chip into her mouth.

"Ha! Yeah, right, everyone has a weird hobby. I'll even share mine first."

She rolls her eyes up off to the side and says, "Well, go on then."

"I like watching a new movie once a month."

"That is probably the opposite of weird, and a hundred percent does not count."

I chuckle and say, "Yeah, except *new* means new to me. So, for example, I'm watching my dad's favorite movies I've never seen. Like old westerns and cheesy nineties comedies."

"I will say it again, that is not weird. In fact, it is very cool. How dare you say that is a weird hobby." I cannot help but laugh at her response. She does not let that feisty demeanor of hers fade a bit.

"All right, stone skipping."

"Excuse me? What? Did you say *stone skipping*?"

I nod, a chuckle pouring out of me. "You heard me. That's my weird hobby. Whenever I'm near a body of water, I look for some rocks and try to skip stones as far as I can throw, trying to make as many bounces as possible."

"Prove it," she says, giving me a squint and then nodding toward the ocean.

I get up and scope out the sand. Not too many rocks are around today, so I walk a bit closer to the water until I find a decent-shaped stone. It's smooth and flat. I can probably skip this a few times. I turn around, waving the rock to Annika as she sits on the blankets. I notice she's moved over to the blanket I was sitting on. She has her legs crossed and her arms propping her up behind. I have a sudden urge to run over and tackle her. She gives me a big thumbs up, which is my cue. I turn around, wind up my arm and skip the rock into the ocean. It takes 6 fast skips before plopping into the water.

Annika starts slow-clapping for me as I return to our spot on the beach. "Wow, very impressive, Parker, but still not that weird. I'm weirdly impressed if anything."

"Whatever, maybe you just think all my weird hobbies are fun and cute 'cuz you like me or something," I say, nudging her shoulder.

She gives me another glorious eye roll and says, "I don't remember when I said they were *cute,* but okay." I notice her face blushing a bit in response.

"Lay it on me. I bet I won't find your weird hobby that weird at all."

"Okay, fine." She looks off like she's thinking about it. Or maybe she is thinking if she wants to tell me the truth. "I like collecting postcards."

"That's not—"

"No, no, not like new postcards. Although I usually pick up at least one from museum gift shops. I like going to garage sales and flea markets and finding old postcards that were already written on and mailed. I like seeing the little messages that people write and the old stamps. There's something nostalgic about it. I think it's sweet, and not many people send postcards anymore."

I can tell she wants to keep going on because she leans forward and starts taking her jacket off, so I stay quiet while she goes on.

"Chloe and I used to send postcards to each other when we'd go away on a holiday break. It's silly, but I like it. For my birthday in October, Chloe took me to a tattoo parlor, and I got a little stamp tattoo on my back shoulder."

"Okay, that has to be the dopest hobby I've ever heard of, especially when it involves a tattoo. Can I see it?"

She nods and turns her back right shoulder toward me. She's wearing a T-shirt, so she lifts the sleeve up a bit, and then I see the little one-inch tattoo peeking out. It's a black line work tattoo of an old stamp. It has swirly edges and an ornate rose on the inside with the number eighteen in the corner. My instinct is to give it a little kiss where the rose is. But I refrain.

"How did you decide what number to pick?"

"Well,." She shuffles back, facing me, putting her sleeve down. "I thought about putting my birth year, but I'll always remember that. But I might not remember when I got my first tattoo, so I thought my age would be better."

"I love it. That's the best tattoo story I've heard. I don't have any myself."

"Well, thanks. Maybe you should get a tattoo of a rock." She falls back laughing at her own joke.

"Ha ha, don't joke, I just might."

"I still think my hobby is weirder. Both of yours are total normal hobbies. So you still owe me a weird fact about you."

"Oh, I probably have a lot of weird facts, but I'll give you one. My car doesn't have a radio."

"And?"

I knock my head back laughing. She's relentless. "Well, since it has no radio, I'll sing songs in my car with no music playing."

This must've hit a target for Annika because now she plops her back against the blanket, laughing hard. She's even holding on to her belly as she cackles. I think I see tears forming at the corners of her eyes.

"Are you crying? Do you pity me that much?" That only makes her laugh even more.

She takes a deep breath and finally says, "What do you sing in your car?"

I lie next to her on the blanket and meet her joyous expression face-on. "Whatever is stuck in my head, which is usually nineties and early aught's rock."

"Like Nirvana? You had a Nirvana T-shirt on the other day."

"Yeah, sometimes I'll belt a little Cobain."

"What did you sing on the way here?"

I love that she is wondering about this. "In Too Deep by Sum 41."

"It sounds familiar, but I'm not sure if I know that one. Sing some for me."

"I'm sure you'll recognize it once you hear it. But I'll only sing it if you dance with me." I stand up and reach down for her hand.

"Looking to redeem your square dancing days?" she asks, reluctantly eyeing my hand before reaching up to grab it.

"You could say that." I pull her up and spin her around while we spin around the beach, dancing hand in hand. I look down at her and start singing the start of the song.

I twirl her around in a big circle as I sing the bridge, and she starts laughing. "Cool it with the twirls, Parker. I just had lunch."

"Do you recognize it yet?"

"No, not yet. Keep singing. This is kind of fun."

I smile and keep singing as I dip my hand to her low back and sway her gently. I'm addicted the euphoria I feel around her.

"Okay, now the chorus, ready?"

"Ready for what?" As I launch into the chorus, I take her arm and draw her out and twirl her back into my arms, dipping her.

As I bring her back up, I meet her face against mine and press my forehead to hers, singing the last line of the chorus again.

She doesn't move her head from mine. "You are a better dancer, but a terrible singer," she says as that signature smirk shows up.

I lean down as she angles her head up toward mine. My nose grazes over hers, and I move it back and forth. We are still holding hands and swaying together to the sound of the waves. I breathe her in and close my eyes, getting lost in the smell of the warm florals. I lean closer with my eyes still closed, feeling the warmth of our lips just hovering over each other.

I wish I could bottle up this exact moment. Seal up the feeling of warmth and new beginnings. I want to always remember the ambient beach sounds and the remnants of her laughter. The smell of her perfume and the touch of her hands against mine. I lean further and press my lips against hers. Soft and smooth. She tastes like strawberries. I think for a moment if I should leave it at a peck until she leans forward more and matches my kiss. I put my hand on the back of her neck and kissed her more deeply, bending her backward slightly.

When we separate, my eyes linger closed a bit longer, and I feel her give me a small peck again on the lips. I open my eyes, smiling at her and giving her another twirl in the sand. Scratch that. This is the moment I want to bottle up and save forever.

ELEVEN

ANNIKA

IT'S BEEN three days since my beach date with Reid, and I am a complete and utter mess.

Every time I think about our date, a swarm of butterflies attacks my stomach, and it makes me sick. I can't stop thinking about him and how he danced with me in the sand while singing a pop-punk song. *Does he think he is some kind of Disney Prince?* My brain is in peril. I cannot help but ruminate on each moment, and then I tell myself I'm overthinking things. It's been one date. The coffee hang doesn't count.

Although I can't help but recognize that since I was nine years old, I've wanted to date Reid. And now it's happened. I made my boy crush dreams come true. However, on the other hand, I wanted to be a single-pringle through college and to, as Chloe puts it, casually date. I mimic her arms as I lie in bed, going through an existential crisis. All right, maybe I'm being a *little* dramatic.

Every time I look over at my stack of textbooks, the loose papers shoved into folders, and the sticky notes littering my desk, I'm hit with a wave of guilt. Do I even have time to date someone? I should probably focus on myself, at least until the workload lets up. We're almost six months into the school year, and yet, I'm overwhelmed with school and now a boy. *I'm in too deep,* as Sum 41 ever so poetically put it.

I lie on my dorm room bed and look out the window. In times of deep contemplation usually, I'd take a drive to the beach and step in the water, staring off into the distance while the sound of the waves crashing on the sand is the only thing to calm my thoughts. That and shopping. If Chloe wasn't in class right now, I'd drag her out to lunch or thrift shopping. I need a distraction from my own brain. I decide to go with the first one and drive to a beach closer to our dorm. It's about a five-minute drive and on the smaller side, so there usually aren't that many people there. In the car, I refrain from playing the song again and instead, turn off the music entirely. This must be what Reid feels like when driving. Silence. Alone with your thoughts. Terrified, I turn the music quickly back on.

AS I HOPED, the beach is nearly empty. Only a couple of people are sitting in the sand. I set my bag down on a spot a few yards from the water and roll up the bottoms of my pants. It is later in the day, so the tide is farther out. I can walk out a bit just as the waves touch my toes gently. It's as if the ocean knows to be chill with me today. I stand about ankle-deep and look at the horizon. A few swimmers pass in the distance.

The sun is about an hour from setting, and the sky is starting to turn shades of cotton candy. I take a deep breath, close my eyes, and think of everything all at once. All my thoughts come tumbling around, and instead of holding them in, I let them all pour out. *Is my major the right one for me? It isn't too late to change it. Should I just drop out of college entirely? I wonder what my mom is up to right now. I should give her a call. Where will Chloe and I live after this year is over? Should I go home for summer break?*

A seagull squawks and snaps me out of my ocean-induced trance. *Right, I came here to get clarity on Reid.* I take another deep breath and close my eyes. The ocean wraps around my ankles like a gentle hug. *Should I go for it with him or keep it casual?* I wince even at the word casual. *Casual, casual, casual. That word haunts me. Is that even what I want? I don't think so. I wish I could say I want to keep dating him, but I'm worried about classes. I can't let school slip. My parents would be so disappointed in me. They are the most important people in my life.*

I open my eyes and look out toward the ocean. I think I also expected Reid to be texting me constantly since our date. But he's only texted me once, and it's been three days.

REID

gm :]

Gm... that's it? He didn't even spell it out completely. Maybe he wants to keep things laid back too. I suppose that would answer my dilemma about how I should approach things. But I shouldn't lie to myself. I've always been into Reid. He's kind and confident. He makes me laugh and forget about my worries. I know I can't be relaxed about this. Especially not after the way he kissed me. No kiss I've ever had has made me forget where I was when I opened my eyes. I wish I could let myself go and fall into my feelings towards Reid, like I did when we were kids. My responsibilities are clouding my ability to be carefree.

Buzzz bzz

REID

Hey :)

I hope you aren't too busy today.

I look up at the ocean suspiciously. He always texts me after I am on a spiral of thoughts about him. His ears must've been ringing.

ANNIKA

Just deep in thought, as per usual

REID

I hope you are thinking about me ;)

Yikes, sorry, that was awfully cheesy

ANNIKA

I walked right into that one

REID

What do you say about seeing a movie with me Friday night? They are screening Mean Girls in the Amphitheater.

ANNIKA

No way! I love Mean Girls. I could watch that 100 times.

REID

Well, perfect because I've never seen it, it will be my new movie this month.

ANNIKA

...

REID

What?

ANNIKA

Did you just say, you've never. seen. it?

I glance up from my phone and realize I have the cheesiest smile on my face. *Gah! See, I'm screwed.* I notice the tide is getting higher and decide to move back over toward my bag and walk up to a bench by the sidewalk. *Buzzz bzz*

REID

Hey...I grew up as an only child with a single dad, Mean Girls wasn't a typical Friday night movie pick for us.

ANNIKA

I'd be honored to escort you to your first viewing of Mean Girls.

REID

:] awesome, pick you up at your dorm? 7pm Friday?

ANNIKA

I'll be there

I'll be there? Of course I will, it's my dorm!

And just like that, all my doubt washes away because I've agreed to another date with Reid without second guessing. It's just one more date, and we'll be watching a movie most of the time. *Casual Annika, don't fall in love with him.*

TWELVE

REID

THE PAST WEEK has been the hardest I've experienced in college yet. Two classes had projects due. One told us we'd have a quiz at the end of the week, and I can't concentrate on my lecture because I keep doodling "Annika" over and over again on my note sheet. I've done it so many times that the double n's turn into a long squiggle. I feel terrible that I've texted her so few times since our date. And I feel worse that she isn't on the top of my mind. Anatomy II is.

I've been thinking a lot about balance. I want to do this right with Annika. I don't want to treat it like it's some college fling. I never thought in middle school that I'd actually get to date her, let alone kiss her. Holding her up so we don't collapse on the beach. I've been comforting my stressed brain by thinking about that date. It was perfect, which is why I want things to only improve. I want to take it slow and make sure she knows how much I care about her. But balance. I can't let my feelings for her cloud my studying. I am on track to finish the year with honors, and I intend to make sure that happens. So if I can't text her right away in order to study, I'll have to wait.

I was nervous to finally message her two days ago, but we fell into conversation with ease. She is effortless to me. Her banter, her expressions. It's a breath of fresh air. I can't mess this up with her. Hopefully, she understands, and we can take things slow. If I'm capable of slow.

The sound of my professor closing his textbook means the lecture is finally over, and I've successfully written "Annika" probably a hundred times and taken zero notes. *So much for balance.*

MY LAST CLASS of the day is over, which means in two hours, I get to pick up Annika and take her to a movie. I am walking light on air back to my dorm. I'm so giddy I start skipping. I feel like I'm in a romantic comedy, but I'm not going to let the puzzled looks of my peers stop me from enjoying this high I am on. I see Isaac, and he starts laughing hysterically at the sight of me skipping toward him.

"Dude! What the hell are you on right now, and can I get some of it?" I meet Isaac's hand and pat his back to greet him.

"I'm on a silly thing called *love,* my dude." *Except I'm not in love, not yet, at least.*

"Yo...love? Don't be throwing the 'L' word around like that. Who's the lucky girl?"

"You know Annika? We went to middle school with her. She was at your birthday party."

I think I notice an expression change in Isaac's eyes when I mention her name. *Interesting.* Maybe there's something he isn't telling me.

"Ya, of course, I know Anni...I invited her to *my* birthday party. You should be thanking me. Shit, call me Cupid!"

Any worry I have melts away as Isaac's big smile spreads across his face, and he pats my shoulder.

"I'm really happy I decided to come to your party. I'm about to pick her up again tonight for another date. It feels like the real thing."

"Well, that's dope, bro. Tell her I said *hi*, and have fun tonight. Go get some!" Isaac forces a smile and strides off.

Is he into Annika too? Isaac is one of my closest friends here, and it would majorly suck if a girl came between us. I shake it off and finish my walk back to my door. I need to freshen up and change out of these school clothes before I pick up Annika.

I STAND at her dorm door and take a deep breath, then lift my arms to double check I put deodorant on. *How should I knock?* Now I'm questioning my knock style? I do two quick knocks and immediately wish I did three. I hear muffled talking from inside and then the door opens.

This is the third moment I'd like to bottle and remember forever. Seeing Anni's eyes light up as she looks up at me. She's done something again to her hair, so it flips out at her shoulders and sways when she turns her head, just like the first night I saw her. Her perfume wafts over to me, and I am instantly transported to our kiss on the beach. I smile and look down at her outfit. She's wearing a black crop top with a big rose on the chest and a black flared skirt. She's not wearing her Chucks today. Instead, she's got on a pair of sexy black platform boots. *Damn.* I shove my hands into my pockets to prevent myself from pushing her back into her dorm and kissing her all night instead of watching the movie.

I look up and see she is also looking at my outfit. "So, do you approve of my movie night outfit?" I say, putting one hand on my head and one on my hip, posing for her.

"Is that your grandpa's sweater?" She looks up and reaches over and touches my arm, lingering on my thrifted sweater. My arm tingles under her touch.

"He had great style, if I do say so myself. Goes great with my crusty Converse."

She turns to say goodbye to Chloe, and we head out toward the amphitheater that is showing the movie. We are quiet most of the walk over. I ask her how her classes are going, and she asks about mine. She doesn't seem too excited to talk about her courses. I notice that she tries to change the subject whenever I ask her another question about her major or classwork. I get the feeling she isn't enjoying it. I remember she did the same thing when I mentioned it on our beach date. I don't want to start our date on a sour note, so I change it and talk about my classwork.

We get to the amphitheater, and Annika insists on buying us snacks since I got lunch on the first date. I appreciate that she is thoughtful about it. Other girls I've dated expected me to shell out every food and ticket for anything we went to.

Annika leads us to a spot near the middle, so we have a central view of the screen. The AV-Club that set this up installed a giant screen that a projector will hit. It's already getting dark, so we should be able to see it easily. Annika puts the popcorn in between us at our feet and hands me my candy of choice, Swedish Fish, while she starts munching on Reese's Pieces. She seems a little off ever since we sat down, just making small talk and joking around, but she doesn't seem as comfortable as she was on the beach. The movie is going to start soon so we won't be able to talk as much and I want to get to know her more.

"So, is Reese's your favorite candy?" *Stupid question Reid.*

"Huh? Oh yeah, I love anything peanut butter and chocolate together."

Her shoulders are turned straight toward the screen while I am leaning toward her. I want to shake her and ask what is going on in her head. It's as if we didn't share a kiss a few days ago. *Have I been overthinking her feelings toward me?*

"You smell really nice, like flowers in the fall," I say, leaning into her. She turns her head and looks me in the eyes.

"Are you for real?" she says with a straight face, and I'm not sure if she is offended by my comment until her lips spread into a wide smile.

"I figure that I think of these things in my head. Why not say it out loud and tell you exactly what I'm thinking? I thought you'd like to know. I'm really happy you said *yes* again, by the way." I scooch closer so our shoulders and knees are touching.

She glances down at them and then rests her head on my right shoulder. I am a ball of nerves. I reach around and put my right arm on her side, holding her close. My hand resting where her small tattoo is beneath her shirt. She reaches in to eat popcorn while resting on me still.

"Hey, can I get some of that?"

She giggles and, without moving her head, sticks her arm up, guessing where my mouth is and feeding me a piece of popcorn. I turn my head and give the top of her head a little kiss. She squeezes in closer and puts her left hand on my leg. We watch the movie cuddled close, taking things slow, just as I hoped we would.

I CAN'T BELIEVE I've never seen *Mean Girls.* It is kind of the best movie I've ever seen. The visual, the iconic lines, maybe four and a half stars for me. I'm definitely going to see if I can find a shirt that says the line Gretchen Wieners delivers at the end.

We were quiet most of the movie, but occasionally I'd put my hand on her knee or bump her shoulder during a funny part. She would poke me whenever I'd try to whisper something in her ear.

As we walk back to her dorm, I link our hands together, gently swinging them and humming a song from the movie. I could get used to this. Having someone like Annika to spend my Friday nights with. I am quite obsessed with her and her raspy chuckle. The way she squints at every dumb joke I make and then makes one back at me. The way she doesn't shy away from my affection towards her and yet takes it slow with me. I don't mind it because I want to savor these early moments of our relationship. When we are years into our relationship, we'll look back at this moment, walking her back to her dorm room from the movie. *Years from now? Maybe I'm getting ahead of myself.*

We get back to her dorm room, and we stand at her door and look at each other. She doesn't race to go inside, and I don't rush her. I am enjoying the view. I take her hand and running my lips along her knuckles and kissing the top of her hand, which makes her eyes roll.

"You are too much, Parker."

I laugh and give her hand back. "I really loved *Mean Girls*, probably the best movie I've seen so far this year."

"I knew you'd like it. It's a classic." She smiles, and her dark eyes twinkle up at me.

I take that as an invitation and reach for her waist, pulling her into an embrace. She stiffens at first, but after a beat, she wraps her arms around my back, pressing them against my shoulder blades. I nuzzle my face in her hair and breathe in her scent. I should probably stop smelling her so much, but she smells too good. I give her a kiss on the side of her head and on her cheek before I separate from her. I'm not sure why I'm nervous about kissing her again, but I am. I don't want to scare her off.

"Next time, I'll take you to dinner at an actual restaurant with a table. This is the second date where we were eating from our laps." I say to her.

She gives me a tight lip smirk, nods, and says, "All right, sounds good."

I'm not sure what to do next, so I put my hand up to give her a high-five. "Okay, I'll text you later! Have a good night."

She squints and gives me the worst high-five back, then turns to her dorm door and goes inside. I just stare at the doorknob. *Did I just high-five her?*

I rub my neck and replay the entire date in my head. She's the same mysterious and witty girl I've always known. I want to break open that shell she keeps around herself.

THIRTEEN

ANNIKA

AS SOON AS I get behind the front door to my dorm, I press my back against it and release the anxiety that's been inside me the whole time with a big exhale. The entire date, I felt the struggle of wanting to get closer to Reid but also struggling with the definition of *casual*. I'm seriously going to scream if I hear Chloe say that word to me again. I take a deep breath in again and close my eyes. Reid was a dream. He is a dream. He wore this chunky thrifted sweater that was soft whenever I'd rub against his shoulder. He smelled like rainy woods and palo santo. His green marble eyes twinkled every time they looked at me. I wanted to sit on his lap and make out with him the entire movie. But Chloe's voice in my head said to keep things light.

"Are you okay? How did the date go?" I open my eyes and notice that Chloe has been staring at me while sitting on her bed reading a book.

She never really likes campus gatherings and always prefers spending time with Dane or me or hanging in the dorm, reading, or painting. She is sporting a concerned expression as she gazes up from her book. I realize I look strange pinned against the door, taking deep breaths, so I shake it off and sit next to her on her bed.

"Unfortunately, I think I'm falling in love with him," I confess to her.

"I knew this was going to happen. What happened to your college fling dreams?" She closes her book and chucks it on the shelf like whatever we are about to talk about is way more interesting than whatever she was reading.

"We both knew I was doomed when my first fling was Reid, the love of my life all through middle school." I rub my eyes with my palms, not caring that I've smeared my eyeliner. "What do I do now?"

"Well, what do you want? Do you want a steady boyfriend?" She leans toward me and starts braiding little pieces of my hair in the hope it will relax me. "Or do you want to be a free bird through college?"

I weigh these options in my head as if my life depends on it. He already expects a third date, and when he said that, I got a pit in my stomach as if that wasn't what I should do. I wish things in my life were clear. I can't seem to put my finger on the one thing I actually want. Whenever I try to search within myself to discover what I actually want to do, I can't help but put everyone else before me. I decide that I'm not going to settle on something tonight and instead drag myself to the shower and go to sleep. Maybe tomorrow, I'll be in a clearer headspace.

11:18 a.m.

Bzzz bzz

I slept in longer than I ever have before. Even in my sleep, I was procrastinating my next steps with Reid. I could barely sleep. I kept tossing and turning. Sure, I got butterflies whenever I thought about him, but also that was followed by a nauseous wave because I can't help but think it wasn't the right thing to do. I don't even know if

I'm enjoying my major, and I am worried that if I start to date someone seriously, I'm going to get even more distracted.

The sun outside is fighting to shine through my drapes, so I stand up and pull them open. Chloe isn't on her side of the room, so I'm guessing she's out with Dane today. It also doesn't help that she keeps reminding me to keep my dating experience light. Yet she's been dating Dane for a couple of months now. My head hurts the more I think about everything, and I feel like it would be easier to just hide from everyone and lock myself in my room.

Buzzz buzz

I reach for my phone and see it's from Reid. My feelings are so confused that I just stare at his name for almost a full minute before opening his text.

It's a video. He looks like he's in his car at a stoplight. When I hit play, he's singing "*Milkshake*" by Kelis. I think of *Mean Girls* instantly and how, on the walk home from the movie Reid stood under a lamp post and did the same dance from the movie. I nearly fell down laughing. We walked the rest of the way back, holding hands. It felt so natural, so easy with him. When I am with him, things are clear, but once I am alone, I struggle with what I want.

In the video, he's belting out the chorus, and the car next to him is laughing until he blows them a kiss, then they give him a scowl and drive off. I play the video three times and laugh each time. He's so unapologetically himself. He's such a goof and is not embarrassed by it all. I really like that about him and find it rubbing off on me when I'm with him too.

I send back a few laughing emojis and decide to go for a long walk today. Hopefully, that will clear my head. I'll take it day by day and go from there and try to trust my gut.

FOURTEEN

REID

MY DAD and Pam's weekend visit disrupt my desire to spend more time with Annika. I've taken them through Balboa Park, to a few museums and beaches, and walked around Gaslamp. Pam always wanted to go to the Long Beach Flea Market, which is a few hours north, so we decided to make the drive up there this weekend. My dad refuses to take my truck, though, and rents a car. He says it's because he doesn't want to put more miles on my pickup, but I know it's because I don't have a radio and he wants to keep tabs on the Giants game while we drive up.

So far, this week has been great. I love spending time with my dad, especially since he and Pam got serious. She showed me her engagement ring almost immediately when I picked them up from the airport. She gave me the biggest hug and teared up when she saw me. Pam fills this void I never knew I had. She will check in on me to make sure I got my flu shot and will send pictures of her garden. She will always randomly send me books that she has finished reading and thinks I'll enjoy. I'm just as happy to see her as she is to see me.

Saturday arrives, and we pile into the SUV my dad rented and make the trek up to Long Beach. Pam insists we get there by eight a.m., so we leave by six-thirty. Five minutes into the car ride, and I'm sprawling across the entire back row getting my extra hour of sleep.

I decided to tell my dad and Pam about my last couple of dates with Annika. He remembers her from when I was in middle school. I told him it is still pretty new, so he doesn't ask that many questions about her, but I know he's probably holding back. I don't have too many answers. She seemed distant this past week. I pull out my phone and look at our last messages to each other.

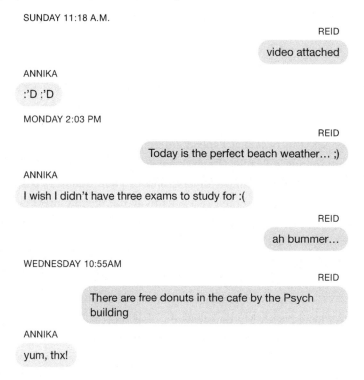

SUNDAY 11:18 A.M.

REID

video attached

ANNIKA

:'D :'D

MONDAY 2:03 PM

REID

Today is the perfect beach weather... ;)

ANNIKA

I wish I didn't have three exams to study for :(

REID

ah bummer...

WEDNESDAY 10:55AM

REID

There are free donuts in the cafe by the Psych building

ANNIKA

yum, thx!

If I was just going off our recent text history, I'd say she isn't into me. But another part of me remembers our dates and the chemistry we had. Maybe she's just a terrible texter. Maybe I'm a terrible texter. She could be busy with school. She did mention she has three exams to study for. I'm probably overthinking everything. Maybe I should talk to Pam about it and see what she says.

We pull up to the Long Beach Flea Market, and it's already filled with cars. Pam wasn't kidding that this is a popular spot. Pam already told my dad that she's prepared to cancel their flights and drive back if she finds stuff she likes for the house. Dad smiles and pulls out the folding cart that they picked up at some point during the week.

"Wow, you guys are really committed to this flea market. When did you get this cart? I could sit in it." I jokingly make a move to hop in, but Pam puts her hand up.

"Nuh uh, no, this is for the rare antiques we find today. I've been wanting to go here for years. This is a dream come true."

She grabs my dad's hand, and they begin their way walking through the maze of vendors and stalls. I decide to wander around alone, checking out some of the clothing vendors. One booth is selling vinyl records that I spend a decent amount of time in, and I end up buying a Beatles album. I can see why Pam was excited to come here. The selection is diverse and of great quality. I pass by them at one point, and their cart is halfway full of stuff already, and Pam gives me a big thumbs up. Yup, they're driving back home after all.

I'm starting to get a bit hungry and walk over to the food truck vendors and order a couple of carnitas tacos. Nothing beats tacos from a food truck, I don't know what they do differently, but they always taste better. My dad texts me that they just finished going through once and are going to start making their way back but going to see if a few vendors will haggle so I make my way toward the front of the flea.

On my way over, I notice a stall selling some maps and see a stack of postcards. I flip through them, and my mind immediately goes to Annika. I'm about to buy one for her when I see something shiny catch my eye on the table next to the postcards. The vendor is selling some jewelry that fits the same vintage theme as the other items in their stall. A few rings, some bracelets, and about ten different necklaces. Each is on a simple gold chain with a pendant on the end. I hesitate for a moment. *We've only been on two dates, and yet I want to buy jewelry for her?* But I can't walk away from this. It's perfect. I'm done taking things slow. I want to show her how much she means to me and that I want to take our relationship further. It's not like we just met. We've both told each other that we've had a crush since we were kids.

I pay the vendor the twenty dollars that's listed on the necklace, and she slides it into a velvet pouch for me. I tuck it into my back pocket, and it feels like I put a brick back there. It belongs to Annika, and I can't wait to give it to her.

MY DAD and Pam drive back to Nor Cal the next day, leaving me with a day to unwind and catch up on studying. I ignore everyone and keep my head down in my textbooks. I notice it's been five hours since I left my dorm room. I reach for my phone to check the time and feel guilty I haven't checked in with Annika. But on the other hand, she hasn't either. It was a mistake buying her that necklace. But, I just can't shake the feeling that we are meant to see this through.

I decide to leave my dorm and go for a walk, maybe stop by the coffee shop, until I see Annika from afar. I stop dead in my tracks at the site of her. It's a bit colder today, so she has on an oversized sweater and black leggings with her Converse. Her short black hair is braided into two pigtails. She looks like the girl I first met on the playground. All my doubts melt away, and I jog over to her.

"Annika!" I wave and smile. She sees me and lights up for a moment then I notice she reins in her expression. "Hey, I'm so glad I ran into you. Sorry, I've been quiet. My dad came to visit."

"Oh, it's no problem. I've been really busy with school, anyway. I hope your dad is doing well." *She isn't looking me directly in the eyes.*

"Yeah, he's great. We went up to Long Beach yesterday to the flea market." I reach into my back pocket to get the necklace but realize I left it in my room. "I-uh-got something for you. Nothing big, thought maybe I could give it to you during dinner? Friday night? With me?" I ask, trying to lay on the charm with a big smile, except Annika isn't smiling back.

She's looking at the ground, avoiding my eyes. *Something is wrong.*

"Reid…about dinner, I don't know…if I feel…if I should…" She looks at me with a look of hurt across her face, and suddenly, I feel my world spinning. *How could I be so stupid?*

"I just feel like we are going too fast. I am so preoccupied with school, I don't think I can handle dating. I don't think I can do this." She starts fumbling with the books in her hand as she looks down at her feet and then back up at me. Her eyes are glassy.

"We can go slower. I… I thought our feelings were mutual. Do you not feel the same way about me that I feel toward you?" *I can't believe I just said that out loud.*

I can't tell if she shakes her head or nods, and I'm not sure what she says after that. Everything turns blurry, and I think I hear, *"I'm sorry, Reid."* I barely register that she turns and walks away when I don't say anything back to her. Maybe the timing isn't right, or maybe the timing will never be right. Either way, I feel like my heart has been ripped out and tossed in a fountain like a worthless penny.

I forget why I even left my dorm, but I turn back towards it and go straight to my bed. I don't know when I started, but I notice that I've been crying into my pillow because it's half soaked from my tears. I'm filled with "don't knows." I don't know if I'm crying because my heart is broken. I don't know if I feel an ache in my chest for the past me who was picturing a relationship with her. I don't know if I feel this dread to leave my dorm because she suddenly seems everywhere.

I don't want to see her for a while. I don't know why she doesn't feel the same way. I don't know why she doesn't feel the tingles every time we touch. I shouldn't have let my heart fall so deeply so soon. I couldn't help it, though. We had a second chance to turn our childhood crush into a reality. Except, apparently, it was all my fantasy.

The necklace pouch sits on my desk, taunting me. I chuck it in the box of knick-knacks I'm going to send up to my parents. They left a few things here before they left, and I don't want this necklace in my sight.

THE REMNANTS of feelings that linger after a breakup are some of the most sour, in my opinion. It's not even that it's on your mind all the time. It's that anything at any point of the day can remind you of that person, remind you of what could have been. The sun reminds me of her because the day after the beach, I got a sunburn on the top of my ears, so I had to wear a hat until it faded. So now that hat also reminds me of her. I can't see someone in pigtail braids without thinking of her. I push the thoughts away, though, because I've convinced myself that it's for the best.

I've spent the past few months head down in school, replacing the uncomfortable void with my biology major courses. With summer courses and keeping the grades I'm at, I should be able to graduate early and do the training needed to work as a Physical Therapist. Being able to help people day to day is something that keeps me trudging along. Although it would be good to blow off some steam, my roommate invited me to his DND match, which I know nothing about, but he always talks so lively about it. I'm sure it's entertaining to watch.

I pivot on my walk home to treat myself to a cold brew with whip. It's been a while since I had one, and I've passed all my finals so far. The campus is alive as the semester is coming to a close. I can feel the relief of summer break like a ray of sunshine after a cold winter. The coffee shop I usually go to by the student store is packed, and I am feeling impatient, so I'll try the one by the dorms.

I grab the door handle, but not before looking inside and seeing Isaac sitting with Annika. He is leaning in, talking to her. What could they possibly be talking about? I know they are old friends, but their body language doesn't look friendly. It looks flirtatious. He puts his hand on her leg. She doesn't move it. I think I'm going to be sick.

"Hey, are you going in?" I realize I'm clutching the door handle, preventing people from entering.

I open the door for them and turn away. I really can't come around this side of campus ever again. Or maybe I can transfer schools. Is that too dramatic?

Isaac? My friend? He knew we dated. How could he go behind my back like that? Even if he asked me first, I'd say it wasn't cool. Dang, I need new friends. Suddenly, I'm even more relieved it's summer, so I can get out of San Diego for at least a little while.

FIFTEEN

ANNIKA

~ Two years later ~

MY THERAPIST TOLD me in our last session that I should take up a hobby. She said collecting used stamps and scrolling on the internet aren't constructive enough to tame my ruminating mind. So that is why I'm wandering around downtown San Diego with a used Nikon I found at a consignment shop. I stop near a pet store and stand out of the way of passersby to look at what I've captured so far. A graffiti wall that *Money is Love*, a pair of Wiener dogs sitting under a cafe table, and about ten pictures of this pretty rose I saw blooming in a flower box. I'm not sure I feel any different from before I started this photo tour.

I thought of photography as a hobby because I took a photo elective class my freshman year and really enjoyed it. The only difference is I don't have a prompt. What am I supposed to even take photos of? I feel like people are staring at me whenever I pull out my camera.

I pass by a cafe and treat myself to an oat milk dirty chai. I haven't been to this cafe before, but it looks pretty cozy. I snuggle in a corner booth away from people and pull out my journal. Aside from photography, journaling is something that keeps me focused and not spiraling. I've been writing in it since freshman year—whenever I feel like I need to get thoughts out of my head and on paper. I flip through the previous pages and read a few entries.

Freshmen Year - March

Hi, I don't even know why I keep writing hello each entry here, but I feel like it's rude if I don't. Hi, how are you? Great? Well, I feel empty. Like I lost a piece of a charm bracelet, so there's an awkward empty space, and it seems unnoticeable until you lean on your wrist against a table and feel the gap. I think I made a mistake with Reid. I keep hoping I'd run into him again so I can take it all back in some kind of grand gesture, but I haven't seen him in weeks since I told him I didn't feel the same way he does towards me. Which was a total lie. I was scared. I feel like shit, Journal. I need to just focus on school.

Freshmen Year - June

Hey Journ, trying out a hyphenated name for this thing. A diary sounds so juvenile. Anyway, Isaac finally worked up the nerve to ask me out. He's been "accidentally" bumping into me for two months now. I think he's always had a thing for me but held off because Reid asked me out first. They were close. *were is the keyword. Isaac told me that Reid saw us having coffee and was pissed at him. Something about bro-code. It makes me queasy just thinking about it because… I don't know. It feels wrong to even admit it here, even though I'm the only one to read it.

Isaac has been nice, but I keep comparing my feelings toward Reid, and they aren't the same. Not even close. Isaac feels like a placeholder.

Summer - July

Isaac and I decided to take a weekend trip to Santa Barbara. He had some friends that went to UCSB and thought it would be fun to go away together. It was fun for the most part until I found out we'd be sharing a bed. It shouldn't be a big deal, but I haven't slept with anyone. We had only been dating for three weeks, but I guess now is as good as any. I'm not sure how I pictured I would lose my virginity. I guess I thought it would be more romantic than on a blow-up mattress behind a folding divider in a stranger's college apartment. Isaac tried to be sweet about it. He gave me a rose at dinner and told me he loved me. I felt so awkward, so I just smiled back. I don't love him, and honestly, I don't know if he really loves me either.

It's been three weeks! And when we were alone at the apartment, we were making out until he slowly removed my clothes. He asked if it was okay, and I said yes. I feel like there is supposed to be so much more build-up and foreplay. At least, that's what it seems like in movies and books. Isaac just pushed himself inside me and lasted a few grunts before collapsing beside me. I don't think I even orgasmed, but I googled later that night that that was normal the first time. Afterward, he said he wanted to cuddle, but I felt hot and sticky, so I took a shower instead. I guess I'm glad I got it over with, but I wish this entry made me feel happier to write about.

Sophomore Year - September

Hey, it's been A WHILE since I've written in here. I went back to Ojai for the summer and worked at an ice cream shop in the downtown area. This journal was packed in with my school stuff, and I only found it after Chloe, and I unpacked our new *off-campus* apartment! We feel so grown up. It is very small, and she and I share a bedroom, but we couldn't be happier. We hung fairy lights around the living room and bought three poufs that we sit on and read books all weekend.

Summer was fun, I guess. Isaac and I broke it off shortly after the weekend in SB. It didn't feel fair to keep stringing him along if I always compared him to someone else. I started dating this guy who worked at the ice cream shop with me, Marcus. He was in my physics class in my senior year of high school, and I always thought he was kinda cute. We would make out during lunch breaks and hook up in the back of his Honda Civic since both of us lived with our parents. I would talk to him about how I wanted to do something in life that made me feel fulfilled, that made a difference in the world. He said he was fine living in Ojai and working at the ice cream shop or any other small business. I was coming back to UCSD, and so we ended things. Funny how the most casual relationship I've had wasn't even at college. Let's see what this next year brings me!

Sophomore Year - January

Sophomore year fucking sucks. Sorry for my language, Journal. But SHIT, my teachers are all assholes, and why do they give so many fucking quizzes and tests. I just wanna quit school. I hate it so much. It would be so much easier if I didn't have to do any of this. But then I think of my parents and how disappointed they would be in me. I think of my brothers, who I want to make proud. I think of Chloe, who is struggling just as much as me, and I would let her down if I just quit.

I can do this. It just sucks.

Sophomore Year - March

My mom sent me my old diaries from when I was a kid. I thought I threw them away, but she said she went after and grabbed them out of the trash. It feels meta to write in here about old diaries, but what I wrote about and the time of year it is got me so emotional. I don't know what else I was expecting. Of course, I wrote about Reid. I was simply obsessed with the boy. And then I looked at the first entry in here, and it was about a month after I broke it off with Reid. What was I thinking?

There's NEVER been another guy that's given me those stupid butterflies like he has. He just had to look at me, and I felt sick. Sick like if I spent any time away from him, I might have to be admitted to a hospital. We only went on a couple of dates, but I've replayed them in my head so many times it feels like my favorite movie. I know every detail, every smell, and feeling I felt. Sometimes I will go back to that spot on the beach and close my eyes, pretending he's twirling me.

Why am I crying? Gah I'm a mess. This year fucked me up. I need to start dating again.

The rest of my entries are just me complaining about school and how I should try and date again. I spent all of my sophomore and most of my junior year so far single as ever. Honestly, it was probably for the best. I needed to focus on myself and my school work before adding another person into my life. This past summer, I told my mom how stressed I've been with school and admitted to her that I might not be enjoying it. She told me whatever I wanted to do, she and my dad would be behind me. But still, I have this nagging feeling that I just need to keep going. I'm so close. Just a year and a half yet. I managed to stay in honors the whole time, which is surprising. My mom was the one who suggested I take advantage of the campus therapist just to have someone to talk out these specific academic stressors. It's been great so far. I go once a month and just unload every thought and worry I have.

I feel in a better place but also still so fragile. Someone could sneeze too close to me, and I might go off on them. I hope this feeling goes away after I'm done with school. I've been so stressed and preoccupied it's been difficult to fit dating into my life. Chloe told me about some dating apps she's been on. She and Dane are "off" right now, so she's been going on a new date each month, it seems like, in search of *the one*.

I look back over at the entry from last year in March. It is still hard to read about Reid and the residual feelings that are lingering. I would be lying if I said I didn't think about how things might be different if I had gone on that third date with him. He said he had something to give me. I wonder if he still has it. I need to shake him out of my mind. Maybe I should sign up for a dating app.

ANNIKA

What was that app you are on called again?

CHLOE

Flame!

OMG where are you!? I need to be with you when you create your profile

ANNIKA

please no, it's fine.

I'll send you a screenshot

CHLOE

deal!!

The app logo is a little orange flame, which is pretty cute. Before I put in any info, I'm prompted to curate my own photo gallery. I select a couple of selfies, one of Chloe and me and one picture Chloe took of me after I got my tattoo. The picture is right after I got it, and I'm turning around with a big ol' dumb smile on my face. Things were so simple back then. The profile is pretty simple. You fill in your name, age, bio, and favorite song.

Annika, 20

San Diego, CA

Bio: If I'm not collecting used postcards, then I'm overthinking everything I've ever said. Libra.

Favorite Song: The State of Dreaming by MARINA and the Diamonds

After sending numerous screenshots to Chloe and ignoring her begs to change my bio to something sweeter, I begin to swipe. The first guy is a typical SD surfer boy, tan, blond, troublesome smirk. He's cute but more Chloe's type, so I swipe left. This app is kind of fun. No wonder Chloe keeps talking about it. I settle into my cafe seat and look up, suddenly self-conscious that everyone in the cafe knows I'm on a dating app. I collect my camera and journal to head out. I walk back to my car and decide to drive through the park. I'm excited to find a quiet spot to swipe the faces of guys. There's a section of Balboa Park that has a big fountain and lots of benches surrounding it. I find a bench against a wall and click on the little flame icon. *Time to swipe.*

George, 23

San Diego, CA

Bio: only chicks under 5' swipe right

Favorite Song: Pretty Fly (for a White Guy) The Offspring

Swiping left, what an ass.

Griffin, 19

Chula Vista, CA

Bio: I enjoy short walks around my neighborhood and a tall glass of orange juice.

Favorite Song: The Motto by Drake

He seems sweet. I'll swipe right.

Jake, 21

Long Beach, CA

Bio: You go Glen Coco

Favorite Song: Blank Space by Taylor Swift

A *Mean Girls* quote? I mean, Jake might be my true love, right? I wonder when I'm going to get a match. I keep swiping left and right to a few guys and almost jump out of my seat when I get a notification. "It's a match!" I stare at the chat screen between me and Griffin. Nothing. *Do I message first? What is the move?* I'll just keep swiping, and maybe he'll message first. I get a little lost in the

125

endless photos to swipe that I nearly drop my phone when I come across a familiar face.

Reid, 20
San Diego, CA
Bio: I'm probably already in love with you.
Favorite Song: All I Wanted by Paramore

I stare at his bio for what feels like hours. His photos bring a smile to my face. His eyes are glowing in the second picture, where he's cradling a pug in his arms. He's grown a little bit of beard stubble in these photos which is really hot. I listen to his favorite song, and my heart breaks in two. I almost catch myself taking a screenshot but then panic that it might tell him that I did, so I don't. I should swipe left. I ended things. I should be confident with my decision. But I want to know what he will do. Did he swipe right on me? I can only know if I swipe right on him.

Swiping right…

IT'S A MATCH! CHAT WITH REID

My heart feels like it's going to jump out of my mouth. I'm fully leaning over this bench with my head nearly between my knees. I stare at the chat screen. He might not say anything. I guess that is the best case. I know my answer. He does still like me. That's why he swiped right. Right? Or maybe he swiped right for the same reason I swiped right. To see what I'd do. Three dots start appearing on the screen, and I audibly shriek, startling an older couple walking by. They glare at me, and I wave in apology.

The three dots are still pulsing on the screen, and I might just collapse and die right here. Maybe he's going to profess his love to me? This could be my second chance with him. Maybe I should just force quit and delete the app before he has the chance to message me.

REID

Are you joking?

Is he saying that in a cute serendipitous way, or like he is upset with me?

REID

What are you doing?

Why did you swipe right?

Shit, well, that answers my question. I think my second chance is gone forever. Maybe I can recover.

ANNIKA

I wanted to see if you would swipe right.

Which you did.

Honesty is best, right? Well, I guess that's not the full truth. The full truth would be something like, *"I fell in love with you when I was nine years old, and I've compared every guy to you since, and I can't get you out of my head, and I think I still have feelings for you, but I'm scared to do anything about it."*

REID

Of course I did. I still like you.

You ended things with ME. You said you didn't feel the same way.

Are you saying you were lying to me?

ANNIKA

What? No, I'm sorry.

REID

Sorry for what?

Why did you really swipe right Annika?

ANNIKA

I don't know why...

REID

Well, figure it out.

- REID UNMATCHED YOU -

My eyes search the screen in panic. He unmatched me. I didn't even realize that was something that could be done. I screenshot our conversation before it disappears and reread it. "I still like you." Present tense. He still has feelings for me too. He's right. I don't deserve to feel his frustrations, his love, and his loss. I'm not being honest with myself. I know why I swiped right. I can't admit the full truth to him. But he would only swipe right if he wanted me to swipe right, too, right?

"Well, figure it out." My life, my love life, my direction. I need to figure it all out. I feel emptier than I did earlier today. I should probably schedule another therapy appointment. I start walking to my car and think of how to spend the rest of the day. I'd like to do anything but be alone right now. My thoughts feel like a cyclone in my head. Spinning around and around.

Bzzz bzz bzz

IT'S A MATCH! CHAT WITH JAKE...

JAKE

Hey ;)

You're so sexy, my zipper is falling for you.

I nearly throw my phone into the fountain but instead, delete the app. Finally safe in my car, I look out at the people around me. I see couples smiling on benches together, having conversations with their arms draped around each other, exchanging little kisses. I envy what they have. Then a group of girls passes my car with inter-locked elbows and giggling. I need to hang with my gals. I wonder if anyone is up to anything. *Bzzz bzz* Well, isn't that a terrifying coin-cidence?

AIMEE

Hi girlie, u up for bar hopping in North Park tonight?

I know you usually tell us no but i figured I'd ask, anyway.

ANNIKA

I'm in, what time?

AIMEE

Omg yay!! Meet us at Grange at 9 pm.

SIXTEEN

ANNIKA

GRANGE IS your run-of-the-mill hipster bar. Dark wood bar-top and metal stools. Pictures of black and white photos of farm animals cover the walls. I spot Aimee and a few of her other friends at a bar top when I walk in. They are already all sipping pink, bubbly drinks, and casually talking. Grange is the go-to place to start bar hopping because it's on the quieter side, and the drinks are cheaper than other bars. So we usually get a few drinks here and then pop around to other places. I head to the bar and quickly flash my fake ID. Matching pink, bubbly drink in hand, I head over to the table, ready to forget everything that happened this afternoon.

AFTER TWO DRINKS, I realize why Chloe and I always say *no* to Aimee's invites to bar hopping. Her roommate and best friend Carly is such a brag. Even though we shared a dorm with them during Freshman year, I've never seemed to warm up to her. She can't stop talking about herself. Every time someone talks about a concert or place they went to, Carly is first to jump in with, "Oh, I've been there too!" I find myself rolling my eyes at the sixth long-winded story she tells and nearly planting a kiss on Aimee when she interrupts, suggesting we move on to the next bar.

Carly suggests we hit up Zano next—a dance club. Of course she does. We get in successfully with our fakes and grab drinks at the bar. I don't even know what Aimee ordered me, but it's electric blue and tastes like four different liquors mixed with pineapple juice. The music is loud techno music that vibrates my brain with each bass drop.

Carly yells to the group, "Let's dance, bitches!"

I smile and shake my head, shouting back, "I'll hang at the bar with our drinks!"

Carly rolls her eyes at me in return and retreats to the middle of the dance floor, where she immediately finds a poor man to gyrate against.

I sip my drink but find myself almost halfway through. The pineapple juice is scarily good at concealing the bitter alcohol taste. I take a moment to look around the club. It is packed with people. I wouldn't be shocked if the entire population of San Diego was here. I turn my attention back to the bar and try not to get lightheaded from the music pounding my head. *Or is that this drink that's making my head throb?* I slip a bit on my stool and adjust so I have one foot on the ground.

I feel a hand on my low back and a hot breath against my neck. I look to my side and see icy eyes glaring down at me.

Trey Roberts

"Hey, you, still falling over me. Look at you, hot as ever." He snakes his hand so the fingertips dip under my skirt waistband, and I jump.

He laughs at my move and takes it as an invitation to stand closer to me.

How does he manage to swoop at the worst times? I came here to have a distraction. And that distraction should not be Trey Roberts. But my tipsy brain is making my weariness blur, and the

ANJELICA ROSE

way his body heat feels against the right side of my body is oddly comforting. Against my better judgment, I lean over towards him and give him an evil smile.

"I'm surprised you aren't in jail yet." I take a long sip from my drink, which only makes the lightness of my head more severe.

He tilts his head back in a laugh and squeezes my hip. "You've always been my little pain in the ass, haven't you?"

He reaches down and caresses my ass before squeezing it a little too hard and leans down to nuzzle my neck. I can smell whiskey on his breath. I close my eyes as he starts kissing the crook of my neck, reaching his other hand to my waist, pulling me so I'm zipped against his body. My mind goes blank. I picture I'm elsewhere. Not in a bar, not making out with Trey.

I picture myself on my bed instead, and someone else is kissing my neck. Someone with warm, green eyes who smells like pine trees. Trey reaches his hand up from my waist to my hair and pulls my head back abruptly, ripping me out of my fantasy. He tilts my head so I'm looking at him directly in his eyes. His eyes terrify me, nothing but evil, and if I stare too long, I'll be under some spell.

"I've wanted you for so long," he says against my lips, and I feel my soul leave my body.

I'm no longer in control, just floating along. The alcohol is seeping into my veins, making the room look fuzzy. It feels like I'm not actually experiencing this but watching from the side. I'm watching him crash his mouth into mine and jam his tongue against mine. I try to tell myself to relax and enjoy myself. An uncomfortably tall, arguably hot man is making out with me. But I can't shake the feeling that I shouldn't be here at all. And yet I'm not pushing him away because this affection feels better than the lack thereof I've experienced for the past year and a half.

I hear Carly in the distance whistle and yell, "Yeah, you go, girl!"

Trey peels himself away from me, and I feel too hot. He whispers in my ear, "Come follow me, sweetheart."

I don't remember when I finished my drink, but it's officially taken over control of my judgment because I push up off the stool and take his hand. He weaves us through the crowd and into the hall. He pushes past a line of people and takes me into a bathroom just as someone leaves. I hear the line of people shouting in a roar. The bathroom echoes the music from the outside, and my ears are ringing.

I can barely register what Trey is saying to me, but he grabs me, pushes me against the wall, and continues mauling my mouth.

I think I can hear him muttering things like, *"You're so sexy."*

"I want you so badly."

"I wanna fuck you so hard."

Before I can react, he flips me around and bends me over the sink. I hear him unzip his pants. He lifts up my skirt and pushes my thong aside in one quick motion while I feel the pressure between my legs as he stuffs himself into me. A sharp pain stings through my abdomen as I clutch the sink. He grabs the back of my hair and starts pounding into me. It hurts and doesn't feel right. I try to tell myself to breathe, I try to tell myself to enjoy this, but I just start looking at the stickers around the mirror, hoping he will stop before I read them all.

I reach down to rub myself hoping to stimulate myself, but he yanks my arms back while he plows harder into me. He is pulling my arms back, using them as tethers to ram into me harder. The pain is gone. I feel nothing now. I just feel numb. I finish looking at the stickers and look in the mirror at Trey's reflection. His ice-blue eyes look evil as he's looking down my back. He squeezes and jack-hammers into me, grunting and cursing under his breath. I can't meet my own eyes in the mirror, so instead, I look directly at the light above it. Blinding my vision until I see black spots. Maybe I'm hallucinating about this whole situation. *When will I wake up?*

After what feels like hours but was probably five minutes, I feel Trey pull out of me suddenly and grunt while I feel a hot stream hitting my thigh. He mumbles something and then leaves the bathroom. No goodbye kiss. Not checking if I finished. No cleaning up the mess he made on me. He leaves me bent over some grimy bar sink with my skirt halfway up my torso and my thong stretched and torn around my legs. It takes me a moment, but somehow I get up and wash my leg off and use the bathroom. I feel like I'm on autopilot, steering myself outside of my body to just get out of the bathroom. I pull out my phone and make a reminder to get Plan B and an STD test at the university clinic tomorrow.

There is still a line of people outside of the bathroom. Some try to give me a high-five, while others just glare at me like I'm the nastiest thing they've ever seen. I get to the main floor, and somehow the number of people in the club has doubled. I don't see Aimee and Carly anywhere. But I see Trey. He's at the bar, leaning into another girl's neck like he didn't just fuck me less than a minute ago and leave himself dripping down my leg. I push my way through and reach the night air.

The cold air hits me like a punch to the gut. I start walking. I pass people laughing and talking on the sidewalk all around me, but I've never felt more alone. I feel wetness hit my chest and think it's raining. But when I look up at the clear night sky, I realize I'm crying. I walk down the sidewalk, sobbing. All my insecurities ruminate in my mind. *Who am I? Where did I go? Why did I put myself in this situation? I need better. I need anything better than this. How can I get better than this?*

Well, figure it out. Reid's last message echoes in my brain, and I lean against a wall crumbling in my tears. Well, figure it out, Annika. I need to figure it out.

I lower to a squat and press my phone to my ear. *Chloe, can you come pick me up?...No, I'm not okay...I'm in North Park near Zano.--- Please hurry. I can't be alone right now.*

PART 3

ADULTHOOD - FOUR YEARS LATER

find your cozy, stay awhile

POSTCARD

Hey Dad!

Auburn Hills is a dream so far!
Working with Uncle Marty is the
best. You and Pam would love it
here, please visit soon and often!
Carrie says hey, hopefully you
meet her soon.

Love, Reid

Sean Parker
638 Hemlock Way
Napa, CA 94559

SEVENTEEN

REID

"HEY, babe, can you grab the reusable bags?" I shout to Carrie from the top of the stairs while I dart around my bedroom, looking for my car keys.

The farmer's market opens at nine, and it's a quarter till. Carrie insists on getting there when they open so she can buy the ripest berries. I honestly don't understand why she doesn't just partner with the local farmers. She owns one of the best bakeries in town. I'm sure they would work with her to deliver the best berries and save me three hours of my life every Saturday morning.

I met Carrie early on when I moved to Auburn Hills, Oregon about a year and a half ago. I liked her feistiness and admired that she owned her own business. After a few months of stopping in for a morning pastry, I finally worked up the nerve to ask her out. Nine months later, I'm still going with her on Saturday morning farmer's market trips. My buddy and coworker, Tyler, can't stand her, but I think their personalities just clash. This is the longest relationship I've been in, and yet it feels new every day. Like I'm still learning who the person I'm dating is. She still feels like a stranger at times.

"I have my own bags...let's go. We are going to be late!" Carrie yells back, and I can hear her opening the front door.

I finally find my keys under a pile of yesterday's jeans and dash downstairs. She's already standing by my pickup truck, one hand on the door handle. I unlock it and hustle around to the driver's seat. We are quiet as I drive the five-minute journey downtown.

The farmer's market is a town event that takes place every Saturday in the parking lot of Auburn Hills High School. Everyone, and I mean *everyone*, is here. Even people from neighboring towns like Medford to towns in Northern California come here. The farmer's market is an event everyone hustles to get to, especially my girlfriend. Usually, she picks me up, or she'll hit it by herself and swing by after. But she spent the night at my place last night, so I am honored with the pleasure of driving us at ten to eight in the morning.

As I take the turn toward the Main Street, Carrie makes a dramatic gasp when she sees the cars lined up to get in. "I *told* you we should have left earlier." She gives me a side-eye that could cut through ice.

"Just get out and head in. I'll circle around and look for parking." I'll probably end up ditching and hitting a coffee shop instead.

"No, because you probably won't even come in." *Dammit.* Is she in my head?

We've been dating long enough that she knows me too well. I don't know if I like it. Then I look over to her to see if she heard my thoughts, and she just gives me a scowl. I'm still unsure if she can read my mind. "Just pull along a side street and park there."

I listen to her orders and start driving along the side streets adjacent to the farmer's market. As I dart around, I start drumming the wheel and humming along to a Bon Jovi song I think I heard playing at work yesterday.

"Can you stop that? *Please.*" Carrie shoots daggers at my hands on the wheel. She looks up at me, and if this was a cartoon, she'd have smoke coming out of her ears. "You know, on second thought,

I can't sit here anymore. I'm going to just walk there. You do whatever you want."

I stop and pull toward the side of the street, and before I can protest, she hops out. Something has been bothering her ever since we got home from dinner.

What did I do?

Being in a relationship is a fucking nightmare sometimes. Half of the time, you laugh and share memories, and the other half, you said or did something wrong during the first half, which makes her ignore you for forty-eight hours until you decipher why she is mad. I drive around the street a few times before I finally find an open space two blocks from the farmer's market. I go to reach for my bags and realize she never brought my bags. She only brought her own. This is some kind of cruel revenge trip she's on.

I thought yesterday went fine, but after she took a shower, it seems like she turned into her alter ego. The version that despises me. When she's this way, I even wonder if she still likes me. What is the point in being with someone if they treat you like shit fifty percent of the time? I feel like I'm giving her all of me, and yet I only get her free trial.

Like our previous fights, I retrace my steps to figure out what I did wrong in her eyes. Yesterday started normally like any other weekday. I picked up a cold brew with sweet cream foam before heading into the wellness center. My uncle had a doctor's appointment, so I was the manager in charge. We had a few regulars in for their routine physical therapy appointments, one new client, and Tyler, who is the massage therapist, saw three people for one-hour deep tissue treatments. Tyler and I went and got sandwiches at this walk-up counter spot for lunch a few blocks down like we do every Friday. It was a standard workday, and honestly, now that I think of it, we are doing great in terms of clientele. I make a mental note to bring up an idea of a member's day to my uncle to celebrate the increase in sign-ups.

After work, I walked down to Carrie's bakery. She was hustling as usual. She closes the shop at two in the afternoon but spends four hours afterward prepping for the next day. Now that I think of it, she was probably prepping for opening staff because she wasn't going to be there in the morning to pick up supplies from the farmer's market. We walked down to a local diner for dinner, and each ordered veggie burgers and beers before heading back to my house.

I let her pick what movie we watched, and she went with *Perks of Being a Wallflower*. It actually wasn't as terrible as I expected. Then we made out on the couch and moved to the bedroom. If I'm being honest with myself, we had pretty average sex, but it wasn't out of the ordinary. We took showers and went to bed. She turned away from me all night and didn't cuddle with me, which hinted to me that she was pissed about something.

Shit.

She was talking about how she wanted to spend more time at my apartment. I got the vibe she was trying to ask if she could move in with me, but I am not ready for that. *Did she tell me she loved me? Double shit.* I don't know if I want her in my space. I don't know if I even love her. My lack of response must have pissed her off.

I reach the market and look around, hoping to see her curly red hair. I spot her by the fig booth. She's laughing at something the vendor is saying to her. He is a big, burly guy with a beard I could never grow, holding up two figs in either hand, bouncing them up and down. *What the fuck is going on over there?*

I catch up to her and stand beside her. "Hey, I finally found a spot. What we got here, some saggy figs?" I crack a smile and shine it over to the vendor and Carrie.

Her laugh immediately drops, and she turns to walk to the next booth.

What the fuck. I reach out to her shoulder to turn her back to face me. "Hey Carrie, what is going on? You can't keep icing me out like this. I can't read your mind." I try to keep my voice down, but this is getting ridiculous.

"Can you not make a scene at the farmer's market? This is my safe space." She glares and looks around to see if anyone is over-hearing us.

Of course, a few people are, everyone in this town is nosy as hell, but that's what you get from a small town. People thrive on gossip like it's oxygen. Nothing else really goes on here, so the young couple arguing at the farmer's market might even make headlines.

"We have to talk about it, Carrie." I keep my voice calm and stern, maintaining eye contact.

She puts her hand up to me and says, "Let me finish up, and I'll meet you by the entrance." With that, she turns away and continues her way along the booths. I go to do the same and head to the entrance. Not before I see that fucking fig vendor hand her a small piece of paper.

I HANG out by the entrance until I see her small, fiery form blaze past me, nearly knocking me over with her armful of bags. She's walking like she knows where I parked, except she's walking in the opposite direction.

"Hey, I parked over toward Magnolia Street." I basically have to break into a jog to meet up with her. "Carrie, what the fuck is going on with you?"

"I can't do this, Reid."

Those words ache in my chest like a nightmare that keeps haunting me. I don't even need her to keep talking to know how the story ends, and yet she continues with her rant. "I pour my heart out to you, and I get nothing in return. I told you I loved you, and you just looked at me. You didn't say it back to me. It's been nearly a year, and you haven't asked me to move in. You haven't done anything to show me you care about me."

With that, everything I've been holding in starts pouring out. "If anyone has been leaving crumbs, it's you. You always find something to argue with me about. I can't do anything without you finding a problem with it. I do care about you, and I am losing energy."

"That's your problem, you give your energy everywhere else, and you don't care to devote any to your own girlfriend." She turns to a car that is pulling up and goes to the backseat before looking back at me. "If it isn't clear, I'm breaking up with you."

"Do you even love me? Or was that just something to say to move in with me?"

She turns back to me and says, "Fuck you, Reid."

"Fuck you, Carrie!"

A stupid, low response, but she flips me off as she gets in the Uber and slams the door. *Fuck.* I rub my eyes, exhausted like I just ran a marathon, and turn to see a flock of older women with their reusable bags in arms glaring at me in disgust. Of course, it's my fault.

I FINALLY GET HOME and feel like absolute shit. I can't even gather myself to tackle my to-do list on the fridge. I sit on the couch and think back to what Carrie said. It felt like we were in the same relationship dating different people. We were dating what we wanted the other person to be. I didn't fit the mold she created for the perfect boyfriend. Maybe she'll find love in Mr. Fig Vendor. Honestly, I wish her the best because the last thing I want for her is to dwell on this relationship.

But shit, I almost spent a year with her, and it's over in an instant. I go by each day thinking about a person. What they are up to, how they are feeling, and within an hour, it's as if all of that doesn't even matter anymore. I couldn't care less about what she is up to right now. I wish I could erase her from my mind. I wish I could rewind back a year and get my time back. I get up and find an empty cardboard box and start going around my house, gathering everything that reminds me of her. A fuzzy pink scrunchie with red hairs tangled around it in my key bowl, a single sock at the bottom of my hamper, and her sugar-free soy milk in the fridge. That's going directly into the trash. I should have known her not liking oat milk was a red flag.

My scavenger hunt for my ex's items turns into a full deep clean of my apartment. I even break out the duster I bought when I first moved into this apartment a couple of years ago. I realize I'm probably doing this to keep my mind busy so I don't think about Carrie. At least my house will get the cleaning it desperately needs. I should burn some of the palo santo that my coworker Nancy gave me for Christmas to cleanse the air. My phone starts buzzing in my back pocket, and I wince when I pull it out, worried it's her already. I really don't want to work things out. I'm done with the guilt she makes me feel. Thankfully, my dad's photo lights up my screen. The picture is him in a jovial, belly filled laugh that instantly calms me down.

"Hey, Dad, what's up?" I sandwich my phone between my ear and my shoulder as I try to dust the tops of all my door frames.

"Hi-what's wrong? What happened?" I swear I can sneeze, and he can tell something is wrong.

I let out a sigh. "Carrie dumped me."

"Oh, son…" He lets out a sigh of his own, "I'm sorry, breakups are never easy. How long has it been since she split?" I hear the sink running in the background. We are both fussing around our houses to get things tidied up. Like father, like son.

"Hm." I look over at the clock on the stove. "Probably two hours now."

The faucet promptly shuts off. "That's it? You sound sad, but not two-hours-fresh-breakup-sad."

"Yeah, I think it was destined to end at some point. We were bickering more, and I was happier when I was away from her."

I plop down on my couch and curl myself in a quilt Pam made me when I moved up to Oregon. She stitched gradients of greens in a spiral pattern and added tassels to the edges. She put a fuzzy flannel on the bottom so it is soft and comforting.

"Well, get yourself some tissues and let it out. You can focus on yourself now. Didn't you two start dating when you first moved up there?"

"About a couple of months later, I walked into her bakery and asked her on a date. And I don't cry over breakups anymore. I realized I didn't even feel that strongly toward Carrie." Haven't felt that way since college.

"Oh, Reid, you never did get over Anni." I immediately wince at the mention of her name. "That was a rough breakup for you. I always thought it was serendipitous how you dated after having a crush on her in middle school."

I never should have brought it up. I can barely unpack my latest relationship, let alone one that barely lasted a month in college. I felt so alone after. I just called my dad and Pam, who took turns on the phone with me for three hours. Probably the most I've cried, and I just felt so embarrassed by it. I'm not going to cry over Carrie.

"Pam! Get in here. Reid needs one of our famous counseling sessions again!" I hear my dad calling out on the other end, which I can't help but laugh at.

"Dad, I'm twenty-four I don't need my parents consoling me. I'm fine, trust me." I wrap the quilt tighter around me and would give anything to teleport Pam here so she can make me some soup. Maybe I do need my parents to console me after all.

"All right, if you say so. And hey, we are going to see you next weekend. So if you need to bottle up your emotions, we'll be there soon enough, and you can let it out. You'll have two sets of shoulders to cry on." I close my eyes and am thankful that the drive from the Bay Area to southern Oregon is more manageable, so Dad and Pam come to visit every other month. "I've got a few boxes of your things to bring you now that you have a house. I'm cleaning up the garage to convert into my retirement workshop."

"I'm renting. It's not my house, Dad."

"But it's a lot more space than you ever had in California!"

That's true. I get more space here for the rent than I ever would in San Diego or in the Bay Area. "I'll see you guys next weekend. Thanks for the chat."

"Love you, Reid," my dad says. "Love you, Reid!" I hear Pam echo in the distance.

I hang up and turn on *The Godfather* for the twentieth time. I'd like to stay curled under this quilt for three uninterrupted hours.

EIGHTEEN

REID

MY DOORBELL RINGS bright and early the following Saturday. I pull my covers over my head and pretend that it was a dream, except my doorbell dings again, and my phone buzzes at the same time seconds later. I stick just my arm out and fish for my phone on my bedside table, knocking over my water bottle in the process. Or at least, I hope that was my water bottle.

9:54 a.m.

I let out a deep sigh. I used to be such an early riser, but this whole week has me in a funk. I'm blaming the breakup, which is a viable excuse. If this were a Saturday in a relationship with Carrie, we'd be on our way back from the farmer's market by now. But now, I'm alone. Finally, I get to sleep in. I feel cozy in my bed, not wanting to peel myself up to answer the door. However, I know that what lies behind that door is most likely my dad with boxes of my college paraphernalia and Pam with an armful of home cooking. I can practically taste the freshly baked cookies on my tongue, and that alone inspires me to fling out of bed. I pull on a pair of black joggers and a matching hoodie to answer the front door. I can see my dad and Pam trying to peer through the side windows and incessantly knocking.

As I swing the door open, they both fling open their arms and say, "Heyyy," while diving in for a group hug.

"It's ten a.m. What time did you leave to drive up here? Three?"

"No, no, a little before five! Your dad can get us up here in less than five hours." Pam squeezes me in for an extra hug after we separate from the group hug.

She and my dad act like they've been married my whole life, but it's only been five years. It wasn't until Pam joined our family that I realized how special it is to have a mom figure in my life. I'm still not at the point of calling her mom, but they are my parents, and Pam spoils me like a son of her own.

Each month, she'll mail me a care package with candy and a book she thinks I'll enjoy. I almost have a tiny library in my house now, thanks to her. Our calls where we discuss the book are some of my favorite things I look forward to. Reading's always been a secret hobby of mine. I never bragged to my friends about my reaching one hundred books read last year or attending book signings for some of my favorite authors.

I found out how big of a reader Pam was when I visited them about a year after they moved into their new house. She turned a whole wall in the living room into a book display. Since then, we have talked nonstop about books. It is the best feeling when you can relate to a friend about a hobby you are both passionate about. I get so much joy from nerding out over font size or cracking the spine, how I prefer dog-earring to bookmarks, and how Pam chooses a pen that matches the cover to annotate.

I help them with the boxes they brought, and we wander into my small galley kitchen. I was right. Pam brought me about four containers of food, and one looks to be in the shape of Snicker-doodle cookies. Those will be gone in a day.

I tell Dad he can put the cardboard boxes in the storage closet off the living room for now, and I'll go through it later, and we head out to breakfast. They love wandering through downtown Auburn

Hills. I've lived here for almost two years and still feel like a newbie. I'm constantly learning about hidden gems and town gossip.

Hopefully, I'm too new not to be the hot gossip that the town physical therapist and baker split up. Although, how would I know? This week, I've just gone from my house straight to the wellness center and back home. I don't think I've seen another soul aside from my clients and coworkers, and none have mentioned anything about my relationship or lack thereof.

We spend the rest of the day bopping around town, in and out of little shops. Dad finds a vintage aluminum sign at an antique store that says *Dad's Den* that he wants to hang up in his new workshop. That evening after Pam heats up some of the food she brought up, gooey mac and cheese with chicken wings, we settle in my living room and put on a movie. It really feels great to have my parents here, not only for their comfort but also just for human connection. It's been nice to chat about what we are up to, any recent news, or really anything that comes to mind.

My parents spend the night on the pull-out couch I have in my living room before they head back tomorrow. Maybe next time they visit, I can persuade them to move up here. My dad already has two family members living here, and both he and Pam are retired. Pam's family all lives in Michigan, so there's nothing really keeping them in the Bay Area other than the perfect weather. My dad worked so often as a kid I feel like he and I barely spent time together. Just the idea of him being nearby so I can go over to his house to work on projects or have coffee with Pam puts an instant smile on my face.

"Hey, kiddo, what are you smiling about?" My dad catches me smiling to myself at the thought of having my folks nearby.

"Oh, just thinking about how nice it would be to have you living down the street from me instead of six hours down the I-five."

"Aye, five hours is all it takes *me*."

I chuckle and try not to think too much of my dad flying down the highway over the speed limit. "But seriously, would you consider moving up here?"

"You really mean that? I don't want to be crowding your space. Plus, I wasn't sure how long you'd be up here. You've lived in three different cities in the past five years."

"Despite having burned one bridge already, I really like it up here. I love working with Uncle Marty, and even though I'm renting, this place is maybe starting to feel like a home."

"Since when did your Uncle start letting you call him Marty? He makes everyone else call him Martin." He narrows his eyes in response. I can sense a phone call later between brothers.

"It's because I'm his favorite nephew...well, think about it. I'd love to have you up here. I'm sure Uncle Marty would too." I pull my dad in for a final hug before he and Pam head back to Napa.

My house still smells like leftovers long after they leave. I treat myself to two cookies while I go through some of my old college belongings. I want to keep this train of nostalgia going. It feels like a time capsule as I open the box. I don't think I've seen some of this stuff in years.

My old sweater from UCSD and the pennant I hung on my wall greets me on top of the pile. They smell like that pine candle my roommate was always burning. I swear I smelled like a tree for four years straight. I start digging through papers and textbooks until my fingers brush against a soft velvet pouch in the bottom corner. I know what it is before even opening it. In fact, I don't even want to open it. An unhealed wound begins to reopen, and my mood turns sour. Looking in this box was a terrible idea. I completely forgot I threw the necklace in here all those years ago.

I sink onto my couch, the velvet pouch clutched tightly in my fist. I feel the corners of the pendent digging into my palm and let my eyes close and drift over memories of Annika. I can't think about her without breathing uneasily. I don't know why this happens to me. We went on *two-ish* dates, and yet I react to her name being said like taking a baseball to the gut. It feels more significant than that.

It feels like a life-altering opportunity brushed by me. We have a history that goes beyond our college fling, if you can even call it that. From being kiddos in elementary school and not understanding the fuzzy feeling she'd give me. To my dizzying crush on her in middle school. When I confessed to my dad about her, he helped me get supplies to make a card I was going to ask her to the dance with. It was hard for him to tell me we were moving before I could give it to her. I don't even remember that whole move because of how sad I was.

Seeing her at Isaac's birthday party felt like a second chance, like it was meant to be. We were meant to reconnect after all these years, to fall in love. If only things had gone differently. I can picture us hand in hand throughout college, and maybe we would have gotten an off-campus apartment together. I don't know if I'd still have ended up in Oregon, but I'm sure we'd have moved out of San Diego. A wave of overwhelming feelings envelope me, sickening my stomach.

I'm realizing this is probably where I went wrong. I was planning what art we'd hang on the wall, and I couldn't even tell you what her middle name is. I fell too hard, and it left a bruise that never healed. I squeeze the pouch again, aching the bruise, just to feel my memories before they fade. I take a deep sigh and put the pouch in the entryway table by the door. Maybe I'll take it to the pawn shop later this week. I'm sure I could get five bucks for it.

NINETEEN

ANNIKA

WHOEVER INVENTED corporate offices can go to hell. I hate coming into this gray office filled with cubicles. I hate the pretentious looks from my coworkers as you walk in on a Monday. I hate them half asking about your day before pressing you for deadlines. I hate the shared microwave that no one cleans. But most of all, I hate being stuck in hour-long meetings just so executives can hear themselves talk.

I can feel the years of turmoil just to get a college degree crumbling away on this job. Being a marketing strategist at one of San Diego's flashiest marketing agencies seems like a dream for anyone two years out of college. Yet I feel more out of place than ever before. I feel like I'm pretending to be someone else when those elevator doors open to the fifth-floor corporate building overlooking Balboa Park.

I can't help but feel like an asshole because what a privilege it is to have a well-paying job that aligns with what I studied in college. I think of Chloe, who keeps getting rejected by agencies just to become a bookstore chain Store Manager instead. And yet, I envy her. I envy the freedom of not having to work in an office and instead being surrounded by books and quiet customers. I realize my eyes are starting to glaze over as the marketing director has been droning on for twelve minutes about the importance of connecting customers to whatever brand we are working on, some surfboard company, I think.

The only thing that is keeping me awake is my 35 mm Olympus film camera with a Zuiko 1.7 40mm lens tucked into my tote bag's pocket. My most prized possession that I dug out of a bin of old cameras at the Long Beach flea three years ago. It took several how-to videos and rolls of discarded film to get it in a functioning state, but it is one of the small joys in my life. At first, I only took pictures I thought were worth taking. But then I felt like I wasn't enjoying the moments, only critiquing them. So now I bring three rolls of film with me along with my camera at all times.

Last year, Chloe pushed me to create a website and start free-lance work. I started out by just taking some new profile pictures for friends and coworkers, but it's expanded to small parties, and even last month, I did my first wedding all on film. I'd give anything just to be able to quit my marketing job to take photos, but there are things like bills and student loans and not wanting to disappoint my family by not having a salaried job.

My parents always tell me how proud they are of me and that I got my degree and work at a job that I can apply it to. I could never quit this job just to take pictures all day. I can't quit the pride they feel. Finally, my coworkers start to shuffle, which means it's time to ditch this meeting and hide in my desk cubby, pretending to work for three more hours. I wonder how many trips to the bathroom I can take before someone starts to notice.

QUITTING time gives me the same relief as the last bell ringing in grade school. *Freedom.* My time is no longer tied to my workplace. I am in control of the next few hours before I have to repeat this song and dance again tomorrow. I pack up my tote and try to make it out before anyone talks to me. Yesterday as I was leaving for the day, my manager Samantha flagged me down to ask me the status of my projects and if I could give her a rundown tomorrow morning. I spent forty minutes last night figuring out what a *rundown* even meant.

My entire work-life balance is thrown out the window. I feel like I am levitating through the office as I make it to the door and down the stairs. Only one more day until the weekend. Is this how the rest of my life will be? Counting down the hours, minutes, and days until the weekend, when I have full reign to do whatever I want but still feel tied to a job I dislike so deeply that it feels like it is crushing my soul. I may sound dramatic, but that's because I am dramatic. I just remind myself that I am still young and I have my whole life to figure things out. I'll just let the older me handle my workplace turmoil.

I WAS GOING to wander Balboa Park to take pictures, but I'm feeling particularly drained after ruminating on my career angst and need to decompress. So I return to the place where I completely feel like myself. Pure Annika.

Pacific Beach is comfortingly always the same. No matter how many years pass, it feels like that day six years ago when I met that floppy-haired boy at the pier and twirled in the sand. The beach isn't very crowded for a weekday in March, so I take a spot on the sand near the pier, making sure it's the perfect distance from the water so no one walks in front of me but also not too close where my blanket might get wet. I don't know why I keep coming here. *Who am I kidding? Of course I know why.*

There are so many other beaches in San Diego, and yet I come back here whenever I feel particularly lost. I lay back and close my eyes feeling the sun setting through my eyelids. A little girl giggles in the distance, and I hear a faint sound of hip-hop music coming from one of the booths on the pier. I easily drift back to that day with Reid and let the pang of missed opportunities weigh in my chest. His touch on my face and his laugh at my salty remarks replay on a loop. The feeling haunts me. However, I keep coming back here. I give in to the ache in my chest so I know I can still feel something. Everyone tells you the path to take after college, but no one tells you that you'll be living life on autopilot, a dullness sweeping over you as you do the same motions every day of the week.

Work infiltrating my brain means it's time to snap out of my waking nightmare. My camera is already loaded with film, so I get started taking pictures and get lost in my viewfinder. The ocean is a constant calm. It will always come back when the tide pulls away. I know it will always be there for me when I come to visit it. It won't flake on you at the last minute, and it won't break your heart.

I take a few pictures of the tide and turn my attention to the other evening beachgoers. A little girl is building a sand castle that looks more like a sand shed, but her dedication is impressive. A man is throwing a frisbee at his Australian shepherd on the beach. I wait for the moment when the dog is reaching up in the air to catch it in its mouth before hitting the shutter. I gaze around, and finally, a couple gets my attention. They are cradling each other, sitting on a green blanket, looking toward the setting sun.

The smaller spoon gazes up to their partner and smiles with their entire face, and I see the love they have for one another wash over their expressions and snap a photo. No matter where they are in their lives, they are savoring this moment together. I turn my attention to the sea. The sun is starting to dip to the horizon, and the sky is swirling its medley of colors. Pinks and corals blend into reds and warm yellows. The blue sky fades behind the transition. I take shots of the sun setting just as it dips below the deep teal water, and a chill washes through the air.

· · ·

CHLOE IS ALREADY HOME as I walk into our shared apartment in the East Village. We moved here after graduating college so we could each have our own bedroom, and it feels like our cozy little clubhouse. All our memories are framed on the walls and displayed on DIY canvas art we've created on drunken weekend evenings. She's humming a song while she twirls around the kitchen. I'm about to call out to her when I hear Dane's voice. This is the third night in a row he's been here. I can tolerate him, but he still acts like he barely knows me, even though he and Chloe have dated on and off for years now.

So I avoid the kitchen and head to my room, but not before seeing a brown bag resting against my door. The perk of living with a bookstore manager, she will surprise me with a book every so often, and it delights me every time. This time she gave me a copy of *Women Who Run With The Wolves,* and I can't help but feel like this is a jab toward my single-and-loving-it lifestyle. Whenever Chloe and Dane are on, she puts on her relationship guru hat and spurts out words of wisdom. I flip over the paperback and read the quote at the top, "She is the Wild Woman, who represents the instinctual nature of women."

Is she trying to tell me I am a wild woman or that I need to start living like a wild woman? It's been four years since my last…encounter. But I still don't feel ready to get back out there. I reached such a low point in my life back then that I really don't want to get to that point again. For the last four years, I've been focused on myself and discovering what I need in life with the help of my therapist. Yet I still feel like I'm aimlessly wandering through life. Perhaps I do need to be a wild woman.

I wait until I hear the common space is quiet to emerge from my bedroom and heat up some leftover pesto ravioli. I take my bowl and curl up on the couch, reading about how I can embrace my womanhood and thrive on passionate creativity.

TWENTY

ANNIKA

I ROLL around in my bed when the revelation hits me. It's the weekend. The weekend is *my* time. I zone out every unanswered email and push away the culpable feeling that I should call my mom to catch up. Maybe I'll try a new coffee shop or buy a new vintage jacket. I think I have some film that is ready to be picked up.

But most exciting of all, Chloe and I have plans this weekend to visit the art museum. I kick my feet in excitement under my fluffy duvet. They have a new film photography exhibit that I've been dying to see, plus Chloe loves wandering through the expressionist painters' section. Second to thrifting, this is our favorite activity to do together. I come out of my room to find Chloe sitting on the kitchen counter, her legs wrapped around Dane's shirtless, tanned torso while he inhales her face.

Just the image I wanted to see first thing in the morning. It's not that I dislike seeing Chloe in a happy relationship, just...why do they have to be in one right in front of me? I can't help but feel grossed out while pushing down the pang of jealousy in my chest. Then I remember the *Women Who Run With Wolves* book, I only got through half of it, but it did motivate me to be independent and go after my passions.

I stomp my feet obnoxiously as I walk into the kitchen, and it does absolutely nothing to deter Chloe from running her hand through Dane's hair and pulling him closer to her.

"Ya know, our kitchen is only fifty square feet, and I'd really love to make some breakfast."

This seems to perk Dane up as he yanks himself away from Chloe and turns to me. Chloe adjusts her legs and sets her head on his shoulder.

"Good morning to you too, Ally. Got enough ingredients to make breakfast for two more?"

He and Chloe both give me puppy-dog eyes, and maybe I'd consider it if it weren't for the fact that he called me *Ally*.

"Sorry, *Derek*, I'm vegetarian, and I don't like to share."

Dane flinches back either at me calling him Derek or that I'm vegetarian, I can't tell. "My name is Dane. I've known you for six years, Ally."

And I truly can't hold back my laughter at the irony of his state-ment, which offends him immensely because he storms out of the kitchen.

Chloe is still sitting on the counter, giving me a frowning pout. She knows I don't like Dane. I really don't know how this happened. When they first dated in college, he seemed fine, and the fact that he spoiled my best friend and made her happy was all I cared about. But now, like he said, it's been six years, and I've seen them break up and get back together probably five times already. It's exhausting, and I don't think it's the best for Chloe. She is the best person in my life. She is the sunshine to my storm cloud and deserves to have someone who basks in her light, not block it. I don't want to see her like she was in middle school when her dad left. She deserves someone who is completely obsessed with her. Dane is comfortable with her, but she deserves so much better than him.

"Dane knows your name, and he's just joking," she responds with a hop off the counter.

"I really don't think he does. He calls me the wrong name every time he sees me. It's pretty pathetic, I'm the closest person in your life, and he can't even get my name right?" I get an eye roll response at that, and she tries to shuffle out of the kitchen to avoid any more of my sass. "Hey, wait, are we still on for the museum later?" She slides to a halt.

"Oh...was that today?" She turns to me, grimacing. "It's just that Dane is revealing his new drink at the cafe today, and he wants me there for support."

I can't help my mouth from falling open. She's ditching me to watch her boyfriend make lattes? Is this what our friendship has come to? Putting our on and off again boyfriends in front of our friendship of literally over fifteen years? Although I shouldn't be surprised, she did this to me two weeks ago when I wanted to try out a new coffee shop. She said Dane would never speak to her again if she stepped foot in another coffee shop. I laughed at that until I realized she was being serious. This whole charade is tiring.

She's never put a guy before our friendship before. This might be a good sign that they are actually starting to get serious and commit to one another. The sinking feeling in my chest is trying to convince me otherwise, however. He's going to do something idiotic, and I'm going to be left wiping Chloe's tears. I am about to open my mouth in protest when all the energy to try drains from me. *What is even the point?* I shouldn't have to persuade my best friend to hang out with me.

"Got it, of course, that's today." I'm trying so hard not to be overly passive-aggressive, but it's hard, so I just turn and prepare a breakfast sandwich. Chloe doesn't say another word, and instead, I hear her shuffle away and her bedroom door close. I guess I'll have another solo weekend. No big deal...

· · ·

THE MUSEUM WAS SPECTACULAR. A part of me is grateful I was alone so I could spend as much time standing in front of a photo staring longingly at it. I love putting myself in the artist's shoes. Picturing what they did that day before taking the photo. *Was it just a normal day for them? Did they go to work at a boring job and, on the way home, snap a photo? Or was it a planned photo scout? What did it feel like to hold the camera in their hands and hold it up just at the perfect moment to capture the art?*

I wandered through the exhibit for over an hour, soaking up each interesting piece. It featured art from photographers in Paris, shot between the 1930s and the 1970s. There was something so romantic about the photos. I loved seeing the Parisian fashion and the settings from so long ago. There was a particular photo I couldn't tear my eyes from. They had a few by Robert Doisneau and his most notable—a couple embraced in a kiss while the streets of Paris hustled around them. The juxtaposition between stillness and foot traffic was so fascinating. Despite the rumors that it might've been staged, there's just something so captivating about the couple. I spent at least twenty minutes digesting the black-and-white photo.

Life seemed both simpler and more complicated back then. I wonder if it ever gets easier. There were moments I wish I had someone with me to share what I loved about certain pieces. I missed Chloe. She would never protest if I wanted to linger a bit longer. I ended up checking out some of the painting exhibits as well and bought her a sunflower pin from the museum shop.

Eager to give it to her and share my favorite pieces, I swing open our apartment door to find Dane's naked ass in clear view while he's grinding into Chloe on our couch.

Our communal couch.

The one in our living room.

Where I sit and read and eat snacks.

I'm going to have to burn this couch now. I don't think I'll be able to sit on it again without having the mental image of Dane and

Chloe in the nude tangled around each other. I slam the front door and bolt into my room, not wanting to witness the front view of Dane but hoping they stop to realize how inappropriate they are being. Chloe has a couch in her room. Why can't they use that one instead? I don't have the energy anymore. Maybe I need to get my own place. Their relationship is affecting my mental health.

I feel so guilty about it. I should be happy for Chloe, but I'm not. I'm bitter. I want her to find someone else who's not an asshole. I want to find someone I can be so enamored with. Next time it's just Chloe and me alone, I'm going to bring up the idea of us living apart. The thought of living away from her feels scary, but maybe it's what she and Dane need if they are getting serious about their relationship.

TWENTY-ONE

ANNIKA

IT'S A THURSDAY EVENING. I should be sitting in my apartment, reading, watching a movie, or literally anything else besides sitting in my cubicle at work. It's after seven, and I'm frantically typing up a marketing outline for a new client we are hoping to get. Even though I don't care about this client, I'm still here after hours. Because I was guilted into staying longer. I want to be promoted so I can make more money and work less. My manager dangled this promotion in front of my face when she asked me to stay after and finish the draft that we will present tomorrow. Everything was last minute, and the worst part of it is, this client isn't even huge. They are an indie brand that has barely been gaining momentum. Don't get me wrong, I think they could totally use the marketing help, but it doesn't need to involve me working overtime so we can present at the last minute.

I hear a buzz from my tote bag, and my heart drops. I had a scheduled client tonight for headshots, and I completely forgot. I grab my phone and swipe open my messages.

CLIENT

Hi, I'm just checking to see if we are still on? I haven't heard anything from you.

ANNIKA

Hi, I am so sorry, an emergency came up. Can I reschedule you for tomorrow? Same time?

CLIENT

Oh no worries. I hope everything is good, and sorry tomorrow doesn't work. I think I'm just going to reuse my old headshots. Thanks

ANNIKA

Of course. I'd be happy to give you a 30% discount, let me know if you change your mind.

I can't afford to give the discount, but I also can't afford to pass up this freelance work. Especially if I want to get my own place. I brought the idea up to Chloe two nights ago, and she nearly broke down in tears. She said she couldn't function if I was not sleeping at least ten feet away from her. And she calls *me* dramatic.

I finish up the outline and head out of the office. The entire place is dark except for my cubicle. I can't do this anymore. I can't keep pretending like I enjoy my life. I'm so young, and yet I feel like my routine is aging me ten years. I need a change. I start crying while I drive home and don't stop until I'm home sitting at my desk. Wiping my tears away, I fling open my laptop and panic apply for jobs. This time, no marketing jobs. I am admitting to myself that I hate it. I hate the major I picked for myself. I hate that I feel guilty that I spent this money on an education I don't want to use, but I can't let it tear me down. I apply for photographer jobs, vintage shop curator jobs, and anything that sounds the slightest bit interesting. I even apply at a local tattoo parlor.

It's nearly midnight, and I think I've applied to twenty applications. I'm so exhausted. Mentally and physically drained. I don't even remember when I managed to take a shower and put on pajamas, but now I'm crawling into bed. I hope I sleep through my alarm and don't wake up until Saturday. I don't know how many more days I can take it before I just walk out of my job without any sort of backup plan.

TWENTY-TWO

ANNIKA

I MANAGE to peel myself out of bed after my mental breakdown and frantic job-hunting the night before. I manage to put on a content face on as I walk into work and sit through the client proposal meeting. As I watch my manager present my outline that I slaved three hours of my time after work to finish. I manage not to combust when the wetsuit company says they can't afford our budget and backs out. I manage to repeat my routine through the next day through the next week.

Midday Thursday, I get pinched awake in the form of an email in my inbox.

Subject: Interview for Film Photographer Position

I nearly fall out of my chair and reread the subject line five times before opening the email. I got an interview. I seriously doubted anything was going to come out of those twenty applications, and yet here is one. A local photo studio that specializes in event photography is looking for a film photographer. This couldn't be any more perfect. I crouch around my phone at my desk and send off a response scheduling an interview for the next morning.

~one week later~

My morning routine is muscle memory now. Get up, do yoga in my room, shower, blow dry my hair pin-straight, fluff it off to the side, apply eyeliner, and eat a breakfast wrap on the way to the office. Today, I decided to check some emails while blow-drying my hair. I've been frantically checking it ever since my first interview. I've had a few more since, and they all seem promising, but I can't tell if I made enough of an impression to get a job offer. I can't stop trying. I need to pick myself up out of this depressing hole. I swipe through some emails, noticing a few stores are having a sale. Very tempting, but I should probably not get anything as I'm on a savings spree. I nearly dropped my blow dryer at the subject line of one email that is different from the rest.

Subject: Position Offer Letter: Film Photographer

I can't believe it. I got offered the job. Out of all of them, this was the one I was most excited about. I would make slightly less than I do now, but I would work fewer hours and could still take on my own clients. I read the email as I get ready for work, screaming and dancing around my room. I can't believe it. I did it. I read the offer and am pleased with their terms. *Fuck it.* I chuck the blow dryer under my sink and scurry to my desk, flinging open my laptop to read over the offer letter one more time. I sign and send it back to the hiring manager.

I feel like the weight that's been draped around my shoulders has suddenly disappeared. I blast some pop music and dance around my room like a wild woman. I jump on my bed like a little kid and sing into my hairbrush. I don't remember the last time I felt so free. I definitely didn't feel this way when I was hired for the marketing job. That was a different relief. Like, *oh good, I can pay my student loans.* This relief feels like freedom.

My phone starts buzzing, and I recognize it as the hiring manager's number. She must have received my acceptance reply. Hopefully, everything is all right. I turn down the music and hold my breath as I answer.

"Hi, this is Annika."

"Hi, Annika! We are so excited you decided to accept our offer! I wanted to just call to go over a few logistics over the phone."

"Of course! I'm thrilled to start."

"Yes, about that. When are you planning to relocate to Oregon? We can determine your start date depending on when you are settled."

I pause my excited movements as my heart drops. *Relocate?* I fly open my mail app and read the offer letter again. Everything looks normal until...the address of the studio is in Oregon. Where the fuck is *Auburn Hills*? How did I miss this? How was this not brought up during the interview?

"Annika, are you still there?"

"Hi, yah. I am sorry, I guess I overlooked the location of your studio."

"Oh....are you not planning to relocate? We assumed you were moving up here when you applied."

"I wasn't planning to move, no, but...."

"How about you give it a day or two and get back to us? We love your work and would love to have you as part of our studio. Let me know what your decision is, and we can go from there."

"Okay, thank you so much. I have a lot to think about."

I hang up and sit on my bed. *Am I moving to Oregon?* My mom would know what to do. She answers after one ring. I fill her in on the entire situation. She knows I've been applying for jobs, so that doesn't come as a shocker. She's so excited that I got offered a job as a photographer until I drop the bomb that it's in a different state. She curses a string of profanities, but I explain the interview process and how this job seems tailor-made for me. How I haven't been excited about anything like this in years. I hear my mom's voice tremble a bit as she responds to me.

She never cries. She takes a deep breath and says I need to promise to come up and visit before I move. I start tearing up. I know I'm an adult and don't need my parent's permission, but having their support means so much. I thought I'd be letting them down. Everything I've done in my childhood and through college, even after, has been for them. I just want them to be proud of me. They never were able to go to college themselves, and I felt like I'd be throwing it all away going this route. I was worried they'd be angry. But for the first time in my life, this feels like something I need to do for myself.

"Annika, I know this is a twist, but you know what I always say, everything happens for a reason. We just want you to be happy, Anni. Go be happy," my mom says just before we hang up.

I guess I'm moving to Oregon. Now I need to break the news to Chloe.

TWENTY-THREE

ANNIKA

IT'S BEEN three days since I accepted the job, and yet I haven't mentioned it to Chloe. I suppose you could say I'm avoiding the meltdown that will surely occur. She was distraught when I brought up the idea of moving to a different apartment in the same neighborhood. I can't even imagine how she'll react when I tell her I'm moving to a different state. A part of me is so sad about it and wonders if she would want to move with me. But I know that would never be the case since she is with Dane.

I'm actually moving, so I need to tell her. I put a deposit down on a two-bedroom apartment that's a block away from downtown and exactly a seven-minute walk to the photo studio. I am starting to love small towns already. That and my rent is the same as the share I pay now. I'm so excited, but it's bittersweet. Chloe has always been by my side, almost my entire life. It feels like I'm about to break up with her.

I have a plan. I'll take her out to her favorite restaurant. Which is maybe a bad idea because then she's going to relate it to negative memories. Okay, maybe I'll take her to *my* favorite restaurant instead. We can have a girls' night, just the two of us. We can have a nice meal, and then I'll tell her gently that I'm moving. I have already worked out that she can come to visit me. There are some flights from San Diego to a few nearby cities. Or I can drive up to Portland when she wants to visit. I'm willing to make it work to still see her. I can't survive without her in my life, either.

MILO'S KITCHEN is my favorite place to visit when I'm feeling a good treat-yourself moment. It's Greek fusion, and the atmosphere is fancy but cozy. I've never felt out of place here, and the staff is always so nice. The setup feels like you are sitting on a balcony in a hillside Greek villa, overlooking the crystal blue waters surrounded by blooming florals and crisp white architecture. A mixture of wicker chairs with plush booths and marble tables with dim lights above keeps everyone cozy while they eat their falafel burgers and Greek tacos. However, at this moment, I find myself grasping for comfort at how startled my best friend is at the news I just dropped on her.

"You're moving? When? *Why?* How? Why? *When?*" Chloe's eyes bug out of her head as she sits across from me at the table.

Thankfully, the hostess sat us in a corner booth so we can have a bit of privacy. I waited until after we ate our main course to minimize the hangry factor. But, of course, she's still thrown off track.

"I know this is a shock, but the opportunity is great. I need to take a chance."

"What about me? What about us? You're going to break up this friendship we have?"

"No, not at all. We can still video chat every day. You can visit me. I'll come to visit you. It will be okay. Chloe...I am so unhappy here."

This strikes a chord. Her body language changes from angry and defensive to sympathetic. As if she didn't even realize how unhappy I am.

"You've been hanging out mostly with Dane anyway. I think you two should consider taking your relationship to the next step. We both need to move forward."

"I didn't know you were unhappy." I knew she was going to be hung up on that.

"Like I said, you've been hanging out with Dane, which is fine, but we haven't had much time to talk about our lives. This is the first time you and I have hung out in what, two months?" I see her eyes start to glass over, which makes my eyes start to water. I don't want us to cry in the middle of Milo's Kitchen. "I don't want you to be upset, but this is something I need to do for myself."

She starts nodding a lot and dabs a tissue at the corner of her eyes. "I get it. I'm sorry for not being there for you. I just don't want you to punish me by moving."

"Oh my god, Chloe, I'm not punishing you! I just said I needed to do this for *me*. This is an entirely selfish decision. I'm sorry I didn't try pushing you more to hang out and talk, and I'm sorry I'm moving. I'm sad not to spend literally every day with you. I don't even want to think about what that looks like."

Our waiter puts down our dessert, and we eat our baklava squares in silence. Each of us waits until the other breaks the silence.

"I'm renting a two-bedroom. You can visit any time and stay as long as you want." That perks her up a bit, and she looks up at me, grinning.

"I'm actually excited for small-town Annika. You always got so sunburnt living down here anyway. Maybe Oregon will be perfect for you."

"I don't really care if it is, but I'm excited to try something new."

I fill her in on all the details. From my nightmares at work to the interview process and looking for apartments over the Internet. She's still in shock that she didn't notice any of this, but I bring up that she was always with Dane. She wasn't around. My mom helped me a lot with apartment hunting. I'd send her listings, and my dad was on the line when I called landlords. I still cannot get over the support they are showing me. I almost start crying again just thinking about it.

"Maybe it is time for Dane and I to take the next step. I could propose that he move in when you move out." She gives me a huge sad face at that. "Actually, I just remembered, I forgot my work keys at Dane's apartment. Can we swing by on the way home, and we can tell him your news?"

I doubt he'll care, but I don't protest. I'll be going along with whatever Chloe wants to do for the next three weeks.

DANE LIVES above a pizza place in Little Italy. I've only been here one time before tonight. It was the second time Dane and Chloe broke up and I picked her up, so not the best memories tied to this studio apartment. We can see his lights are on, so Chloe walks up the stairs and goes to let herself in. She has a key to his apartment, which makes me wonder if she gave him a key to our apartment. Thankfully, not something I'll have to worry about for much longer. I decided to hang out in the car, waiting for her. I'm not too interested in going up and told Chloe I was feeling tired. We can tell Dane the news tomorrow or maybe never. I bet he won't even realize I moved.

I hear a shout followed by the roar of profanities and a crash coming from the apartment. I don't even think. I jump out of the car and rush upstairs. The door is still open, and I can see Chloe waving her arms around and about to throw a book. I grab it out of her hand and look over to see what she is angry about. Dane and his ivory ass are in my face once again, but this time Chloe is not underneath him. Instead, it's another girl who looks petrified. She is scrambling to pull a blanket over herself. Chloe is yelling at Dane at the top of her lungs, calling him a man whore and trying to grab different objects to throw at him. I pluck each object out of her hand before she chucks it.

"Will you just let me throw something at him?" She whips her head back to me before trying to lunge toward him, clawing her hands.

"No, he's not worth it," I shout, grabbing her waist, pulling her back to me.

Dane doesn't even protest. He just stands there and shrugs, barely covering his junk with his hands. I've never been so baffled at how nonchalant he can be in every situation. His girlfriend just caught him cheating on her, and he acts like it was a simple miscommunication.

I pull Chloe out of his apartment and make a mental note to cuss out Dane tomorrow and collect her things. Chloe is limp and lets me lead her down the stairs and to my car. She's fuming and crying. I can tell she's not sure which emotion to let control her actions.

She slumps in the passenger seat of my car as we ride back home. I look over at her as she starts to mutter something. "I'm going to be alone." I see a tear fall down her cheek. "I don't have Dane. I won't have you. Maybe I can move back up to Ojai and live with your parents."

"No, you're moving to Oregon with me." I don't hesitate. "We are going to start a new chapter together." She turns to me, tears falling down her face as she reaches for my hand.

"But you said you were doing this for you, not for anyone else."

"And I want you to come with me. A lot is going to be new and different. I can't think of another person I'd love to share this journey with. Take the week to think about it. But remember, every small town has a bookstore." I give her a little smile which perks her up, and I squeeze her hand. "We're in this together. Always."

TWENTY-FOUR

ANNIKA

BOXES ARE SCATTERED around our two-bedroom bungalow on Beach Ave in Auburn Hills. The street name may or may not have factored into my decision to pick this place. I'm simply obsessed with the beach, and if I am going to be a two-and-a-half-hour drive from it now, at least the street I live on will remind me of it.

As soon as we pulled our moving van up to the house, I squealed in excitement. The neighborhood is filled with grand old trees that canopy all the houses. And the air is still. No obnoxious commercial airliners are flying by every half hour or shrill young college students in the distance. My parents followed us up here to help us unpack and move into our house. Chloe's mom was busy with work but made sure to say goodbye before we drove up. I thought it was nice that she made an effort, even if it was a small one. My dad had already introduced himself to all of the adjacent neighbors before we finished unloading. We had been in Auburn Hills less than an hour but it already felt more like home than Southern California ever felt.

The house itself is perfect. It is a one-story, two-bedroom, two-bath bungalow with pale blue siding, a yellow front door, and a white picket fence around the front yard. The vibes it's giving off are fun-grandma's-house. There is a big oak tree on the right side that shades a part of the house from the afternoon sun. The backyard is small but just what it needs to be. There is a dirt planter box begging for veggies to be planted in and a patch of grass. Our landlord is an old woman, Sheela, who lives a few streets down. She used to live in this house, and when she entered her seventies, she moved to an even smaller house so she had less to maintain. She decided to rent out this house instead of selling, and boy, am I grateful. She said the previous renters had lived there for five years and had just moved up to Portland. It was only on the rental market for a day before I applied.

The day after we moved in and our parents left, Sheela appeared at our doorstep with a basket of, according to her, famous apple crisp muffins. I don't know how famous they are, and I don't really care. They are the best muffins I've ever eaten in my life. We invited her in, and she gave us each a big embrace and proceeded to tell us all her favorite spots downtown. Sheela gives granny energy like a well-needed hug and surprise gifts on a Tuesday. The kind of granny that leaves sweet treats at your doorstep and sends letters in the mail of newspaper clippings from articles she read that reminded her of you. She noticed I had a framed poster-size collage of my favorite postcards I've collected through the years, so now whenever she gives us a basket of treats, there's also an old postcard tucked behind the muffins. I am so grateful to have her in this new town.

It's been a week since we moved in, and our living room resembles a shallow maze of cardboard boxes. Our kitchen and bathrooms are the only rooms that are fully unpacked. Chloe and I each get our own bathroom, which has already improved our friendship. I no longer get my feet tangled around her curly blond strands after she brushes her hair. My bedroom is set up mostly except for two boxes of clothes I still have to put away. I hung up my postcard collage above the couch in the living room, and Chloe made a little painting corner in the breakfast nook that overlooks the backyard.

The biggest difference between SoCal and Oregon is the weather. There are some sunny moments, but it tends to be overcast. I suppose we are still in spring, and things might brighten up as we get closer to May. Chloe seems both happier and sadder. She walks around with an empty smile on her face. The mask I'm familiar with has returned. I can tell she hasn't fully grieved from her breakup with Dane. Even though they've broken up before, it's never been from cheating. It's for real this time. She donated all her romance books to a bookstore in San Diego before we moved and boldly announced that she was abandoning the genre entirely. She's been sulking around reading books on the Roman Empire and thriller novels. If she gets a hint of a romantic subplot, she leaves the book on my bookshelf instead and ceases to finish it.

Luckily for Chloe, there is the same chain bookstore that she worked at in San Diego, in Medford, which is a twenty-minute drive from our house. She was able to transfer easily. The store manager had actually just left that store, and they were looking for a replacement. I feel like everything is perfectly falling into place. We are bound to have a misstep eventually.

TWENTY-FIVE

ANNIKA

OCCASIONALLY, I'm swept up in the feeling of adolescent guilt. My parents swear up and down that they are happy about my decision to move up here, but the look on their faces when we parted ways after moving in replays in my head.

My mom and I have a standing Saturday morning call where we catch up on each other's weeks, and she proceeds to pass the phone around to my dad and my younger brothers. Joey and Wes still live at home with my parents since they are seniors in high school, so I'm glad I get to see their faces on the weekly call. They are inseparable, but that is a given since they are twins. They take the same classes, they both play baseball on their high school team, and they even dated sisters once. I thought that was kinda weird, but thankfully, that didn't last.

They never wanted to tag around their big sister and yet I always felt the need to lead by example. Always trying to excel in school and go to college, so they knew a good example to follow. However, now that my path has shifted, I've taken a one-eighty on my teachings to my younger brothers. I tell them to follow their dreams and don't think they have to do the thing everyone else does. They always just roll their eyes and then tell me about some big play from their last game.

I want them to be happy. They want to come up and visit me during their spring break from school, but my mom is afraid to let them drive alone. Last week, Joey told me he started looking at colleges in Oregon so he could be closer to me, and I almost cried. I love my family so much. I think this is why the guilt of moving weighs so heavily on me. Even though I'm in the same time zone, I don't want them to slip away.

The weekly calls are the most I've spoken to my family since I moved away to college. Even though I lived only a couple of hours away back then, I would only see them on holidays or summer break. Only calling my mom when I was stressed or heartbroken. Another pang in my chest of a bruise that never heals.

This week, I take the call from my front yard. Last week, Sheela pulled up in a pickup truck with two white Adirondack chairs in the back. She said we needed a "chair moment" on the outside lawn. The spring weather in Auburn Hills is the definition of crisp. Sunbeams push their way through the dense cloud cover, and the air feels like a pinch on the cheeks. I'm bundled in a hoodie and blanket while I ring my mom on video chat. She picks up on the second ring.

"Ah! My little Anni bug!" My mom recently reverted to calling me nicknames from my childhood.

We have our normal catch-up about how we've spent our week. We've been here for about three weeks now and are feeling settled. The box maze in the living room has transformed into a box stack in the corner. I started my new job two weeks ago, and it's scarily perfect. I can walk to the studio located a few minutes downtown. I spend my days talking to clients, editing photos, and planning photoshoots. I am shooting exclusively with film, and we are working to turn a closet into a dark room so I can develop the photos in the studio. I have a little experience developing film photos, but I'm excited to have this new skill to master. I told my mom about the shoot I had this week. A couple just got engaged, and we took pictures of them walking throughout the town. It was so sweet, and seeing their burst of love made me crave it for myself.

"I think I'm starting to warm up to the idea of dating again." I pull my blankets in closer after I confess this to my mom.

She gives me a concerned look. "Take it easy, Anni. Follow your heart and trust your gut. Also, one call, and I'm up there ready to kick anyone's butt for hurting you."

My mom has always been nervous about me dating again since the incident at the nightclub. She drove down that weekend and didn't leave my side for two days.

"I know. I think I'd like to find someone to share my life with. I know I have Chloe, but someone I can be intimate with, you know." I can feel my cheeks blushing at sharing details about my lacking love life with my mom.

"Be patient with both of you. Give her time." My mom lets out a sigh. "I am always worried about her. Maybe you two can go do something for yourselves. That reminds me, I was looking up what little shops are in your town. I saw a coupon for a couples massage. Take Chloe and go *relax*."

"Mom, you don't have to buy Chloe and me a couples massage." I laugh and shake my head at the thought of her and me in a room together.

Then I think about how nice it would be to get a massage. My right shoulder still has a pinch from lifting moving boxes.

"Honey, let me spoil you. Okay?"

"Sheesh, all right, no need to yell."

"I'm not yelling. I'm raising my voice. It's different."

I roll my eyes at that, and we finish our conversation with her passing the phone to my dad, who tells me about some new planter boxes he built for my mom. Then Joey shows me the science project he has finished. It looks like a more complicated contraption to water a plant, but he said something about physics that made my brain twirl. Wes told me that he and Joey got accepted to three colleges so far, two being in Oregon, one of which is in Auburn Hills. I had no idea that they applied to the nearby private college. They have been offered a baseball scholarship to each school so far and just need to decide which they are going to attend. He said mom agreed that dad would take them to visit the colleges during their spring break next month and would stop by to visit me.

Not five minutes after hanging up the call, I get an email from my mom forwarding the gift certificate for a couples massage tomorrow at three.

TWENTY-SIX

REID

I PARK my pickup in the lot behind the center and head in. I don't always work on Saturdays, but my uncle asked me to fill in for Tyler, who called in sick today. They have a few clients today, and he didn't want to reschedule them. Since I started working here, Tyler's never taken a sick day, so he's either playing hooky or he's actually sick. I make a mental note to swing by his place later. It's not the most creative to have your closest friend also be your co-worker, but we met in the first week I moved here and got along instantly. He's still trying to get me to go to his rock-climbing gym, but overall we have a lot of similar hobbies. We both love music and books and will constantly trade records. Tyler plays some guitar, and when he's had a few beers will be bold and play in the open mic night at the local pub. He's been really supportive through my breakup with Carrie and distracting me with obscure movies to watch and hikes during the weekend. He didn't dare hide his smile when I told him the news.

The center greets me with Zen music playing over the speakers and the smell of lavender eucalyptus in the air. You'd think it was a spa, not a physical therapy office. I appreciate Uncle Marty having this place feel like a retreat rather than so clinical.

The staff today is slim. I guess two people are out sick today. There's only the receptionist, Claire, one other therapist, and my uncle today. I checked my schedule, and I have two PT appointments in the morning. Then my uncle added a memo asking if I could help fill in for a massage this afternoon. I don't usually give massages, but my uncle made me get my certification when I joined in case, I had to fill in. I've only had to fill in a handful of times. It isn't too bad, and usually, those clients leave hefty tips.

I read over the appointment. Two women are coming in for a couples massage. Me and the other therapist working today are assigned. Shouldn't be too bad, it's only an hour Swedish massage. I set my belongings in my locker and prepare an office for my first PT appointment of the day, a sweet old woman named Sheela. She is in her eighties but has the gusto of a fifty-year-old. She walks everywhere she goes. I saw her trying to carry two lawn chairs down the street and begged her to take my truck to wherever she was trying to haul them. She's come in weekly since I started, and we are working to increase the mobility in her shoulders. She's improved greatly, but carrying two lawn chairs herself isn't doing her any favors.

"How's the shoulder treating you today?" I motion for her to sit in the chair at the center of the room and get to work gently rotating her shoulder joints, seeing her range of motion.

"I think I slept on it funny, so it's a little sticky today."

"Did you look into that pillow I suggested you swap to?"

"Yeah, yeah, no pillow is going to make me live past one hundred." I chuckle at her bluntness, and we do a few exercises to open up her shoulders and some subtle stretches.

"I'll have you know that I convinced everyone in my poker club to boycott Carol Breads."

I shake my head, laughing. "You really don't have to do that."

"You know Missy? The librarian at the high school? She's in my poker club. She said she saw the whole thing at the farmer's market.

She said Carrie was swinging bags at you and screaming. You deserve so much better, kid."

I let out a sigh and help her to her feet. "Thanks, Sheela."

"I just moved some new tenants into the Beach Street house. Two young girls, they are pretty, and the dark-haired one is a little sassy. I think you'd get along with her." She gives me a wink and nudges my arm.

"Appreciate you trying to play matchmaker, but I'm going to take a break from dating for a bit."

"Suit yourself! See you next week. Tell Tyler I'll swing by to give him some muffins." She slings her slouchy tote bag over her shoulder and heads out.

Half of my clients are older folks, and the other half are recovering from an injury. The best feeling is seeing them improve week to week. Sheela's already improving after a few sessions. The second appointment is for Clark, who runs an auto repair shop in town. He had a nasty slip in his shop last month and has been coming in to fix his back. The day passes pretty easily, and I pivot to prep for the massage. The massage therapists have to wear a different smock uniform and softer shoes, so we don't make too much noise. I hear some voices come in and make my way to the bathroom to change quickly.

Annika

The massage is at a wellness center downtown. It's only a couple blocks from the photo studio, so I walk there after work, and Chloe meets me out front on her way back from work. She looks the happiest I've seen her. My mom was right. We needed this.

"I am so excited to have all my problems massaged away. I can feel Dane like a knot in my neck. I want to feel like a new woman," Chloe exclaims as we head inside.

We both fill out a few forms with some information and circle a diagram of a human to point out our pain points. The receptionist leads us to the massage room, and the calming music follows us inside. Chloe and I giggle as we put our clothes in baskets and go under the blankets on each of our massage tables. The room is large, with two massage beds on either side. I notice a hot stone container and some massage oils on a counter. The blankets on the massage table are soft and cozy. I snuggle my head into the opening for my face and take a few deep breaths, letting the lavender scent in the air relax my ruminating mind.

We hear a knock on the door, and a therapist enters. She says her name is Nancy and that the other therapist will be in shortly. I hear her shuffle over to Chloe. Shortly after, another pair of footsteps comes in and heads over to me. They don't say their name, but I don't question it. They seem eager to get the massage going, so I take a few more deep breaths and relax.

I can tell it is a guy massaging me because his hands are large and move with firm pressure. He asks me if the pressure is good, and he sounds like a warm cup of apple cider. I can feel goosebumps prick up under his touch. He asks again, and I nod my head quickly. I suddenly lose the ability to speak, flustered by a man's voice. I don't even know what he looks like, but if the sound of his voice and the way he moves his hands along my neck is any indication, he's the most beautiful man on Earth. He starts the massage with a blanket still covering my back. It feels nice and warm as he eases into the massage. He works my shoulders and down to my lower back. Pushing against diagonal points, stretching my back out. I don't mean to let out some moans, but it feels amazing. I need to get a massage every month. This is a heavenly experience.

He starts to pull away the blanket, and I feel him pause at my middle back. *Oh no, do I have a pimple on my back? Is he absolutely repulsed at the sight? Oh god, I just realized I forgot to shave my legs! This hot man is going to rub my hairy calves.* He suddenly drops the blanket, mutters something to the other therapist, and leaves the room, leaving me stranded on the table. *What the heck just happened? Are my hairy legs really that hideous?*

I feel the female therapist's hand gently touch my upper back and say the other therapist wasn't feeling well and had to step out. She offers to put some hot stones on my back while she finishes the massage with Chloe, and they can reimburse my appointment. I'm honestly enjoying just lying here with this yoga music playing on their speakers, so I accept the offer. I am just glad it was my therapist that wasn't feeling well and not Chloe's. She needs this massage more than I do.

Reid

I lose track of time and shuffle into the room quickly. The two women are already lying down, and Nancy, the other massage therapist, started her massage already. The woman I start massaging is tense as I try to relax her with the blanket on her back first. She lets out little moans and sighs that make my body react very inappropriately. I pull the blanket back and see a little tattoo. It's a small little box on the corner of her back. *No way, it can't be.* Is that a stamp tattoo?

That tiny stamp tattoo is etched in my brain. Of course, I'll never forget the first time I saw it, sitting on the beach in San Diego as she turned her shoulder around to show me while I tried to refrain from giving it a little kiss. I remember having my hand over it as I pulled her closer to me during the movie night.

It feels like an eternity passes as I freeze in place, looking at the cutout edges and slightly faded ink with the little number eighteen on the inside. My eyes trail up to the woman under the tattoo. She has shoulder-length black hair in two pigtail braids, and I nearly collapse. *It can't be her.* That's when I look up to see the other woman, a young blond girl with wild hair gathered in a large bun. I feel like I've been hit by a bus. *It's her.* I panic, drop the blanket, and motion to Nancy that I'm not feeling well, dashing out of the room and seeking refuge in the break room.

Annika

The hot stones feel nice, but after about five minutes, I'm starting to get a bit antsy and decide I want to step out of the room to change. The other therapist quietly apologizes again, and I mouth to her it's no worries. I mean, yeah, I'm disappointed, but I can't control if someone isn't feeling well. It's not Nancy's fault the other therapist left her hanging. Nancy helps me get a warm robe on and says I can take my basket of clothes to the women's dressing room around the corner to change and relax until Chloe is done.

I quietly slip out of the room and head down the hall to find the dressing room. Just as I turn the corner, I see someone head toward me and stop in their tracks. From the look of their shoes, it must be my massage therapist because Nancy had the same shoes on. As my eyes trail up, a familiar flutter awakens in my stomach. This feeling has been dormant for a long time, but I'll never forget it.

My gaze dances around the stubble of his chin and the sweeps of brown hair curling out from under his logo cap. Finally, they land on his green eyes. He is so grown up and yet the same boy I was smitten with at nine years old. Then it hits me, he was my massage therapist. *He touched my butt!* My cheeks burn, and my eyebrows jump up on my forehead, which must signal Reid to turn and flee. I do the same and run into a room I hope is the women's dressing room.

That can't be him, can it? I try to remember where he moved to after college. I remember hearing he moved north to work with a family member, but Isaac and Reid stopped staying in touch around the time Isaac and I briefly dated.

I change back into my clothes and leave the robe in the basket against a wall in the dressing room. Now to plan my escape. I am a

twenty-four-year-old woman, still running away from her childhood crush. Sheesh, I need to grow up. But that day can be
tomorrow because I am not ready to face the uncomfortable reality
that the boy whose heart I broke just had his hands roaming all over
my body only twenty minutes ago. Possibly the most intimate
moment he and I have ever shared. The reminder of his hands
pressed along my back warms my skin, and I feel a pulse in my
core. My lack of sex is starting to catch up with me. I need to get
some fresh air. I peek out from the dressing room and see the hall is
empty. Quickly, without looking side to side, I dash for the receptionist.

"Oh, Miss Gomes, how was your massage?" The receptionist,
Claire, as the name tag reads, asks before I make my great escape.

"It was all right, my therapist left early, but Nancy said she
would fill you in. I'm going to go for a walk and come back when
my friend is done." I wave and bolt out the door before Claire has
the opportunity to respond.

Reid

Well, shit.

What is she doing here? Did she track me down? I highly doubt
it, considering she looked just as surprised to see me as I was her. As
soon as she looked at me, I saw the color drain out of her face, and
she quickly ran into the Men's dressing room. I let my cowardice
take over and turned to flee to my own safe space, the break room. I
feel dizzy, and like I'm catching a fever. I should be angry at her.

I know she felt the same way about me, and she just couldn't
own up to it. She didn't know what she wanted, and she just took
advantage of my feelings. Then when she matched me on Flame, it
felt like she grabbed the knife that was already stuck in my heart
and twisted it. And yet, when I see her bundled in the spa robe, her
shiny black hair pulled into two braided pigtails, reminding me of

the spunky girl I crushed on but now in a woman's body standing before me. I want to pull her towards me and into my arms. Kiss her and twirl her around, singing and laughing. I want what we didn't end up having.

It's been about ten minutes of me sitting alone in the break room, trying to let the meditation-bowls music settle my nerves. I contemplate never leaving the break room for the rest of my life. There's a couch I can sleep on, and people leave their lunch in the fridge for sustenance. It wouldn't be an exciting life, but at least I would be safe and never get heartbroken ever again.

I take a deep breath and peek out the door. Hallways are empty, so I quietly walk down to the reception. I quickly decide in the thirty-second walk that if I see Annika, I will own up to it and say hi to her. I don't have to make a big thing out of it. So we went on two and a half dates in college, and that was ages ago. We are adults now. For all I know, she's married by now. I wouldn't know. I abandoned social media after that Flame interaction we had. I hear some conversation happening in the reception and just bite the bullet and walk right to the entrance. As I do, Claire, the receptionist, and the woman she's talking to turn their head over to me.

Claire gets up and leans in to make sure the other woman can't hear. "Oh, Reid, Nancy told me you weren't feeling well." But she's cut off after the woman, clearly eavesdropping, squeals and shouts my name.

"Reid!? Like *the* Reid Parker? What are the odds?"

That's what I'm saying. I look up and see it's Chloe, of course. She and Annika are an inseparable duo. Chloe flies over to me and squeezes me in for a hug. I think I've hung out with Chloe only a few times, at parties or between classes, and each time she would give me the biggest hug. It is endearing, but I'm not eager to return her hug. She must sense my tension and pulls away from me.

Smiling and collecting her ash blond curls back into a giant bun on the top of her head, she says, "It's so good to see you. This place is amazing. Nancy gives the best massage. Have you seen Annika? I think she ran out of here. She must not have been feeling well."

"I'm glad you had a great session, and no, I haven't seen her." I try to step back slowly so I can go back to living in the break room.

Chloe pulls out her phone and turns quickly to look out the window. I follow her gaze and see Annika across the street at the coffee shop, the Human Bean. She's sitting at one of their tables outside with her head angled down to her hands on the table. There are two coffee cups next to her. I'm guessing one is for Chloe. I see her check her phone and look up toward the center. The windows of the center are mirrored so we can see out, but anyone on the street cannot see in. I'm suddenly grateful for the windows because I can't tear my eyes away from her. Even from here, I can see her dark brown eyes that I always seem to get lost in.

"Do you want to get some coffee with us, Reid? I'm sure Anni would love to catch up. You can tell us your favorite places in town." She motions her arm, wanting me to follow her.

I reluctantly move my eyes away from Annika and over to Chloe. She looks actually genuine that she wants me to come with her, but I can't. I need to process everything about today. A part of me wants to burst out from these doors and go to her, and another part of me wants to start this day over and tell my uncle I can't cover the shifts today.

TWENTY-SEVEN

REID

I DRIVE DIRECTLY past my house on my way home from work and instead head into the hills where Tyler lives. He's an Auburn Hills native and lives on his family's property. He left Auburn Hills to study at the University of Oregon but moved back about three years ago after his parents passed away and has been fixing it up ever since. It's really a charming land, and I always enjoy the twenty-minute drive through the rolling hills from downtown. The road winds through the charming craftsman houses and bungalows of Auburn Hills before starting to sparse out when you get deeper into the hills.

When I first moved here, I wasn't sure why it was called Auburn Hills. The hills are green. Or in the winter, they have white at the top from the snowfall we get. The first time I drove up to Tyler's house, I realized the name is for all the redwood trees you pass through along the hills. The bark is a rich red with deep green ferns covering the expanse. Tyler's place juts off a long driveway off the main road that takes you through the hills and opens up to spacious grassland. It has a great view of the town and the sunsets from here are unreal. His place is a large stone ranch house that sits on three acres and a small guest house to the side. He has a soft spot for animals and so far, has a llama, chickens, and a little beagle pup named Scooter.

Normally, I love the drive, but today it's different because I am preoccupied with the events of earlier today replaying in my head. If Tyler came into work, I wouldn't be in this mess. Who knows if Annika and I will ever run into each other? I don't even know if she's just visiting or what her story is. Sure, it's a small town, but there are plenty of people I probably haven't met before. Who am I kidding? We can't seem to stop running into each other. As if she's my opposing magnet. Drawn together despite the forces surrounding us.

I head up the gravel driveway to Tyler's property, giving the llama named Lucy a wave as I pass. I swing my truck next to Tyler's 4Runner parked in front of his garage and hop out, jogging to his front door, pounding aggressively until he answers.

"Hey, okay, hey, I'm here," Tyler says as he swings the door open.

I immediately squint at him. He doesn't look sick. In fact, he looks like he more handsome, if that's even possible. His dark red waves are trimmed and flopped stylishly to one side. He's wearing new, clear brown wayfarer glasses that match his eyes, and I think he even has a new flannel on.

"You don't look sick," I say to him.

"And happy Saturday to you too, Reid. Please come in. Grace me with your lovely presence." Tyler sarcastically bows and swings his arm as if he's presenting his home to me.

I enter and pivot back around to him as he closes the door just before Scooter comes bounding in, trying to make an escape.

"No, Scoot, not today. Lucy doesn't want to see you."

"He and Lucy have a thing?" I ask, bending down to give the beagle scratches behind his ears. He flops down on the tile floor, rolling to his back so I can rub his belly.

"Puppy love," Tyler says, shrugging. "So, what did I do to

deserve this sudden visit? Not even an 'I'm heading over' text warning."

We head into his living room, which has plush oversized couches surrounding a fireplace. The walls are all wood paneled, which gives the house a cabin vibe.

"I filled in for you today. Because you were '*sick*.'" I exaggerate the quotation marks on the last word, so he picks up my angst.

"That's so kind of you. Thank you so, so much, and you're right. I'm not sick."

"So, you played hooky while I had the most traumatic experience of my life today?"

Tyler's head shakes in disbelief.

"Traumatic? I hardly believe Parker Wellness is a facility to produce trauma, especially under Martin's guidance. Did you know he's starting to study Buddhism? He wants to get an acupuncturist on staff."

"You're avoiding telling me why you weren't at work if you weren't sick." I squint at Tyler. We've been friends long enough that I know when he's hiding something. He will tap his left foot a little too fast until he realizes he's doing it and then swings his left ankle to his right thigh, trying to play it cool. But I see right through it.

"All right, I'll tell you, but it's kind of nerdy." He uncrosses his legs again, tapping his left foot.

"You are already a nerd, but a cool nerd," I reassure him.

"I appreciate that because I was 'sick' today because I booked my personal appointments and every check-up all on the same day so I don't miss too much work because I enjoy it too much."

"You're kidding?"

"Nope, remember last year? I was 'sick' one day, and Nancy filled in for me. I went and got a doctor's check-up, teeth cleaning, vision check-up, new glasses, a haircut, and even picked up a few more clothes today because I was near an L. L. Bean."

"Wow, well, your haircut looks great, man." Tyler's stressed appearance melts away, and he relaxes.

"Thanks. I'm sorry you had a shitty day today. Was it Sheela? She can be a handful."

"Sheela was an absolute delight compared to what happened."

"Okay, spit it out already. What happened?"

I tell Tyler about the events that played out today. It feels so far away, as if it happened months ago rather than two hours. I leave out the full details about the appointments at the beginning because I know he'll want a rundown on the client's status which we can get into on Monday. He stops me halfway through to let Scooter out to the backyard. I finally get to the part about walking into the massage, and the moment I realized it was my ex, my childhood crush. Tyler doesn't know every detail of my past, but one night we had a bit too many beers sitting on his porch, and I was reminiscing. He calls her "the one that got away."

"So, what did you do afterward?"

"I left through the back and drove straight here." I sink back into the couch. Hoping the cushions will suck me into the depths of the fluff, and I will just be stuck enough to never leave.

"Well, you better get your ass off this couch and go try again." I sit up at his response.

"What do you mean *try again*?"

"How many times in life does a person leave and reappear in your life? Especially a person with which you clearly have a connection. Not that often? I think you should take advantage of this serendipitous opportunity."

"I knew we should've watched the newest Avengers movie, not *Love, Simon*, last weekend."

"Hey, it was a great movie, and that's beside the point. I'm just telling you what I would do if I were in this situation."

"It's not like I don't want to. You didn't experience what I did. I'm still so embarrassed by the situation. We had big crushes on each other as kids, and then I blew it in college. And then I blew it again when we matched on that dating app."

"Wait, what dating app?"

"Oh, did I forget to mention? Two years after she dumped me, we matched on that app, Flame. I basically said to get lost."

"You are an idiot. She matched with you, and *you* turned *her* down?"

I shrug. "I know, I'm an idiot. I guess I was still bitter about the whole situation."

"Clearly." Tyler gets up to let Scooter back in. The pup flies in, zooming around the couch before launching himself onto my lap.

"I still think you should try again if you still want to," he says, sitting back on the couch. Scooter abandons me to get pets from his owner.

I shake my head. "I'm just hesitant about it. It isn't that long since Carrie and I broke up."

Tyler rolls his eyes at the mention of my ex's name. "Maybe take it slow? If you run into her again, try to just be friends."

"Honestly, a part of me wishes that's the last time I'll see her. But I doubt that's the case. What are the odds she's visiting and coming in for a massage at the place I work?"

"I mean, she could just be passing through. Do you still have her number?"

"There is no way I'm texting her. Are you crazy? I basically ran out of the room when I realized it was her."

Tyler knocks his head back, laughing. "Boy, I wish I was there to witness. See, this is why I don't like missing work!"

"Yeah, I'm never covering for you again."

Scooter jumps off the couch again, barking toward the door to be let out. "You need to put in a little doggie door for this guy."

"He's obsessed with the chickens. He thinks he's herding sheep or something."

We transition from our recap of the day into a regular weekend of eating carne asada tacos on the back patio while Scooter barks at the chickens who roam the yard freely.

I suppose I could use another friend in this town, even if it's possibly the girl who stole my heart.

TWENTY-EIGHT

ANNIKA

TURNS out the wellness center and the photo studio are not only on the same street but on the same block. Like maybe forty steps from one place to the other. Parker Wellness is 3402 Main Street, and Golden Hour Studios is 3410 Main Street. So, it will be inevitable that I will run into Reid again. I have no idea what his life is like now. I wonder if he has a girlfriend. A part of me hopes not. In college, he was charming and delightful. He looked kind of like a puppy flopping around, always smiling at things. It's been so long since I've seen him, but he still makes me feel uneasy.

If this was me a year ago, heck, even four months ago, I would awkwardly try to avoid his side of the street for the rest of my life. But I didn't move here to run away from my responsibilities. I moved here to face my fears. To discover what I want in life. The first step was taking a job I never thought I'd even get an offer for. All because I decided to try.

Even though Reid and I have a rocky past, he's the only other person I know in this town besides Chloe and our landlord, Sheela. Besides, it isn't like we dated for years. It was a couple of dates and a little kid crush. I believe we can move past our history and start new now that we are living in the same town again.

So, I ignore the voice in my head that is yelling at me, *"No, don't go to him,"* and decide to stop at the coffee shop across from the wellness center on my lunch break. I am going to be a bigger person and make amends. This whole new journey I am on is to figure out what I want. And I want to be his friend.

The last time I got coffee with Reid, he had an iced black coffee with whipped cream on top. I thought it was the weirdest order, so it always stuck out in my head. I even ordered it a few times myself since, and it's actually really tasty. The sweet, whipped cream mixes with the coffee, so you get these two intense flavors with each sip. It is bold of me to assume he still likes this order, but indecisive Annika is taking a back seat. I take his drink and march across the street. The same receptionist is working, and she immediately recognizes me. I guess this town is small enough for her to remember. That and probably because I'm the first person to ever run out of there after a massage.

"Hi, good afternoon!" I give Claire a bright smile to hopefully erase the weird impression I left last time. "Is Reid working today?"

"Hi, nice to see you again! Yes, he is. Would you like me to get him?"

"That would be great."

"No problem, feel free to take a seat. I'll let him know you are here."

I wonder what she's going to tell him. "Hey, Reid, that crazy chick from the weekend is back, and she's asking for you." I half expect him to just bolt out the back door. *What if he thinks I'm stalking him?* Oh no, that idea never even came to mind. He must think I'm on a mission to ruin his life. I wonder if it's too late to leave. I can back out and go back to the studio. I could avoid this side of the street easily. Except the Human Bean gives you little chocolate-covered coffee beans with each drink, and I would miss that a lot.

The door to the back area of the wellness center opens, and Reid strides out. He's wearing the same black cap he wore this weekend, and instead of a matching cotton outfit, he's wearing a relaxed dark green button-up shirt that's perfectly fitted around his muscular arms and shoulders. He has slim dark jeans on that I wish I could see what the back looks like. *Goddamn.* Snap out of it, Annika, *friend*, remember I want to be his *friend*.

I can tell he is unsure what to do, but he walks over to where I'm sitting and quietly takes the seat next to me. I feel the air around him press into the right side of my body. I'm suddenly glued to my chair and have lost all of my ability to speak. He is looking down at his shoes. He still wears worn-out Converse. Me too.

He smells like fresh air and spice. No more pine tree smell as he did in college. This must be his Oregon scent. I open my mouth, and still, no words come out.

"What did you order?" He knocks me out of this fantasyland I'm living in my head and points to my drink. The whipped cream started to emulsify with the iced coffee.

"Oh, this is for you, a truce." *A truce? Who says that?*

He cracks a grin and says, "I didn't realize we were in battle."

I hand over the drink, and he holds it up while inspecting it. His eyes flick up to me as he raises the coffee to his mouth. *Who knew keeping eye contact with someone as they drank an iced coffee was my biggest turn-on?*

"Did you order me..." He takes another sip. "A cold brew with whipped cream on top?"

"Yes, yes I did." I can't decide what to do with my legs, so I keep crossing and uncrossing them. I think he notices because he looks at me fidgeting. I take a breath and try to summon the confident Annika I was this morning that made this plan. "Your coffee order is the weirdest thing I've ever heard of."

This confession must have broken through because I can see Reid relax an inch. He leans back a little in the chair and keeps drinking, closing his eyes.

I shift in my chair again. "So...truce? Can we start fresh? You're the only person I know here besides Chloe." He turns his head to me, closing off his wall again.

"Wait, wait." He gets up and shakes his head. "Why did you even move here? Of all the places in the world." *Ouch.* I don't think I was supposed to take offense to that, but I can't help but feel hurt by his words.

"I got a job offer and decided to take it. I wasn't vibing with SD anymore."

"I'm pretty sure there aren't any marketing firms in Auburn Hills. Where do you work?"

"Oh, yeah, no, marketing was a bad call for me. I decided it was not what I wanted to do after all. I work at the photo studio on Main Street, Golden Hour Studios. I'm a film photographer."

"You're kidding? You ditched your degree to take pictures?" Again, I can't tell if he's making a dig at me. We haven't spoken in years. The last time I knew Reid, he was the nicest boy in the world. Maybe I ruined him. He might be an asshole now. I sit up straight a little, and he starts to backtrack. "I just realized…what I meant was, why the change? I don't think I remember you liked photography…"

It seems like he was about to say *when we dated.* I realize I was only taking an elective class when we went out.

"I took up photography later in college. I was crazy, stressed with school and started going to the campus therapist. She recommended I start a hobby. I found an old film camera at the flea market, and it just went from there. I applied to this place on a whim, and when they offered me the job, I didn't realize it was in Oregon. But here I am, and of course, Chloe came with me. That's the short version of the story."

Reid nods through the story, like he is tucking each word into his mental journal.

"I'd love to hear the long version." Reid meets my eyes again, and his entire face smiles. The corners of his eyes curl up, and I can tell I have another friend in this town.

The butterflies awaken in my stomach, looking for an exit, filling my chest and fluttering up to my head. "I'd like to tell you. How about you, Chloe, and I get some drinks this Friday, and the three of us can catch up." Perfect. I'll use Chloe as the buffer while we start this new friendship.

"Sounds like a plan. Hey, can I bring a friend?"

"Of course!" I say a little too cheerily, but I can't hold in my excitement that the coffee truce worked.

He gets up to leave, but before he heads back to the center, he turns to me and says, "Thanks for the coffee." He takes another sip without breaking eye contact. *I'm screwed.*

TWENTY-NINE

REID

WE ARE TANGLED in the layers of my duvet, and I'm giving Anni sweet, little kisses around her face. She closes her eyes, and I softly kiss each one and then kiss the corners of her mouth. I feel light as air, relishing in this perfect moment of bliss with her. Her hands fall along my body, and she squeezes my ass. She giggles, and I nuzzle my nose against the side of her hair while my hands trace up her torso and land on her soft breasts. I gently squeeze and flick them.

She lets out a soft moan against my neck like she did when I was massaging her, increasing the heat between us. I lean my hips down and grind into her abdomen, and she treats me to another moan, urging me closer. *"More,"* she whispers. She kisses my neck and nips at my shoulder as I line my hips with hers. She swings her legs around my back and arches up to meet me as I enter her in one swoop, both of us buckling in instant pleasure that shoots from my toes to my head. I close my eyes and rock against her. Her moans turn into gasps as I pick up the pace, and she is digging her nails into my back. This is a moment I've been waiting for years. We are finally connected. I open my eyes, and I'm sitting naked in a college lecture.

Shit…it was just a dream. I open my eyes now, and I'm drenched in sweat. I definitely did not have sex, but you can't tell my penis otherwise with the force at which it levitates. I glance at the window before checking the time. The sky looks like a peach smoothie outside.

5:13 am

A little earlier than I prefer, but not the worst. I get up and start running a cold shower to calm down from that dream. I haven't had a sex dream since college. Not a good mentality to start our new friendship. I don't know where that will go. We planned to get drinks on Friday with Chloe and Tyler. I'm hesitant, but I could use a couple more friends here as well.

It sort of feels like I'm living in a daydream. The girl I dated in college moved to the same small town as me, brought me my favorite coffee order, and asked to be my friend again after all these years. When will I wake up and realize she was never there?

Turns out she and Chloe have the same numbers as they did in college. It took less than a day for Chloe to start a group chat with the three of us. I decided to leave out Tyler until they meet him. Then I'm sure he will be added to the mix. All of this is so sudden it is going to take some time to get used to.

Also going to try to refrain from having sex dreams about her. I can't help it. Especially now that I know it was Annika I massaged. I picture running my hands down her spine and along the soft curves of her hips. The goosebumps raised as I exposed her skin. I'm getting hard again just thinking about it, dammit. She's always had a spark about her, but there's something different about her now. Maybe something bolder or a mystery she's holding in. I admire her for just quitting a steady job and pursuing a creative passion instead. I don't even know how I would start to do something like that.

I shake my head under the cold water. *Friends, we are friends.* I can't let myself get swept up in her again. I can't help it. I think of every moment we've ever shared every time I look at her. It feels like I am flipping through an old journal, getting hit with waves of nostalgia. It feels both comforting and distant. Like coming home after a long trip. She feels like a reminder of home. I need to force myself to change this mindset. If she wants to be friends, I need to remember to take it easy, and if I want her as a friend, I don't want to chase her away again. My heart (and my sexual fantasies) need to take a back seat on this one.

I haven't been on a run in weeks, but this accidental early rising seems like the perfect opportunity to get out, breathe in some fresh air, and clear my head.

Quickly, I realize why I don't like going on runs in my neighborhood, there are way too many hills, and I never learned my lesson about going slow at the start. I just start running way too hard, and then it comes to bite me in the ass ten minutes into it. Probably a metaphor for my love life. I decide to head toward the Main Street since it is relatively flat, and I feel like my heart is going to fall out of my chest after that last hill. I head past the wellness center and notice a familiar mop of red curls in the distance.

I totally blanked that Carrie gets into the bakery before the town wakes up to start baking. I've thankfully avoided running into her since we broke up. When was that? A month ago? Two months ago? I've lost track of time, honestly. I ran into Annika only a few days ago, but it feels like it's been a lifetime. I need to make a game-time decision to run by and hope she doesn't notice me, or I can run down the nearest alley in the hope that it's not trash day. I'm closing in on her. All right, I'm going to start sprinting as soon as she walks into her bakery.

I slow down and see her grabbing a box from her Subaru parked out front. She passes the sidewalk, thankfully not noticing the man struggling on his two-mile run, and heads inside. That's when I book it. My fear of running into my ex propels my legs into gear as I take off down the sidewalk. I probably look insane since I was running at a snail's pace and then picked up to cheetah speed.

Although, I probably look more like a zebra about to be hunted by a cheetah. I push past and am so close to passing the bakery when a bearded man emerges. We collide, and my momentum flies me shoulder-first into the sidewalk, skidding to a stop. I look up at the man I ran into, and he's angrily gazing down at me. He dramatically squeezes his shoulder as if I'm not the one with sidewalk burn on my entire left side.

"Hey, dirtch, watch where the fuck you're going." The bearded man flips me off and heads inside. He looks so familiar to me for some reason.

The box he's holding is unscathed from the collision, but he acts like it's precious cargo. *Did he call me a dirtch?* I need to remember to ask Claire at the front desk what that means. She just graduated high school so is more in the know with the lingo these days. I manage to peel myself off the sidewalk and start to hobble away. Except when I hear the jangle of the bakery door flying open again.

"Babe, this is the moron who ran into my fresh figs and made me spill your latte." *Shitshitshit.* Did he say fresh figs? No way she ended up going out with Mr. Fig. Is it too late to take off sprinting? Honestly, I don't think I could even try to sprint because my ankles decide to give out, and I trip just as Carrie emerges from the cafe with Mr. Fig behind her, his arms crossed in front of his chest. Carrie wears her signature bitchy scowl on her face. I always thought it was just her morning face, but maybe this is her default.

"Reid, what the fuck are you doing here? Can't you just leave me alone?" Whoa, is she serious right now?

"Hey, trust me, I hate this as much as you. I was just going on a run. I didn't realize the entire Main Street was off-limits. Besides, your meatball man ran into me too. I think my shoulder is dislocated."

She turns back to me aggressively. "Everything has to be about you, doesn't it? You can't think of how your actions affect other people."

"I don't know where this is coming from. Have you been sitting on this for a month?"

"It's been three months, Reid. Wow, you are unbelievable. I can't believe I wasted nearly a year on you. And his name is Griffin. He's a fig farmer." Confirmed, the bearded man is Mr. Fig, after all. "And at least he wakes up at five with me every morning to help me set up the bakery. At least he drives me up to Eugene to get me the special flour for my scones. At least he makes me come more than once."

I shake my hands before me, trying to get her to stop her rant. She's letting everything she's been stewing on fall out of her mouth. Good thing Missy and poker ladies aren't around again, they'd spread this like wildfire.

"I don't want to finish this conversation or talk to you ever again, Carrie, so if there's anything else you need to get off your chest, go for it, and I'll make it my life's mission to avoid you."

She reaches into the box she is holding and chucks a muffin at me. I duck just in time and avoid taking a bran muffin to the head.

"Hey, what the hell?" I turn to run far away from them just as I see her reaching in to get another muffin to throw at me.

"Fuck you, Reid!" I hear Carrie yell and hear another muffin plop behind me, missing me again.

I really can't believe *I* wasted a year of my life with *her*. How did I ignore all the red flags of toxicity dripping from her? The woman is a walking double standard. She yells at me, saying I am self-involved, and yet her only complaints are that I didn't stop what I was doing so I could fulfill her every want. I woke up with her every weekend and would drive her to Eugene every other month. It is a four-hour drive. No one wants to do that drive every week. Also, I most definitely made her come more than once unless she was faking it. But then, how is that my fault if she doesn't tell me what's going on in her head? I realize I'm fuming and talking to myself as I reach the end of the Main Street. The train tracks cross over both ends of the Main Street like bookends. It's probably three miles from my house, and I'm sick of running.

It takes me an hour and a half to get back to my house, and I have twenty minutes to shower and change before heading to work and turning this day around. I shower quickly and pull on my work uniform, black pants with my light blue "Parker Wellness" polo. I never wear this polo, but I can't be bothered to think about fashion in this time crunch. Besides, I need to bring my new friend a coffee.

IF I CAN RECALL, Annika's coffee order is an oat milk dirty chai latte with some kind of syrup. I don't know if she follows the same order now, so I decide to keep it simple and ditch the syrup. There's still a chill in the air as I walk from the cafe to Golden Hour. Even though it's creeping into late spring, Oregon gets its last wave of winter before we are hit with the sizzling summer sun. Thankfully, our workplaces are three blocks from Carrie's bakery, which I will be avoiding for the foreseeable future. I liked picking up cards at the stationary store across the street, but I guess I can make my own. Oh, but that one bookstore that stocks special edition hardcovers is two doors down from the bakery.

Shaking Carrie out of my head, I head into Golden Hour Studios. I didn't even realize this place existed until Annika told me she worked there. The building itself is tucked at the corner of the block in a brick building. It has a clean and industrial look to it. Dark wood and metal accents in a big open loft-style space. I think this part of the building used to be an old fabric mill. There's a main area where guests can sit and meet with photographers and a few studios segmented in the back. I see a room off to the back corner with a sign above that reads, "Annika's Lair." I wonder what's behind the door. I wait a moment, and when no one comes out, I head over to the door in the corner and knock.

"One second." I hear someone shuffling and walk over to the

door. "Hi, sorry I didn't hear the bell-oh! Reid!" She cracks open the door and emerges from the dark, crimson room. Ah, a film developing room. She's the film photographer on staff. That makes sense. The sign makes much more sense now. She heads past me, and the smell of her floral shampoo flashes images of my sex dream in my head. Annika's hair tousled, her lips gently parted as I thrust into her. Shit, she's staring at me. *Snap out of it.*

"Hey, good morning. I am returning the truce." I hand her the coffee, and her face lights up. "I decided I could use another friend too."

After she dropped off the coffee, I texted Tyler, who responded with a series of raised hands emojis. I'm not sure if he's rooting for this friendship or something more.

She motions us over to the front of the studio, and we sit on plush leather couches, sipping our coffees in silence. It seems like she's the only one here so far, at least that I can tell. I suppose it is still pretty early.

"So, how's your morning been?" She looks up at me, fluttering her dark lashes and slowly sipping her drink. "Mmmmm, a dirty chai? This is my favorite, and the Human Bean does it like no other place."

"I tried to remember that sweet syrup you'd get with it, but I thought it was too risky. And my day, well honestly not great, but it's getting better already," I say truthfully.

The distant comfort returns as I sit next to her. I want to pull her to my chest and nuzzle my face in her hair, but friends don't do that, Reid, so stop being a creep.

"What happened? It's only Wednesday."

I exhale and run my hand through my hair. "Well, not to make this new friendship awkward, but I ran into my ex this morning, and she sucks."

I notice Annika shift slightly at the reaction to the two-letter word but can tell she's trying to play it cool. "How long were you two together?"

"Too long. Like almost a year. I think at some point, it just seemed like a routine rather than a relationship, and both of us stopped trying. She was bottling all her emotions up and turned into a busted fuse. It's better now that we aren't together, but I can never set foot on the same block as Carol Breads ever again."

"You dated the bakery chick? Sheesh, talk about small-town drama. Is she the girl with the big red curls?" Annika lifts her hands up, motioning the volume of Carrie's hair. Her eyes get all wide, and she scoots a little closer to me. I can't contain the smile that spreads across my face.

"Yeah, have you been there?" I scoot a little closer too.

"Once, like the first week we moved here. My landlord, Sheela, told me about it, so Chloe and I got breakfast there one day, but I found a long red hair in my breakfast sandwich. I am never going back. She should wear a ponytail. Who does she think she is? Baking Ariel? Sorry, I didn't mean to trash talk your ex so bluntly." She sips her chai and smiles a little. *She's not sorry.*

"That is the nastiest thing I've ever heard. I'd say I regret it, but I try to remember everything as a learning experience." I am about to ask her about Sheela when a couple walks into the studio, and Annika swiftly stands up and floats over to greet them while setting her chai down on the front desk.

"Hi, Mr. and Mrs. Hutchins. Take a seat, and I'll be right with you." I stand to head to the door, but she catches me just before. "Thanks for the drink, Reid. See you Friday for happy hour."

She starts to lean in like she's going to kiss my cheek, then pulls back suddenly. Instead, she raises her fist, and I return the gesture, bumping fists and cackling as I head back to the wellness center with the goofiest smile on my face. I love having a new friend.

THIRTY

REID

TYLER and I walk over to the Irish pub at the end of Main Street after work on Friday. It feels like we are about to go on a blind date. My nerves are heightened, and it feels like I float through the large wooden door to the pub. The air inside is cool. Thankfully, the sun is starting to heat the valley, and it's only a matter of time before we are sweltering in the summer. Tables are starting to fill up with folks of all ages, huddled around tables and the bar, chatting and laughing. I scan the room looking for a tall girl with straight black hair and a shorter girl with a tangle of blond curls. I spot Clark, my client from last weekend, and give him a wave as we wander around the bar.

"Is that them?" Tyler asks, and I swing my head around.

He's pointing to a pair of ladies sitting at a booth in the corner. They are sitting on the same side, and Annika has her head in her hands while Chloe is shaking her shoulders.

We walk over to the table, and they don't notice us approaching right away.

"Hey!" I say. Annika snaps her head up, and a bright, wide smile appears on her face.

Chloe turns to look at me with a smile, then I see her eyes move to Tyler, then back to me, then back to Tyler.

"Hi, hi, Reid!" Chloe says and jumps up, giving me a hug. "Please join our booth. We got the best one in the place."

I slide into the booth so I'm sitting directly across from Annika, and Tyler sits next to me, across from Chloe. We just stare at each other, smiling for a bit until Tyler clears his throat.

"Oh, this is my friend, Tyler. He works with me at Parker Wellness," I say.

"Nice to meet you, Tyler," Annika says, giving him the same bright smile, she gave me. Just as a familiar ache bubbles up, she turns her dark eyes to meet mine, giving me a smirk, my favorite smirk. "How long have you been in Auburn Hills?"

"Me?" I say, pointing to my chest.

She laughs. "You, Tyler, Chloe, anyone really, just so we don't sit in silence the whole time." Tyler laughs at this comment.

"I like you better already," Tyler says, and I kick his foot. He clears his throat. "I mean, I grew up in Auburn Hills, lived here my whole life but went to college in Eugene and lived there after I graduated for like a year, but I moved back about three years ago. So let me know if you need an Auburn Hills guide."

I see Tyler give Chloe a wink. I think I see Chloe blush a bit but turn to Annika quickly to hide it.

"Why did you move back? Miss it too much?" Chloe asks.

"Sure, you could say that," Tyler replies with a forced smile.

"I moved here two years ago, right after graduation," I say, taking the attention off of Tyler so he doesn't have to delve into his history. "My uncle took me under his wing, and I did some fast-track training. I'm still learning as a PT, but I love it here."

"Well, Chloe and I just moved here a few weeks ago. I got a job offer, and we decided to move up here," Annika shares.

"I already heard the short version." I look directly at her.

"What's the long version?" She gives me a tight smile and squints her eyes.

"The long version is, I hated my major and worked at a marketing firm after college, hating my life, so I went home one day and panicked, applying for jobs in the middle of the night."

"She didn't tell me any of this, by the way. She kept it all to herself." Chloe jumps in. Annika gives her a side-eye and continues.

"Anyway, a few weeks later, I was getting rejection emails, but then one came in asking for an interview. They didn't bring up the location until after they offered me the job. After talking to my mom for, like, three hours, I decided to go for it."

"And Chloe came with you." I nod along, following her story and admiring her ambition to drop everything and chase a dream.

Chloe takes a deep breath. "I didn't have a lot of options. I'm not going to get into it, but I broke up with my longtime boyfriend, so I was kind of in limbo. It made sense to join Anni."

I scan my brain from our past experiences and remember the bleach blond guy Chloe dated, wondering if it is the same guy.

"It's so fun that you live here too, Reid. What a coincidence?" Chloe says.

"I don't know if it is," Annika says. "I don't believe in coincidences. Things happen, shitty or not. I have a feeling we were always meant to come up here."

Tyler taps his fist on the table. "Chloe! Do you want to go to the bar and order some drinks and snacks for the table?"

"Sure," she says with a bright smile. They slide out of the booth and walk to the bar.

Annika lets out a sigh and smirks up at me. "Despite the way you and I ran into each other, I'm happy to see you again."

"Me too." I smile. "I'm looking forward to our new friendship."

"Is Tyler your only friend here?" she asks.

"I'll have you know, I'm very friendly and know a lot of people here," I say.

She chuckles. "Yeah, I know. Everyone loves you, Reid. You know what I mean."

"Yeah, Tyler is my closest friend here. Sometimes we hang out with his buddies from high school. Everyone in the town, well, most people in town, are friendly. Don't tell him, but he kind of feels like an older brother. I go to him for advice and to get a warm meal."

Annika nods along, her gaze following my words, waiting for me to continue.

"I moved here and only knew my uncle. Tyler had been working at the center for about a year, and he took me under his wing right away, showing me the town. We went to a few places. He took me to Carol Breads about a month or so into me living in Auburn Hills, and that's when I met Carrie."

Annika's face scrunches at her name. "Right, redheaded Rapunzel?"

I laugh. "Exactly. We started dating early on, and I started spending more time with her. Tyler and I still would hang out, go on hikes, or check out a new band. If I went out with Carrie, we would hang out with her friends. Tyler never really stuck around."

"Why not?" Annika asks, turning her head and looking at Tyler at the bar.

He's leaning on the side, chatting with Chloe. He has this weird look on his face I haven't seen before and is giving Chloe a goofy smile.

"To be frank, he despised Carrie. He was thrilled when I told him we broke up. But since we did, I realized I didn't branch out to make other friends."

Annika's eyes bug out. "Well, Tyler and I have hating our best friend's ex in common."

"Was Chloe dating that same guy since freshman year?"

Annika nods several times, turning to Chloe and Tyler. "On and off since freshman year. It was a messy breakup, but I think it's for the best. I hope it is, at least. I'm a little worried about her. I can tell she's lonely."

"But she has you."

"She's always had me, and she always will. But it's different from having a friend to having a companion." Annika looks back at me.

Tyler and Chloe slide back into the booth, interrupting my conversation with Annika. Tyler slides a beer to me, and Chloe gives Annika a clear red drink with a cherry on the bottom.

"Is that a dirty Shirley?" I ask. We raise our glasses and say, "Cheers" to the new friend group.

"Mhm, it's my favorite," she says, meeting my eyes, taking a sip of her drink.

A MONTH PASSES, and Friday happy hour at the pub becomes a tradition that our new friend group keeps up each week. We take our beers and cocktails to the same corner booth. Chloe gets a basket of mozzarella sticks which Tyler always steals one or two, and Annika and I split the nachos. Tyler is very punctual every Friday afternoon, making sure we are out the door and on our way to the pub when Annika and Chloe arrive. I almost think Tyler is more excited about this new friend group than me. But even I find myself looking forward to our casual chit-chats. We talk about things we've been up to since college, Annika keeps us clued in on what's going on in pop culture, and Chloe shares new book releases.

Last weekend, we drove up to Medford and tried out a new brunch spot. If any of us wants to do anything, we ask the group chat if anyone is up for it. So far, we've all tagged along to each other's plans.

We all reluctantly went with Tyler to his climbing gym after he had been begging us for weeks now. Annika, Chloe, and I all had to take a class to even use the gym while Tyler did his usual climb. I'm not sure if it's my thing, but Chloe seemed to have a good time and said she'd go back with Tyler.

Most recently, Chloe sent the group chat a series of cat gifs followed by, "I'm at the animal rescue with Tyler. I'm adopting a cat."

Annika and I pulled up to the shelter at nearly the same time, and it was clear they were getting a cat. Good thing Sheela is such a chill landlord. Chloe had a small white fuzz ball cradled in her arms, her face soft with bliss. Tyler was scratching its little head. Of course, he went with Chloe. He loves animals more than humans.

I recalled our conversation at the bar about Chloe needing a companion. I didn't think she meant a cat, but having a little buddy can't hurt. Tyler and I met them at their house after, bringing a little cat bed we picked up on the way back. The little fur ball was bouncing all around their living room. We sat on their couch and chairs, staring and giggling at the kitten.

As we took turns giving the kitten pets and cuddles, I took in the decor of their apartment. I've never sat in their living room yet. It definitely feels like two best friends live here. They have pictures of each other on the walls and brightly colored art. House plants are stacked on window sills, and I notice an easel tucked in the far corner past the kitchen. Annika has some photographs she's taken framed on the wall. I recognize one as Pacific Beach, the same spot where we had our first date. I tear my eyes away from the photo and over to a large framed poster of postcards above her couch.

"Hey, Anni, do you still collect postcards?" I point up to the frame.

She smiles, a spark lighting in her eyes. "Sometimes, it was getting a little out of hand." She laughs.

"She donated like three shoeboxes before we moved," Chloe adds.

"It was heartbreaking, but I decided to frame some of my favorites and display them, so I can see them every day."

Tyler asks, "Can I ask why you collect postcards?"

Annika opens her mouth to respond, but before she does, I chime in, "She likes seeing the notes people write and the old postcards. Like a little time capsule on six by four paper rectangle." I look over at her, and her eyes soften, blush blooming on her cheeks.

"Exactly." She stands up and walks over to the frame. "Like this one. Someone was so excited to write to Linda Anne, they took up the entire postcard. And this one, I love the green color of the stamp. Oh, and this on up here." She reaches up, pointing to a postcard in the top corner. "Chloe sent that to me one year my family visited Brazil." The postcard has "Southern California" in block letters with a retro beach scene.

"Yah, these are cool. I never would think of collecting them. That's a pretty cool hobby," Tyler says.

Annika spins to look at me, and we both start cracking up.

The kitten suddenly jumps off Chloe's lap and starts dashing around the living room.

"She looks like a dandelion flying around in the wind," I say as the kitten tumbles through the coffee table and twists between our legs.

Chloe looks up at me. "She does! I'm going to call her Dandelion, Dandy for short."

THIS WEEKEND, Annika has a big photo shoot out in the woods. She is taking photos of a couple who are celebrating their fiftieth anniversary. Her studio scouts the location, and she works with the set designers to plan the shoot. She asked the friend group to tag along, so naturally, we did.

As we pull up, all piled into Tyler's SUV, our casual chit-chat stops. We are speechless about how they've transformed the area. The location is a popular hiking spot, an easy twisting path through the redwoods, surrounded by ferns and wildflowers. I remember hiking here with Tyler last spring, but they've transformed the park into a fairy meadow. They have a spot set up just off the entrance and textured fabric drapes from the branches mixed with twinkling lights.

The couple both are wearing wildflower crowns and a matching off-white suit and dress. I realize this was the couple that walked in that first day I went to the studio to see Annika. Crazy to think how surreal it felt to see her again after all these years, and just a month later, we are building a friendship again. It feels different this time. I can picture us staying close friends for years.

"Reid! Chloe! Tyler!" Annika chants off and appears from behind a redwood tree.

Annika quickly shuffles over to us as we get out of Tyler's SUV, which is filled with cat hair now because Chloe refuses to leave Dandy at home. She spent the entire trek to the photoshoot telling us about how Dandy learned to climb their new cat tree.

"Hey, this place looks incredible! I feel like I'm in a Wes Anderson movie," Tyler says.

"You wish you were in a Wes Anderson movie," Chloe fires off a reply.

The two of them have a unique banter. They are always quick to say a snarky reply, which I know Tyler enjoys. With Chloe, on the other hand, I can't tell if she despises Tyler or also enjoys their banter. She always scrunches up her face in her retorts.

I greet Annika with a fist bump that's become our special handshake.

"Anni, this is so magical. Dandy likes it too." Chloe lifts the flap from the sling she has wrapped around her torso where Dandy is curled up.

I must say, it is a pretty well-behaved cat. Most of the time, no one realizes she even has a cat with her.

"Thanks, guys…" Annika's smile lights up her whole face, and she turns to the set and then back to us. "It is so fun. I didn't realize work could be enjoyable."

"Seriously, Anni, you were always meant to do this. You are capturing those precious moments in life. I can't wait to see you in action today." Chloe looks like she's about to start crying.

"Okay, sappy hour is over. I can't be crying into my viewfinder," Annika replies, moving her arms to the side as if to wave off the emotional sentiments out of the air. "There's a bench a few yards off to the side if you guys want to set up there. We are about to start soon, and the shoot should last about an hour, depending on how many poses they want to do."

The three of us take a spot on the bench Annika pointed to. We all sit quietly, watching Annika do her thing. Chloe is right. Annika should've always done this. I'm sure she wishes she had started this sooner. I don't know the *whole* story, but I know she started it as an outlet recommended by her therapist. We aren't really at the point of our friendship to unpack any trauma we've experienced in the years since we last left off. And we haven't addressed the fact that we are probably the cause of some of each other's trauma, at least for me.

Annika gently coaches the Hutchins around the redwoods into romantic-looking poses. At one point, they are looking into each other's eyes between two giant redwoods with lights and fabric draped around them. Annika is saying things like "gorgeous" and "absolutely radiant" to them, which makes them relax and smile more naturally. The studio assistants have giant windscreens and are flapping from the side, which makes the branches and fabric ruffle around the couple. I can feel the love they share for each other radiating.

Mr. Hutchins brushes a lock of his wife's hair out of her face and presses a kiss to her forehead. "Yes, pretend I'm not here," Annika says as the couple leans into each other, softly swaying along with the branches. As they pull apart, I have a clear view of Mr. Hutchins' look into his wife's eyes. His eyes are glassy, and his facial expression is something I can't put into words. I've seen it on my dad's face when he looks at Pam. I've seen it on my Uncle Marty's face when he looks at a pastrami sandwich. I don't know if I've ever had that look on my face. But I want it. I want that feeling.

Like a magnet, my magnet, my eyes get pulled over to Annika. She has her hair pulled back in a headband today that makes her straight hair flip toward the back. She looks up from her camera and over to meet my gaze. We stay staring at each other for a couple of seconds before she ducks back behind her viewfinder. I exhale. We tried this song and dance already. It didn't work.

She wraps up the shoot, and the four of us go to a drive-up burger joint for a late lunch. Chloe and Annika are talking about how they want to change the style of decor in their living room from minimal to boho, and Tyler mentions a few flea markets in the area, so we plan to visit some next weekend. I chime in here and there, but I'm mostly distracted by the afternoon. The emotion of the photo shoot affected me more than I realized, and I am starting to wonder if I'll ever find my person. When do you even know? Have I already passed them at a grocery store, or are they my barista? I have no idea. Do I just go around smiling at every person in the entire world until I feel sparks and flutters in my stomach?

"Hey, Parker?" Annika snaps two fingers in front of my face, and I turn to her. *Flutter.* "You're drifting off into your fantasy land again. Come back to earth and give me some of your fries."

"What happened to your fries?" I shake my head and slide my tray over to her.

"I got sweet potatoes, and I want to try the crinkle-cut ones." She pulls out a fry and dips it in ketchup. "What were you thinking about, anyway?"

Hmm, how truthful should I be? Chloe is preoccupied with

Dandy, walking her around in the sling and humming some song. Tyler is leaning with his back on the table, scrolling on his phone.

"I was just thinking about the Hutchins. Their love is admirable. Tyler was right. It felt like I was watching a movie." Feeling vulnerable, I stand up from the wooden bench, brushing off invisible crumbs from my shirt.

"Reid is such a hopeless romantic," Tyler chimes in, turning toward us. Annika stands up, too, collecting our plates and tossing the wrappers in the trash. She sets the trays on top of the bin.

"That is not true," I counter.

Tyler laughs. "Yes, yes, it is. You fall harder, way sooner than you should. Remember when that new bookstore opened up? You went there like every day because you were obsessed."

"There's nothing wrong with falling in love with a bookstore."

"I fell in love with a vintage shop once," Annika says, giving me a wink. "Happens to the best of us."

Tyler laughs. "To your defense, you aren't wrong. The shoot was beautiful, Annika. Makes me want to catch the love bug myself." Just briefly, I notice his gaze glance at Chloe and then back to us.

"Thanks, guys," Annika says. "And I agree with Reid. The Hutchins' love is so special. They were radiant. I had to hold in my tears at times. It was an honor to capture it." With that, she turns and motions over to Chloe, who is lifting her cat to sniff different flowers. "Hey, crazy cat lady, we are leaving!"

Tyler and I wave as the girls head to Annika's car. We head back into town. I sit in the passenger seat, replaying the events of the day, adding to the Annika-sized sunburn on my chest.

THIRTY-ONE

ANNIKA

TOWARD THE END OF MARCH, my dad and brothers came to visit us during their Spring Break. I almost cried when I saw the two of them come running toward my house. They somehow got even taller since I moved. They stand probably a full five inches above me. Wes always looks like such a typical California boy in the summer. His light brown hair gets lighter, and his olive skin deepens to a golden brown.

Joey could pass as my twin more than Wes. We don't get dark in the spring and summer like Wes and Dad. Instead, a constellation of freckles appears on the tops of our shoulders and cheeks. I definitely wasn't expecting Joey to show up with a buzzcut, but he said he couldn't stand how hot his thick black hair gets during their baseball season. I took my dad and brothers around town and showed them where I work. The twins are deciding on what college to go to, but they both agreed they want to come to Oregon, where it's less hot than SoCal and closer to me.

IT'S BEEN three months since Chloe and I uprooted our lives in San Diego and moved to Auburn Hills. Summer is in full swing as mid-

June rolls by. In a rare occurrence, Chloe and I both have a free Saturday. Lately, our schedules have been booked by summer weddings and Chloe training a new flock of employees. It was Chloe's idea to spend this weekend doing something we both love and haven't done in ages—thrift shopping! Just the idea of stumbling on a gem in a vintage shop fills my soul with giddy anticipation.

"So I asked Tyler if he could send me a list of his favorite thrift spots." Chloe strides into my room wearing bright yellow flowing linen pants with embroidered white flowers and a just as whimsical, breezy white tank to match.

"He really loves a curated list," I say, shimming my denim cutoff shorts on.

I dive into my small closet, looking for my favorite band tee. It's a dark gray shirt that's perfectly worn in from Beyonce's *Dangerously in Love Tour*. Though I didn't attend, I was too busy climbing monkey bars and fawning over the new boy. It is still one of my favorite thrift finds and, hopefully, my good luck charm for today's trip.

"Oh my god," Chloe says. "I mentioned to him the other day about how I like pancakes. The next day, he sent me a list with all the best places that make buttermilk pancakes."

I emerge from my closet, thinking about her response.

"When did you two see each other?" From my experience of the four of us hanging out, Chloe and Tyler keep things neutral. Though I can tell he might have a thing for her, she effortlessly brushes him off, still not wanting to wander into dating territory.

Chloe shrugs and says, "He came into the bookstore the other day, and we chatted for a few minutes. Nothing really."

"Ah, okay," I say, keeping my response short, although Chloe reacts as if I told her a monologue.

"Whatever, okay, are you ready yet? I want to hit all seven places."

"*Seven*? San Diego didn't even have that many we could hit in the same day."

"Well, who knew that rural Oregon would be a gold mine for vintage and consignment shops."

I hop in the passenger seat of Chloe's sedan and send a text to Reid. Chloe is still nervous about leaving Dandy home alone, so I suggested asking him to stop by and check on the place.

> ANNIKA
>
> Hey can you do me a favor?
>
> Chloe and I are going shopping today, can you stop by the house in a couple hours and check on Dandy?

> REID
>
> A favor? Do I get one in return?

I roll my eyes. He can never just oblige.

> ANNIKA
>
> Depends on the request.

> REID
>
> This reminds me of a ping-pong game I played one time.

A weird, sinking feeling starts bubbling in my belly. Reid and I are still avoiding discussing our past relationship. I'm not sure if it's part of a truce or if both of us are just so horribly immature at communicating we are delaying the inevitable.

> REID
>
> Have I mentioned I am the worst texter alive?

> ANNIKA
>
> No need, I've experienced it firsthand.

> REID
>
> I'll swing by, you buy drinks this Friday.

ANNIKA

deal

I tuck my phone back in my purse, successfully ducking the uncomfortable conversation that might've occurred if we continued. Besides, it's girls' day.

The first store on the list, titled "Tyler's Thrift Crawl," is more of a consignment shop, and the price tags were a bit steep for us. Still, it was fun to look through some designer pieces and old furniture. The second place is a few stores down and more up our alley. We are flipping through the racks of clothes, I look up, and Chloe already has four articles of clothing slung over her shoulder. She is furiously flipping through the hangers, quickly scanning each one until finding something satisfactory and flinging it over her shoulder with the others.

So far, I have found a pair of old Levi 501s and a sweet, oversized denim jacket in a beautiful sage green color. The previous owner sewed patches along the shoulders. There's a patch with the space needle for Seattle, one of the rolling beach dunes, and even one with palm trees for California. This is a gem, for sure. *Thank you, Beyonce.*

We are in the fifth store of the day when my phone buzzes in my back pocket. I didn't find anything that interests me, but Chloe is making the thrift store worker bring down a painting of a cat that they have displayed on a shelf.

REID

Dandy is alive and well, sleeping on the middle of the couch.

ANNIKA

I just realized, I forgot to leave a key, how do you know this information?

REID

I peered through the front window like a proper weirdo. I hope none of the neighbors saw me.

ANNIKA

that explains the text I got from Miss Smith across the street, police are on their way.

REID

Come visit me in prison

ANNIKA

I'll sneak in a can whipped cream for your prison coffee

REID

I can always count on you <3

Hey, sorry if I made things weird, with the ping-pong thing.

ANNIKA

no worries, it's cool. I know you're still upset I beat you

REID

lol ya right, i demand a rematch!

but maybe we should talk about that, the whole thing, at some point.

I am about to respond but am halted by Chloe's shriek.

"It's perfect. It looks just like my Dandy!" Chloe turns to me, beaming a smile from ear to ear.

"Let's hang it next to the postcards. We can make a gallery wall."

WE ENTER through our front door to a giddy kitten jumping from each of us. We set our haul down and sprawl on the couches, taking turns trying on our finds and doing our best catwalks down the hallway leading to our bedrooms from the living room. Chloe found a stunning sundress in aqua with a white and pastel yellow print that brightens her eyes.

"This was the best weekend I've had in years," Chloe says, plopping down on the couch, a fuzzy Dandy in her arms.

"Same. We need to have girl days more often," I say.

"Agreed," Chloe says, yawning, eyes batting softly until she sinks into the couch, clearly tired from the long day.

I quietly head into the kitchen to make a snack and remember I never texted Reid back.

ANNIKA

for you, i'm available...at some point :)

～

REID'S BIRTHDAY is on the Fourth of July, and we all agreed we would spend the day doing whatever he wanted. He made sure to say at least three times that he wanted to avoid all the Fourth of July festivities and spend the day wandering different bookstores and record stores. Chloe surprises him and says that he can pick out as many books as he wants from her bookstore within ninety seconds. I've never seen him so excited before. Like a little kid in a candy store. We let him take five minutes to look around before pulling him back to the entrance. I have the timer ready on my phone and hit start. He swiftly darts around the aisles, grabbing as many books as he can. Tyler lists his selections as he picks them up, trailing behind Reid, darting from shelf to shelf.

"Fantasy! All three in the series!" Tyler says as he is on Reid's tail. The sight of two grown men pacing around a bookstore is the funniest thing.

"He just took one of each of these graphic novels. Hope you got stock in the back, Chloe!"

Reid isn't saying a word, concentrating on the books in front of him and darting over to the nonfiction section.

"*Millennial Money* and *History of Film Photography* were just added to the pile." The last one is an interesting choice, I think. The timer goes off, and Tyler holds Reid's shoulders to stop him from grabbing books. He saunters over to the registers with his haul and looks like the happiest boy in the world.

After our bookstore charade, we find an independent record store in a neighboring town that also has a cafe attached. Probably the best cafe fusion place I've been to yet. We sip lattes and flip through the stacks of records.

I am flipping through pop punk albums and stumble upon a Sum 41's record *All Killer No Filler*. *Is it strange if I get this for him?* We have been edging around the topic of our past. This could be another poke in the direction. Sure, I've been avoiding it, but it feels like it needs to happen. I'm just going to go for it. What the heck? It is risky, but if that day on the beach is a memory for him like it is for me, it's a happy one. Just to be safe, I'll throw a couple of other records on the stack.

We end the day at his Uncle Martin's house, who lives near the hills. His house is a spacious craftsman with a big backyard and patio. Reid's parents even drove up from the Bay Area. It is my first time seeing Sean Parker since I was a kid, but he recognizes me instantly when I walk in and pulls me in for a big hug.

"I'm so happy you're back in Reid's life," he says as we pull away.

"I am, too. It feels like no time has passed," I say.

"Has he shown you the card he was supposed to give you yet? I found it going through some old things. I just dropped off another box of his stuff when we got here yesterday. Can't wait to move up here with Pam later this year."

The card? I suddenly remember Reid saying he made a card to give me in middle school. "No, he hasn't."

"Well, remind him, it is the cutest thing ever. He has—had such a crush on you." Sean smiles and pats my shoulder, walking back to tend the grill.

We gather around the porch as Reid opens his gifts. Tyler gave him a shirt from L.L. Bean, which makes Reid double over in laughter. Not sure why nautical New England apparel is funny, but it's clearly an inside joke between the two. The cutest bromance I've seen.

My fingers tingle as I hand him his gift. He opens the gift bag and is pleased with each record. Pausing at each, flipping them around. He stops at the Sum 41 record, pausing a beat longer, then looking up at me.

"*But still, we're trying one more time.*" He recites a line from the song that I've memorized better than my family's birthdays. The butterflies inside me panic and swirl around, tensing my shoulders. "Thanks, Anni. This is perfect."

Reid stands up and gives me a hug, his body warming and relaxing me.

We separate, "You're welcome, we'll have to play them at your place soon."

"Definitely," he says, giving me a fist bump.

I NEVER THOUGHT ANYWHERE ELSE COULD BE hotter than Southern California, but I was wrong. Today is nearly one hundred degrees, and I feel like I'm melting. I don't think I can exist outside. My fair skin is too sensitive to this sunlight. I hope August cools the valley down.

I slather on my SPF80 before heading out. I don't know why I thought it was a good idea to tell Reid I'd walk to his place today, but here I am. Stomping down the sidewalk while wearing a comically large sunhat. I look like a flying saucer, but I have enough freckles on my face and shoulders and do not need more.

Chloe is working at the bookstore today, and we decided to drive up to surprise her. Selfishly, because the air conditioning in there is equivalent to north pole temps. Unfortunately, Tyler is booked at work and can't join us, but he sent us a list of books to pick up on his behalf.

Reid only lives three-quarters of a mile from us in a little townhouse. His place is cute and simple. It fits his personality perfectly, really. Everything he could need on two floors. His living room has a large squishy dark brown couch, and his walls are covered with music posters and records. He has about three giant bookcases filled with books, and even then, he has books stacked along corners of walls. I think his collection qualifies as a library at this point. There's a little galley kitchen off to the side of the living room that has light green cabinets and a window above the sink that overlooks his neighbor's garden. His bedroom and the bathroom sit on the second floor, directly above. I've never been in his bedroom, but I peeked inside once and noticed he painted one wall a dark jade green. Clearly, he has a favorite color.

I turn the corner heading down Reid's street, and I see him bolt out of his house to meet me on the sidewalk.

"Whoa, someone is eager to get to the bookstore." I head to the passenger side of his pickup truck and slide in.

"The air conditioning in my house is busted. I'm leaving sweat puddles around my house."

"You are revolting."

"You love it." He winks at me as he cranks the air conditioning in his truck.

Shivers cascade down my arms, and I'm not sure which is the cause, the wink or the cool air blasting through the vents.

There is only one long seat in the front. So, nothing divides Reid and me except for about ten inches of the seat. Sometimes when he turns corners too fast, I'll slide a bit over to his side.

Even though I'm trying to be just his friend, it still feels like too much to be that close to him. And yet, I don't want to lie to myself about how I actually feel. But we are trying this friend thing, so it's going to be ten inches of distance and fist bumps for the foreseeable future. Neither of us has brought up the last conversation we had on Flame. That was technically our last inter-action, but that memory is tied with other embarrassing ones, and I try to bury it as deeply as I possibly can. Reid clicks on the radio, and I'm hurled out of the misery tornado forming inside my head.

He keeps flipping through the channels until he lands on a station he deems acceptable. It sounds like alt-rock, Reid's favorite. He has posters of Blink 182, Sum 41, and Smashing Pumpkins all through his house. I can recognize the song playing, but I'm not sure who the band is. Reid is drumming along on his steering wheel and belting the lyrics. I love that about him. I mean, I don't love him. I just like that. *Oh, whatever, never mind.*

He sings and side-eyes me as I join in on the chorus. We sing along together. He reaches for the volume and turns it up higher while we both shout the bridge.

I try not to think too much about how these lyrics are a scary parallel to the thoughts I was just having, and the tornado starts spinning again. I shake those thoughts away and let the impromptu karaoke moment bury those thoughts down as I swing my head around. I pull my fists to my chest as if I wrote these lyrics myself and sing with all my might.

The song ends, and Reid starts cracking up and lowers the volume. "I had *no* idea you were so passionate about Papa Roach."

"Oh, is that who sings it? It's like one of those songs that I just happen to know all the lyrics, but I couldn't tell you the band that sings it or even what the song is called."

He throws a sideways smirk my way. "Well, it's 'Scars' by Papa Roach. For future reference."

I realize his truck has a working radio, and I remember his car in college didn't. "Your radio works? Did you get a new car?"

He quickly flashes his face over to me, and I can't quite read his expression, but he just as quickly faces the road again. "This is the same car. I got the radio fixed before I made the road trip up to Oregon. I couldn't handle all that quiet anymore."

Our conversation is on the brink of teetering to rocky territory, but thankfully, Reid pulls into the parking lot, and I'm rescued by the sight of Chloe's waterfall of ashy blond curls through the window.

We hear her squeal before we see her as we walk in and get hit like a slap in the face with the icy air of the store. I can feel the heat radiating off my limbs as Chloe rushes over, greeting us with a hug.

"What are you guys doing here? I won't get off for another hour."

"I think the earth is melting, and a bookstore is our only salvation," Reid says as his face relaxes, and he does a small spin with his arms at his side as if he's praising the lord of the books.

"We'll hang here until you're off, and then we can go get some ice cream."

"You don't have to ask me twice. Let me know if you guys need anything. I'll probably be stuck at the registers because it looks like the whole county figured out that we keep it cold in here." Chloe turns to shuffle back to the registers, where four more people have joined the line since she greeted us.

Reid and I both get large iced green teas from the connected cafe and aimlessly wander the book aisles. We spend ten or fifteen minutes not saying much. He and I follow each other in content silence, occasionally pulling out some books to look at or show each other. He picks up a paperback from the historical fiction section, and I grab the third book in a series I've been reading. We take our respective choices to the big armchairs in the corner of the store. We comfortably settle into the chairs and read, not expecting the other to strike up a conversation, just peacefully reading.

I appreciate that he is not saying anything and that we can both happily sit in quiet reading our books. I've felt a sense of calm wash over me recently. I recall being so self-conscious of each movement not that long ago. I felt like everyone was always watching me and calculating my moves, judging me. As if my life choices didn't measure up to the expectations of passing strangers. The feeling now brushes past me, a distant memory. I feel relaxed here. It feels like my place, my home.

I settle deeper in my seat and flip to the next page of my book. As I do, I can't help but peer up from my book every so often and look over at Reid. Our chairs are side by side with a small table in between, but the chairs are slightly angled toward one another. Depending on what page I'm reading, I can gaze up at him naturally. A motivation to read faster, I suppose. His hair is shorter now since it's summer, and he can't stand his hair getting in his face.

I gotta say, I do miss the way his hair would curl around the baseball caps he wears to work, but his shorter hair looks good too. It's short on the sides, and the top has enough volume that it still flops in front of his forehead. He pushes it back every few minutes. I'm not sure if he is enjoying the book he is reading because his nose is scrunched up, and his thick eyebrows are knitted together. I refrain myself from reaching over and smoothing the tension between his brows. I keep trying to keep my eyes on the book in my hands, but my eyes flick up to Reid each time he fingers his hair from his forehead.

He catches me taking one of those stolen glances and meets my gaze with a soft smirk.

"Whatcha lookin' at, Gomes?" *I love it when he calls me by my last name.*

"How adorable you are," Is what I want to say. But instead, I say, "Are you enjoying your book?"

His smirk falls, and he glances over the pages before closing them and setting the book on the side table between our chairs. He turns his body so he's facing me directly now. "Meh, it takes place in the 1700s, which is the period I'm least interested in for some reason. Give me the 1600s, heck, even the 1900s, and I'm all about it. But something about this pre-United States era is just a big bore to me. What about you? How's your book?"

I glance down and realize although I've read through several pages, I can't recall any of the words. "It's good. It's the third in the series, so I know all the characters. Not much has happened, though."

"Is that one of those romance books with a cute cover so no one realizes you're just reading porn in public?" He makes a move to try and grab the book out of my hands, but I pull the book to my chest so he can't swipe it. I can feel my cheeks getting warm.

"So, what if it is?" I lower my head and bat my eyelashes heavily in his direction. He seems to squirm a little, which pleases me. "I like to live vicariously through characters in the books I read."

I can see him pause to form a response. I am entering a danger zone, but we still have a while to wait for Chloe to finish up work, so why not shake things up? Maybe a year ago, I would have felt too empty, too unmotivated in life to even bother. But I'm on a warpath to do exactly as I want. And I want to flirt with my new friend. *Is that a crime?* If it isn't, it should be because I feel an excitement rush through me, I haven't felt in years. I could very well ruin the friendship we've established in these short months, but maybe I'm willing to risk it.

"When was the last time you were with someone?" Oh, so he's going straight to the point. I always appreciated Reid's directness. I look around, and no one in the store is near us. Not like anyone would care. I doubt my sex life is big news in this town.

"Uh, let's just say it's been a while."

"Oh, come on, you know about Carrie. Let me in on your past, a lil' Anni." He leans forward and softens his eyes. He's asking as a friend, I assume.

"Well, you were with Carrie in the last six months...for me, it's been...." I pause, drifting my eyes up, pretending to do the math as if I don't know that the last time I let anyone inside of me was the worst night of my life. "...it's been about four years, give or take..." I quickly open my book and bury my face in it.

He chuckles and reaches for my book again, this time swiping it away from my hands. "That's nothing to be ashamed of. It just means no one was worth your energy."

"I mean, the last guy definitely wasn't worth my energy."

His stare bores into my soul. "Okay, you gotta elaborate. You can't leave me hanging on that."

I swallow and fidget with my fingers. I don't know if I've said my last experience out loud with anyone besides my mom or Chloe, which was immediately after it happened. I've grown a lot since then, and I feel like it's part of my healing journey to not let the experience claw at my insides. I'm bigger than my trauma, and I refuse to let it stop me from finding happiness.

"It's just so embarrassing and a bad memory..." He sits up and opens his mouth as if to say, *never mind*, but my mouth decides to word vomit the rest out. "I got really drunk at a club and hooked up with Trey Roberts in the club bathroom. You remember Trey? The yeti? You saved me that one time he had his grimy hands on me. Well, he came at me again four years ago, and I let him. And after, I was alone and embarrassed and felt gross."

I feel my eyes go glassy and suddenly realize I just told my crush-turned-ex-turned-friend-turned-crush about my last hookup in the middle of a bookstore. I feel sick and decide to curl up in the chair and pretend I'm anywhere but here.

"Hey." I open my eyes, and Reid is squatting in front of my chair, his hands hovering out to the side.

He smiles, "I thought I told you to call me if he bothered you again."

When I don't smile in response, his expression falls. "I couldn't. I mean it was after we matched on Flame."

Reid braces his arms on either side of my chair. "Oh, I—I didn't realize, it was then."

"It's okay."

"No, it's not. I'm sorry for what I said to you. I'm sorry you went through that with Trey."

I'm quiet for a moment, studying his face. More freckles are speckling along his nose because of the summer sun. I'm sure an abstract drawing would form if I connected them. His face is soft as he kneels next to me. I wish he would move his hands from the chair to my legs.

"Yeah, it sucks, but it happened, and I am stronger from it, I suppose." I press under my eyes to shake the tears trying to form and take a sigh that lasts an entire year.

"You're the strongest person I know, it takes a lot of guts to follow your dreams."

I nod and avoid looking at him directly. I really don't want to cry in public. "I think Chloe should be off soon. I could use some mint chocolate chip ice cream after this trauma dump in a bookstore."

Reid's expression morphs into a smile that doesn't quite meet his eyes, but he extends a hand to me as we rise and gather our books. I go to grab mine, but he swipes it away. "Hey, I want that one."

"Well, you're going to have to get another copy because this one is mine," he says.

"Dude, you have to read the other two beforehand. You can't read out of order! That's like the biggest book crime."

"Fine, I'll buy you this one. You buy me the first book." I am beside myself, giggling as I lead us to the romance section.

"That makes no sense, but it's a deal. I hope you like reading about rich kids in Philly."

"You said Philly? I love their cheesesteaks." We head to the registers after grabbing the books Tyler requested, where Chloe checks us out and raises an eyebrow toward Reid's book purchases.

The three of us head out to a local ice cream shop, and no talk about past relationship trauma is mentioned again, which I'm grateful for. Although, since telling Reid, a part of me feels a bit lighter. Like a chip of the weight from that night was broken off. A lighter load to carry on with. I feel like I can walk a little taller and smile a little bigger. I hope I can keep chipping away at the bad memories.

THIRTY-TWO

REID

I CAN'T SLEEP the night we get home from our bookstore and ice cream adventure. I'm buzzing. I'm furious. It's not because of the heat that I can't sleep, although that doesn't help either. I'm fucking pissed about what Annika told me. I spent hours searching the internet, seeing where Trey Roberts was and how I could punch him in the face. Four years ago, she dealt with this asshole, and clearly, it affected her so badly that she hasn't dated another guy since. I wish I could have been there for her again. I wish it could have been me at that bar with her. How differently things would have gone. I'd have treated her like the phenomenal woman she is.

Four years ago.

I reflect on the past. Where was I four years ago? I was desperately trying to get through college, ready to move to Auburn Hills. I didn't end up studying abroad, so I was even more antsy. I stand up and pace my room and decide I need to just get out of my bedroom. Maybe I should take another cold shower and blow off these nerves. If it hadn't happened so soon after we matched on Flame, then maybe I wouldn't be taking what happened so personally. I was still fuming at her for rejecting me and then playing with my feelings like a puppet.

Now, we've established this friendship, and I care about her and am upset that she told me some douchebag asshat took advantage of her when she was in college, probably in a sad spiral, drunk, and vulnerable. *Dammit*, I'm fuming again. I'm probably miss judging the timeline. She didn't mention how much time had passed since we matched on the app. She wouldn't have spiraled like that from our little dating app interaction. It was nothing.

I sit on my couch and run my hands through my hair, thinking and searching my memories. *Did I take a screenshot?* I must've if it was Annika. Who would I even have sent it to? Maybe my dad. I guess it's worth a shot to go through my camera roll. Good thing I don't delete any photos ever.

It feels like I'm on an endless scroll through my screenshots folder until I find a familiar orange and yellow app background. The funny thing is, I wasn't even on it very long, before or after. I think I downloaded it the day before we matched. I was just so angry that out of all the women in San Diego, I matched with the girl who broke my heart, so I deleted it the day after. Okay, so maybe our interaction affected me after all, but I assumed it was one-sided, that she just went on continuing not to care about me.

I reread the chat. It's hard to absorb. I feel the anger I felt at the time in my messages. I hated San Diego. I wanted to leave so badly. I was incredibly lonely and ached for any sort of human connection.

IT'S A MATCH! CHAT WITH ANNIKA...

REID

Are you joking?

What are you doing?

Why did you swipe right?

ANNIKA

I wanted to see if you would swipe right.

Which you did.

REID

Of course I did. I still like you.

You ended things with ME. You said you don't feel the same way.

Are you saying you were lying to me?

ANNIKA

what? No, I'm sorry.

REID

Sorry for what, why are you sorry?

Why did you really swipe right?

ANNIKA

I don't know why...

REID

Well, figure it out.

- YOU UNMATCHED ANNIKA -

Damn, I feel attacked by the past me after that last message. I shouldn't feel guilty about sending those messages, but a part of me does. At the time, I didn't hesitate. I just said what was on my mind, what was brewing inside me. All the confusion about why she ended things when our dates felt perfect.

I need to shake these feelings off. We are starting fresh, a new friendship, which I love so much. I love having her as a friend. And Chloe and Tyler. It's the best to have this new friend group. The four of us. The four musketeers, four amigos, the four cool rats. *Is that last one a thing? I think I've heard Annika say it before.* Regardless, I need to shake off the past. It seems Anni is trying to do that, too, and I need to respect it.

A cool shower sounds like just what I need, after all. My apartment is still so hot that I don't even put my pajamas back on and pass out on my bed. I have another sex dream with Annika because my brain likes to torture me weekly. I force myself in the morning to release the tension that was built under my shower head while I mutter to myself that she's just my friend.

THIRTY-THREE

ANNIKA

I'M OFFICIALLY SCREWED. I'm pretty sure I'm in love with my best friend. And that's not Chloe, although that would be a lot easier, and we'd probably live a long, happy life together. Unfortunately, it's my other friend I'm in love with. The one with whom I have so many layers of unpacked conversations that keep getting buried under bookstore friend dates, brunch on the weekends, and after-work hangs. It's like the nachos we share at happy hour. We never reach the bottom. We always skim the good stuff on top and ignore the crunchy-gone-soggy chips at the end.

I woke up the day after exposing the lowest point of my life to Reid between the bookstore's Young Adult and Non-Fiction Sections to a chain of texts from him.

> REID
>
> Hey, I just want to tell you I'm proud of you
>
> Also, good morning.
>
> i'm always here for you by the way :] if you need to talk about anything else.

Which feels like an invitation, meaning he and I can—and

should—discuss our college relationship, but I take it as Reid solidifying our friendship. He's not going anywhere, no matter what curveballs I throw at him. Even though it's been a few weeks, I've gone back to his messages and reread them repeatedly.

I feel like I'm betraying myself when I think about him all day. I see a mug at the store, and I think, "Hmm should I get Reid a matching one?" I came here to focus on myself, and all I can focus on is the rush he makes me feel. The butterflies in my stomach are taking up a permanent residence. Maybe being his friend was a terrible idea. I can tell how much Chloe loves when the four of us hang out together. It feels easy. Each time we are together, I get to know a new layer about him that I never saw before.

I love the way the dimples on his cheeks show up only when he laughs a certain way, and I've made it my life's mission to unlock that laugh. The kind of laugh where you forget where you are and what you are supposed to be doing. Once I do, I want to photograph him smiling with those dimples so they can live on forever. I can look at the photo and see what pure joy looks like.

I can't wait for it to get cold again so that he can grow out his hair and it can curl up under his caps. Those tousled brown waves flop around his face as he bobs his head in the car or runs his fingers through his hair when he's thinking hard about something. They should carve that moment out of marble and put it in a museum, but in a special room that only I can view.

I love how he knows Tuesdays are my least favorite days, so he always brings me a dirty chai with oat milk to cheer me up.

I love how he fills up Dandy's water bowl every time he visits our house.

I love that he eats the crusts from my pizza.

I love that we've moved from fist bumps to side hugs because the side of my body he touches tingles for at least five minutes afterward.

I feel like I'm in middle school again, eager to run into Reid during the passing period. Stealing glances and smiles in his direction.

Except this isn't a crush. He's one of my best friends, and I think I'm in love with him.

And it hits me suddenly that this yearning in my chest is apparent and clear because everything else in my life is as it should be. Is what I've always dreamed it to be. Now is a reality. Happy, fulfilling, and still exciting. I wake up each day happier and enthused about what will unfold. I don't feel like a walking zombie at work. It feels like an actual workplace family. Not the toxic language that would be thrown around the office floor when someone new joins the team.

Everyone at the photo studio understands the dynamic and is supportive of one another. We go to each other's shoots and help out where need be because we love doing it. I love seeing the joy in people's faces and capturing them. Each client is a new project I'm excited to tackle. They built an entire dark room just for me when I started this position. Tiffany, another photographer, put a sign above the door that reads, "Annika's Lair." I don't feel guilty if I need to come in later one day for an appointment or leave early on a Friday because no one takes things too seriously. We even do team outings once a month, where we go bowling together. I keep pinching myself to wake up from this dream, but it's real. I made it happen for myself and need to accept that life can be good. I'm allowed to be happy.

I love living in this small town where everyone knows everyone. Nature, the trees, the rolling hills of deep reds and greens. It all contributes to the healing in my heart. I wake up to peace. The sounds of chirping birds and the branches swaying outside my bedroom window whisper me awake.

Though, I worry about Chloe. I don't know if she is thriving as much as I am. Outside of our house, she puts on this bright, happy face, but when it is just her and I, I see her with the mask off. The mask I haven't seen since we were kids. Even the edition of her new kitty has only softened the hard edges that formed since we left SoCal. I suddenly feel guilty about being wrapped up in my own heart and for not recognizing my best friend's feelings. I dragged her up here with me because I didn't want her to be alone. Yet I haven't been paying attention to how she is adjusting to our new town. Does she feel the same way about her job as I do about my job? I can't imagine she feels like working at a bookstore for her entire career is her dream. But maybe it is, I don't know, and now I feel like a terrible friend that I don't know. I need to talk to Chloe about everything. About my feelings toward Reid, about her, and how she's feeling.

I exhale and realize I've been lying in my bed staring at my ceiling while thoughts shuffle around my head. It's another Saturday Chloe, and I both have off. We'll have to make the best of it.

THIRTY-FOUR

ANNIKA

I EMERGE from my room to find Chloe curled on our couch, reading a new release she brought home. Hardcover. I don't know how she reads such monstrosities. I won't even look at a book unless it's a floppy paperback. Dandy is curled up on Chloe's shoulder, snoozing away as she reads. She looks at peace and calm. I hope she's happy here and not pretending for my sake. She seems happy.

I head into our kitchen and make myself a dirty chai latte on our little espresso machine. It's not the same as the Human Bean makes it, but it will do. I need the energy and courage to have a serious talk with my best friend. *Why am I nervous?* Chloe and I have been friends our entire lives and lived with each other for the past six years. I'm worried she'll say she's unhappy and we'll have to move again. I don't want to leave, I want to stay here with my happy life, and I selfishly want her to stay here too.

Joining her on our small sectional, I take a spot on the other end of the couch and sip my chai, staring at her until she feels my eyes burning a hole through the book she's reading.

"Good Morning Anni," Chloe says to me without looking up from her book.

"Hey Chlo, whatcha wanna do today? We have an entire free day today. We can do whatever we want. Whatever you want."

I will myself to stop fidgeting, but I at least get her attention, and she closes her book and sets it down, careful not to disturb the purring cat still on her shoulder.

"Why are you giving me so much attention this morning? What book do you want?" My mouth flies agape. Is that who I am? Do I not ask her what she wants to do, so when I do, it's only for my benefit? I push aside my defenses and remember it's not about me right now.

"I just am curious if there's anything you wanna do today. I feel like we haven't had a day with just the two of us since our thrifting day in June."

She lets out a deep sigh. *That can't be good. Sighs are never good.* "Well, honestly, I don't want to leave the house today. I know it's sunny and gorgeous outside, but I just wanna stay in this spot, sitting on my butt, reading my new book. I feel like I see enough of the public during work that I just want a break from it."

She goes to reach for her book again, but I keep talking. "We can have a day in. I can order us some breakfast if ya want."

"Ooo yeah, let's get pancakes." She shimmies in excitement.

"Of course, pancakes are one of your major food groups," I say. "Hey, speaking of work, how is it, by the way? I realized I've just been happily going to work and rudely never even asking you if you like your job, and all the feelings rushed to me this morning when I woke up, and I feel like a terrible friend, but I'm trying not to make this about myself so I want you to tell me if you hate it and we can try again. We can move somewhere else that you like too. We can find you your dream job. And–"

Chloe's mouth falls open, and she reaches for my arm, cutting off my panic rambling. "Whoa, whoa, Anni, chill. Is that what all this is about? You're trying to butter me up because you're worried I'm unhappy?"

All I can do is nod. I feel like if I open my mouth, I'll start rambling again, and I'm trying to push the tears away that are forcing themselves up.

"I love you, and you didn't force me to move here. You were going to move alone, remember? But you took me with you, and I am so grateful for that. Sure, I am not the *happiest* right now, but it's not because of where we live or my job. In fact, I'm kind of living the same life I was living in San Diego but in Oregon and single." Dandy flops down onto Chloe's lap so she can get some belly rubs.

"You're unhappy? When, why didn't you say something?"

"I didn't say I'm unhappy, but yeah, I could be happier. You are so happy here. I don't want to ruin that with my storm cloud. I just haven't recovered from what happened with Dane, and I miss him. Which I hate. Or I miss having someone to show affection to, at least. And, yeah, being a bookstore manager is not my dream job."

"What could you do? If someone waved a magic wand and gave you your dream job?"

She is quiet for a bit. Almost like she's wondering if she should even tell me. "You know the shelter we got Dandy from?" I nod. "I emailed them last week asking if they have any openings. I feel so much joy from Dandy, but being able to rescue her was a different kind of comfort. I want to help the other animals there too. The ones that don't get adopted. They need someone to give them love too. I think that's what I'd do if I could have a dream job. To have my own shelter and take care of animals, find them homes, and give them my love. Have them sit while I paint portraits of each one, so when they do get adopted, their owners can take home their portrait too."

My heart warms and breaks from her response. "What did the shelter say?" Now I reach for Dandy because I need something to comfort me.

"They don't have any paid openings, but they said I can volunteer on my days off. They said if something comes along, it's easier to transition into a paid position from a volunteer position."

"That's great! Are you going to do it? I'm sure there are other shelters around, too, that we can look into. Maybe you can cut down hours at the bookstore."

"Anni. Look, I love you, so I'm going to tell you this straight. Stop trying to fix everyone. You need to focus on yourself, okay? I'll be okay. Yeah, I don't *love* my job, but I'm doing a lot better than I was a few months ago. You helped me a lot. But please, let me try to fix myself, myself. Why are you tearing up?"

I realize my eyes are getting glassy, and I exhale a deep sigh. "I just want you to be happy."

"I want the same for you. I'm getting there, okay?" Chloe reaches for my hand and squeezes it. I don't know if I can let her go completely. I want to help her, but she wants to try to help herself. I need to respect that. I know so deeply how that feels.

"You've been there for me my entire life. You were there for me when my dad left, when my mom didn't care about me, and when my Birkenstocks were ruined at a party. Not to mention through the worst breakup of my life. You picked up my pieces and glued them together for me. I don't know how to do it for myself. I need to try."

"Okay, now I'm full-on sobbing. I'm sorry, I just want-"

"No! Don't be sorry for being my best friend, my sister. I love you."

I can't take it, and I just reach over and squeeze her, tears streaming down my cheeks. Dandy nearly misses getting squished between our hug and jumps out to safety. Chloe's curly hair tangles around me, and I hug her tighter. I am so thankful to have this girl by my side and someone who's been there for the majority of my life. She's my sister not by blood but by soul. I don't want to lose her, and I'm afraid if I let her figure out her life, she will realize she needs to move away from me.

"Okay, can we order pancakes now? I think I'm going to tell the shelter I want to volunteer, but I need carbs in me."

"Please do not hesitate to ask me for help. I'm happy to."

"I know you are." She smiles and squeezes me tighter.

WE SET up a little brunch moment out on the front porch, spreading out the pancakes, scrambled eggs, and veggie sausage we got delivered from a local diner so that we can serve as we wish. I bring out Chloe a glass of her favorite guava juice because I still need to confess my feelings about Reid. I'm worried about how she will take it.

I hand her the glass and give her a big smile. Her face turns from happy to suspicious as she sees the light pink juice. She keeps my gaze as I sit down, and she takes a sip.

"This is guava juice. You only get guava juice for special occasions. What's going on?"

"I, uh, don't know what you mean."

Chloe keeps squinting at me as she gulps down half the glass. "Spill the beans."

I take another deep breath, willing the heat in my cheeks to subside. I open my mouth, but she cuts me off before I can start.

"It's about a guy. O-M-G, you're in love with someone! I know it's been a while, but I remember you getting all flushed like this the last time...."

I just stare at her and give her an uneasy smile. She is putting the pieces together without me saying a word. She knows me too well. When I dated Isaac and Marcus, the relationships were short-lived, flings, not something I thought about day and night. Chloe rarely heard me talk about them. I've thought about how unfair it was that I never gave them all my heart. I could never meet them at the level I should have. The level I feel when my heart longs for Reid. My thoughts are consumed by him. I don't want to picture a day where he isn't in my life.

"Annika, you need to speak because I don't want to guess."

"You already know. I know you do. I don't want to say it."

"Again?" She spears half a pancake and shoves it into her mouth, furiously chewing and swallowing before continuing. "Are you sure? I don't need to remind you how everything went down last time. Do you think he even feels the same way toward you?"

Ouch, I wince at that last hypothetical question, and she sees it in my face. I knew it was a mistake to say anything. I should have just let this crush simmer in my life forever until one of us eventually moved away. But I know I will always compare anyone I'll ever be with to him.

"I'm sorry, Anni, to be brutally honest. I just don't want to see you at your lowest like that ever again. I didn't know how to help you. I was so scared. I'm worried it will happen again.

"Also, selfishly, I'm warming up to this town. And if you try something with him again and it doesn't work out, do we stay? Leave? This town isn't huge."

"He dated the baker girl down the street, and they broke up. It's not impossible. I just, I don't know, maybe it's stupid, but I want to try for real. I was afraid to let myself go toward my feelings back then. I was self-sabotaging every aspect of my life. I never followed my heart toward what I actually loved. What I loved doing and who I loved being with. I was doing everything in my life for the wrong reasons."

"Okay, so what if it does work out? Are you going to move in with him? Are you leaving me alone? Or is he moving in here? Because we've already decorated the place exactly how we like and I can't imagine where we are going to fit all his books in here."

"Whoa, okay, wait. You were just saying you want to figure things out on your own."

"Yeah, but that doesn't mean I want you to move away from me. I need you close! At least for the start of it all."

"I'm not going anywhere. Even when we are old and wrinkly. I'm going to bother you for your whole life. I want your support, but I get where you are coming from."

"Just maybe, don't do anything drastic yet. Feel it out for a little bit. It might just be a crush."

I nod in agreement, even though I've thought about this for a while. Honestly, ever since he brought me the dirty chai a few months ago, I knew this was a sign to try again. The third time's a charm, I suppose.

MY WEATHER PRAYERS WERE ANSWERED, and so far, August is cooler than July. I can't wait for the fall in Oregon. Tyler said the view from his house when September hits is picture-perfect. I can already imagine all the landscape photo shoots I'll take once the oak tree leaves turn amber and mix with the dark emerald redwoods.

I've been taking Chloe's advice and not making a move on Reid. Instead, I've spent the last few weeks texting him about books and stealing glances. I admit it's not that creative of me to have a crush on the same guy three times in my life, with two of those times not working out. The first time wasn't my fault, however. If he hadn't moved away, we could have gone to the dance together in middle school, married, and lived happily ever after. But no, now we have gone through a different kind of dance where we twirl around, brushing shoulders or missing each other completely. Reid is my closest friend besides Chloe and Tyler. Tyler is nice and great, but no one makes me feel as equally relaxed and overwhelmed as Reid does.

A part of me is definitely saying not to make a move. Our life is so lovely now. I can't help but notice the emptiness I feel when I look to my future without trying again. Even if he still rejects me, I'll know I at least tried one more time.

Chloe has been eyeing me since I told her. I feel like my every move and glance is being cataloged and criticized. Chloe doesn't want me to do anything about my crush, which hurts because I know I won't be able to hold it in for much longer. So, I'm ultimately going to betray her, but for the first time in what feels like my entire life, I am finally doing something for myself.

The four of us are sitting in a corner booth at the Human Bean, sipping on our iced drinks, enjoying the mild weather and bright sun. Iced hazelnut latte for Tyler, iced matcha for Chloe, iced green tea with honey for me, and iced black coffee with whipped cream for Reid. He never strays. It's a Sunday afternoon, and it never feels old that I don't dread going to work tomorrow. I have two client meetings tomorrow and a bunch of photos to develop. I can't wait.

"Yo, no way, Chloe, bringing soup to the theater is weird as fuck," Tyler says to Chloe.

"Sometimes I just want something hot and comforting while I watch. I put it in a thermos and sip. Plus, they always crank the air conditioning in the theaters, so I get chilly."

"You're telling me you *drink* chili because you're chilly?" Reid doubles back, laughing at his own dumb joke.

"Oh, and please tell me what book you are reading, Reid!" Chloe retorts, making Tyler snort laugh. Reid can't help but laugh at her joke himself.

I snap out of my thought cloud and try to pick up the pieces of their conversation.

"She's brought soup to the movies at least three times in the past year. She's obsessed with soup," I interject.

Reid chuckles and shakes his head. It hurts to look at him as each day goes by, knowing I shouldn't do anything about it. I want to lean into him, feel his body heat against mine. To run my fingers through his hair and pull him into me, running my lips along his neck. I peel my eyes off him and realize Chloe sees me staring. I give her a little smile and focus on my green tea instead.

"Hey, Anni." Reid bumps my wrist, and I look up at him again. *Sigh*, I could get lost in those green eyes for the rest of my life. "Whose car do you want to take to the concert?"

"Well, considering your truck only has one bench seat, we should probably take my hatchback so the four of us can fit. Unless Tyler wants to drive," I reply, and I hear Chloe clear her throat.

"Yeah, about that, I can't go to the concert." This is news. She would have mentioned to me earlier that she couldn't go. "Tyler can't either."

"What? Since when? We already got our outfits picked out."

She gives me a weird look and bugs her eyes a bit. I look at Tyler, who also seems confused but hasn't said anything.

"I got roped in at the last minute to oversee an event at work. The other manager is going to be out of town, and they need a manager there, so that leaves me. Plus, Tyler said he'd volunteer to help."

I squint my eyes at her, then to Tyler, who is slowly nodding. *That is total bullshit.* First of all, Chloe is the only manager at her location. Second of all, what kind of event is it, and why is she just mentioning it now? We'd all be down to go to the event to keep her company. She's up to something. I go to open my mouth to protest, but she waves it off.

"You guys go without us, please."

We look over at Tyler. "I totally spaced that I said I'd help out. You know me, I can't go back on my good word. It would ruin my glowing reputation," he says. Reid is also squinting his eyes at his friend.

Reid looks over to me and lifts a shoulder. "Do you mind if we take my truck then? No offense, but your driving scares me."

My mouth falls agape. "What? I'm a great driver." Now they are all wincing.

"No offense, Anni, but I'm always holding on for dear life when you are driving. You act like you are a race car driver just because your car is red," Chloe says.

"Ever wonder why I take my SUV and drive separately when

you volunteer to drive?" Tyler asks with big eyes, looking away and taking a sip of his drink.

I give them both a dramatic eye roll. "Fine, we can take your truck. But I want to leave early so we can check out the merch booth ahead of time. Plus, it's an hour away."

Reid reaches up to give me a fist bump, and I return it to him with a smirk.

IT DOESN'T TAKE me thirty seconds before we are past our front door to turn to Chloe and say, "What the hell are you up to?"

She returns a sly smile and plops down on the couch just as Dandy finds her and curls around her, wanting pets. "I've been watching you two closely since you confessed your love for Reid to me."

"I don't love him. Okay…maybe a little bit, but go on."

Now she's the one to give me an eye roll. "First of all, Miss Delusional, you love him a lotta bit. You always have. Second of all, ten thousand percent he feels the same way. I can see it when you two look at each other. It's different when he looks at me or anyone else. Or when Tyler looks at you. When Reid looks at you, his whole demeanor softens, and his eyes get all sparkly. Like what you are saying or doing is the most important thing in his life. He leans closer to you and it pains him to look away."

"Are you reading romance books again?"

"No…maybe…whatever, it doesn't matter. What *does* matter is that I am right, and I saw my chance to finally help you. I meant it when we cried over pancakes a few weeks ago, you always help me, and not only do I want to help myself, but I want to be there for you when you need it."

"So, you lied. You don't have an event."

"Of course not. You know my work schedule better than I do. I was worried you were going to ruin my whole plan."

"Wait, if there's no event, then why did Tyler go along?" I ask.

"Tyler was a wildcard I threw in, and I am pleasantly surprised he followed my lead. I have a feeling he is picking up on the feelings between you and Reid too."

"Pssht, doubt that."

"He's Reid's best friend. Reid definitely told him about your history. I think he's on Team Annid."

"Annid?"

"Your couple's name, or it could be Reika. Oooo, that's kinda beautiful. Maybe I'll name my firstborn after you two."

I am so flabbergasted by these events that I can't help but fall back smiling, Chloe joining in.

"Chloe, are you sure? Am I sure about this?"

"Do whatever feels right. Even if you don't do anything yet, you and he can have a few hours alone, and it should help you decide what to do."

A bundle of emotions builds up in my stomach. I don't know if it's nerves or excitement or joy or gratitude or maybe all of it at once tumbling together. "Thank you, Chloe. I'll buy you some merch."

"It's the least you can do, honestly. I'm absolutely gutted that I'm missing the concert for my fake work event. Okay, Dandy, your fur is too warm, and I'm melting, get off of me, please."

"Will you help me pick an outfit? Because now it's just me and Reid. I want to look hot and confident."

"Duh." And with that, we scurry off to my bedroom, and it feels like we are freshmen in college again, planning outfits while giddy feelings bubble through me.

THIRTY-FIVE

REID

JUST ME AND ANNI, going to the concert as friends. This is not a date at all. We are two cool pals, going on a friend-hang to a concert.

So, what if this will be the longest amount of time she and I will have spent together since our newfound friendship? If she and I are hanging out, it's for maybe twenty minutes, an hour tops, and even then, it's because we are waiting for our friends. This is different. We have an hour's drive to the concert and a two-hour set, then an hour's drive back. I release the breath that I've been keeping trapped in my chest and am suddenly self-conscious of the outfit I pulled together. I felt weird asking Chloe and Annika how my outfit looked, so I just sent it to Tyler. Who, by the way, I'm intensely suspicious of because this whole concert was his idea.

He seemed to approve of my navy chino shorts and a band tee. I almost put on a new pair of Vans, but I am so nervous for some reason that I put on my Converse. My security blanket shoes. I went against Tyler's suggestion to wear white ankle socks and instead picked a pair with yellow and black smiley faces. I figured it's a concert, so why not be fun, but now I'm worried that I'll be under-dressed.

I pull up to Annika's house and almost get out to knock on her door, but that feels too much like date behavior, so instead, I hit the horn on my steering wheel a couple of times. A few more minutes go by, and I hit the horn again. *Didn't she want to leave punctually?* But then I see the front door swing open, and she hurries outside and over to my truck.

She is wearing a white high-neck tank top tucked into short light denim shorts. Her legs look a million miles long, and they go down to a pair of white Converse, just like the ones I have on. And she's wearing some funky socks. I can't help but chuckle at the coincidence of our outfits.

She has on a light green oversized denim shirt with little patches sewn on the shoulders and about four gold necklaces around her neck. She'll need the extra layers later. Late August is still warm, but we are reminded that autumn is around the corner as the sun dips below the horizon.

Her hair. Whenever she does anything to that black shoulder-length hair, I go nuts. Today, she did two small braids on either side of her face with little green clips at the bottom. She's so fucking adorable. I breathe out another sigh and chant silently in my head. *Friends, friends, friends.*

I keep searching her facial expressions to see if she feels anything else for me but push those feelings away. I don't want to ruin this again. I fall too hard for her. Every. Time.

But she hasn't given me anything other than wanting our friendship to be mutual, so I follow suit. I don't even know if I would make a move on her. Not until we unpack our baggage. I know I was harsh on her in our last interaction, and I guess I still have a fear she will reject me if I wear my heart on my sleeve like I did freshman year.

She circles my truck, swings the door open, and slides in. I give her a nod, and we share a fist bump. Even though we are more comfortable with each other, it's become our little handshake.

"I figured we could listen to the album on the way there." I go to switch on the radio, but she surprises me and turns it off.

"I thought we could just sing songs to no radio, you know, like the good ol' days?"

This makes me burst into laughter. "Good ol' days? I don't know about that. There's a lot I don't miss about San Diego, and the lack of a radio in here is one of them." I glance over, and she shifts in her seat a bit.

"Alright, let's sing to no music. I know it's just because you love my singing voice."

She looks up at me, her little smirk on display. "You are the worst singer alive."

I start beating on the drums and singing Neck Deep's *'Parachute'* at the top of my lungs.

Annika joins in, and that's how we spend the hour car ride. Singing at the top of our lungs, windows down as the air starts to cool down, drumming on the dashboard, humming along to the parts we don't know, and feeling like this whole moment could last forever.

AFTER STANDING in line for twenty minutes at the merch booth and each getting a T-shirt, and one for Chloe and Tyler, of course, we find our seats. I leave for a second to grab us each a drink and come back to some tattooed shirtless dude chatting up Annika. She is smiling at him like she never smiles at me, and I don't know why that pisses me off. I stalk up the stairs and approach them, staring the guy down.

"Hey Anni, here's your drink." I hand it to her and slide onto the seat next to her.

The shirtless guy pays me no attention and proceeds to ask for her number.

"Sorry, I don't give my number out to random guys I meet. But maybe if we come across each other again at a farmer's market or something, I'll know its fate." She shrugs her shoulders and plops down on the seat next to me, leaving the guy stunned in the aisle and me trying to hold in my laughter.

"You can leave now, bro. She doesn't want to give you her number." He finally notices me sitting next to her, grunts and shrugs, then walks down the aisle.

"Not gonna lie, it felt kinda nice, though. I haven't had a guy ask for my number in, well, a long time."

"You can do way better than a shirtless dude," I say while taking a sip of my beer.

"I know," she says.

THE CONCERT COULDN'T GO any better. Once the band comes on, we rarely sit and are instead drinking beers, singing, and dancing along to the music. We feel so relaxed together, and I realize it might not feel this way if we were to try a relationship again. We work so well as friends. It feels effortless. So instead of overthinking every bat of the eyelash or nudge to my arm, I sing and dance with my friend.

THIRTY-SIX

ANNIKA

I DECIDE the last song is when I'm going to do it. I'm going to make a move. Chloe told me before I left to feel it out and let my gut take the lead. I want to try. I want to show him that I want to try. If I don't try now, I'm not sure if I'll get this courage again. I want to do it for real. No second-guessing, no overthinking. I've loved him since I was nine years old, and just being his friend these past few months only made me fall in love with him again.

The band finishes the song they are on, and the venue goes dark while the crowd shouts, "Encore, Encore," until the band runs out on stage again.

Okay, this is it.

The band starts singing the song. One of the most popular songs on their album. The crowd starts bopping around the most they have the whole concert, including me and Reid. I take a deep breath and slip my hand behind Reid's back. His body is warm and hard. I feel like my whole body—my whole world is shaking. I've never made a move like this on anyone before. Anyone that mattered. I could collapse down the aisles of people right now. I can barely control my legs. With my hand on his back, I stand up on my tiptoes and reach up to kiss Reid on the cheek. He flips his head over to me, and I just go for it. I lean in to meet his lips, closing my eyes and breathing in.

But I'm left in the air. I open my eyes and see Reid pulling his head back, shock on his face, and I realize I've made a terrible mistake. Time starts moving in slow motion. My heart drops out of my butt. I wish I could form wings and fly out of the venue. I wish I could crumble into ash and be swept away by the cleaning crew. I wish I had never done any of this. *What have I done?* Chloe was right. I shouldn't have done anything. I should have ignored my stupid feelings. I should have taken that shirtless guy's number. I ruined my friendship. My heart. It feels emptier than before. Great, now we have to move again.

Reid stands frozen in time while everyone around him jumps to the music.

"I'm sorry!" I blurt out, but the music is too loud. We stop dancing, and he leans closer to me. I almost think he's going to kiss me back until he says,

"We are so good as friends, I—"

"No, no, you're right. I'm sorry. I read the situation wrong. We are friends. And I'm…" I realize my vision is blurring, and I can't be in this room anymore. I feel like everyone is closing in on me. I need to leave.

I break away from Reid and head toward the exit. I don't stop running until I hit fresh air. A slap in the face, it feels like, as I burst through the exit doors. I'm not alone. Reid is right behind me. Of course he is.

I wipe away my tears quickly, hoping he doesn't see, then plaster a smile back on my face. "Seriously, it's okay. I think I just had too much to drink. I'm going to be so embarrassed tomorrow." I try to laugh it off. "We should head out to beat the rush."

Reid doesn't say anything. He's just looking at me with his

eyebrows scrunched and the corners of his mouth turned down. I wish I could read his mind and figure out if I've devastated everything. I hope I can recover our friendship after this, although I don't know if I'll be able to recover. How can I ruin a relationship with a person so horribly, multiple times in my life? I wouldn't be surprised if he never wants to see me again. I know one thing, I'm never going to try ever again.

WE DRIVE BACK to Auburn Hills in silence. I turn my body as close as possible to the passenger door, away from Reid. I can't face him. I actually think I might have had too many beers, too, because it feels like bees are buzzing around my skull. He still hasn't said anything to me, and I don't expect him to. I expect him to drop me off and never see me again. The shame and embarrassment crawls around me, and I close my eyes, hoping the drive goes faster. I want to be at home already with Chloe. I want to take back this whole situation. I want to beg Chloe to come with us. I don't want to lose my friend in Reid.

We finally make it back, and he pulls in front of my house. Before he can say anything, I fly open the door without a word and run inside.

I close the front door and lean against the other side. Chloe is on the couch with Dandy watching TV, and she knows as soon as she sees me. I can't hold it in anymore. A sob breaks out of my chest, and I slide down the door, cradling into a ball. I can't feel anything. I thought I was doing what I wanted, and he didn't feel the same way anymore. I suppose it's karma. *How can you not feel the same way I feel about you?* His words from six years ago replay in my head. Chloe wraps her arms around me as my sobs turn into soft cries.

She pulls me up into her arms and takes me to the bathroom, where she proceeds to remove my makeup and brush my hair out. I manage to shower and put my pajamas on, but I don't know if I can sleep. I keep replaying the events in my head and their alternate endings. I've fucked things up once again. Can I ever get anything right? Can I ever get the timing right?

THIRTY-SEVEN

REID

I LET her get out of my car without saying anything. I lost the ability to speak when she knocked the wind out of me.

I'm trying to form words that can explain how I'm feeling, but I can't. I am at a crossroads. I love her as a friend. I do, but maybe also more than that. I just don't want to lean fully in that direction.

Should I have kissed her back? Should I have made a move earlier? I was so scared she didn't feel the same way and that I'd lose her. But now I'm second-guessing everything. Every smirk in my direction. How she looked at me after rejecting the shirtless guy. She always brings me my favorite drink at work. Our long texts through the days and nights about random topics.

I'll let her cool off this evening, but I want to talk to her tomorrow. We can't let this end us. We have to talk. About everything.

I CAN'T SLEEP. I am lying in my bed, rewinding the events in my head over and over again. I felt her hand on my back and didn't think anything of it. We were dancing, and the crowd was getting rowdy. I thought she was trying not to stray too far away from me, plus I loved the feeling of having her close. Then she kissed me on the cheek, and I was so surprised. I almost didn't think it was her. I turned and saw her leaning in for more. I reacted instinctually, backing away because my friend was trying to kiss me. *God, I'm so stupid.* I am an asshole. The look on her face made me want to crawl into the nearest hole and live there for the rest of my days. I hated that my reaction made her feel that way. But I was so confused. I still am.

I need a snack. I need to do something instead of lying here. I don't know why, but I want a bean and cheese burrito. Something warm and cheesy will be sure to comfort the turmoil I'm experiencing. If only I could find the can opener. I swear I had one. I open every drawer in my tiny kitchen and I can't find it. Maybe it's in a different drawer. I start searching my house, looking for a can opener. It's not until I reach the small drawer at the table by the front door that a little velvet pouch catches my eye. The necklace.

Her necklace.

I grab it and collapse on the couch, clutching it to my chest. Every feeling I ignored rushes out of me at once.

I love her. She's the one. She always has been. No matter how many times we push each other away, we always make our way back to each other. She'll always be the one for me. I can't hold back my tears as I press the pouch to my chest. I only cry when I lose her. No one has ever made me feel as comforted as she does. She feels like home. She is my home. I want to spend the rest of my life with her.

THIRTY-EIGHT

REID

IT TAKES every ounce of restraint to wait until after the sun rises to check in with her.

9:10 AM TO ANNIKA

REID

Hey :)

10:00 AM

Do you want to get a bite to eat today?

MESSAGE UNREAD

10:13 AM

Outgoing Call to Annika - No Answer

I'M STARTING TO PANIC. What if this is it? Our friendship is over. I just need her to give me one more chance. I just need to talk to her. I get a text from Tyler just before I'm about to send Annika another message.

10:18 AM
TYLER

Has she responded to you yet?

REID

No, she's giving me the silent treatment.

TYLER

You're screwed

REID

Gee thanks, I'm freaking out

TYLER

just wait a bit and try again

REID

okay.

What if I fucked it up? What if I missed out?

TYLER

you always come back to each other

REID

thanks for the reassurance

TYLER

try Chloe

I decide to try her one more time before resorting to her best friend. Although if I was M.I.A., I'm sure Tyler would be the first person most people would reach out to as well.

10:34 AM TO ANNIKA

REID

Hey, I just want to see how you are doing?

please text me

MESSAGE UNREAD

11:26 AM TO CHLOE

REID

Is Annika there?

MESSAGE UNREAD

NOTHING, silence. Both of them are ghosting me. I feel like I'm the one who should be doing the ghosting, but no, I want to make things better. Not the time to nitpick, but I'm frustrated. I want to talk this out, and I'm being ignored. I know it is a sucky situation, but I can't let it go. Maybe I should give her space, but I don't want to lose her. I can't lose her. Especially since I need to tell her that I should've kissed her back.

That's it. I'm driving over there.

I see Chloe's sedan parked around the corner, but Annika's car isn't in her usual spot. I'm hoping she is parked somewhere else. Except I saw her car in front of the house when I dropped her off last night. So, she's not home. Where did she go?

I jog to the porch and bang on the front door.

"Hey, don't break down the door. I'm right here." I push through the door as Chloe opens it, and Dandy starts circling my feet. The cat can't help but be so cute even when I am frustrated. I pick her up and give her head some scratches, which seem to calm me down a smidge.

"Is Anni here? I've been texting and calling, but she hasn't answered."

"Reid, she needs time. She feels, well, she feels like shit and is embarrassed as hell."

"I know. I just need to talk to her."

"What are you going to say? How are you going to fix things after that?"

"I can't let her be alone after her making a move and me just leaving her hanging. That's not fair to her. I was surprised, obviously, but I know now."

"Oh, you know now? Not four years ago when you guys matched, and you could have tried again?" Chloe steps closer to me, pointing her finger at me. "You weren't there to pick her up off the street." She has tears welling in her eyes as she lays into me. I let her because I feel like I deserve this. "I found her against a wall, sobbing into her knees." Chloe's volume startles Dandy, who jumps out of my arms. "You weren't there for her after the worst night of her life. I was! She keeps trying, and it doesn't work with you. You expect her to be okay after this time too? I honestly don't know if she will be okay, but it won't take twelve hours, that's for fucking sure, Parker."

I'm fighting my own tears, clenching my jaw, guilt pouring over me. "Where is she, Chloe?"

"I don't know. She wanted to be by herself."

"That's bullshit, Chloe. You two know when each other's next dentist appointment is."

"Why Reid? Why should I tell you?"

"Because every time I go to reach out to her, she's already falling. She's slipping out of my fingers, and I can't grab her fast enough. I'm not letting the girl of my dreams, of every waking moment of my life, slip away again."

I rub my hands over my face, and I feel like I'm going to start crying again. This is the most I've cried in a while. All over this girl.

"Chloe, please, I just need one more chance."

Chloe pulls her phone out of her pocket and types something on the screen before I feel my phone buzz in my pocket.

"I sent you where she's at. I swear to god, Reid, that's it. If you hurt her again, I will hurt you."

I don't even take a second to respond. I'm out of the house and in my truck. It's going to be a long drive to catch her, and I can only hope she's still there. This crazy girl is driving three hours just to breathe.

THIRTY-NINE

ANNIKA

OREGON BEACHES AREN'T like SoCal beaches.

First of all, I didn't realize the nearest beach was nearly three hours away, but I feel so numb from everything that has happened in the past day that the time went by fast enough. Every time I stopped crying, I would remember the events of last night and get upset again. It's been a long time since my head felt this cloudy. I hate feeling this way, and the only thing that made me feel better in the past was going to the beach and stepping into the ocean. I missed hearing the waves crash and the sand in my toes. So this morning, Chloe helped me find a beach I could drive to. She wanted to come with me, but I protested that I needed to do this alone. She understood but made me promise to text her when I arrived.

I pull up to the parking lot and text her before sticking my phone in the side compartment of my car door. I don't want to be distracted. I just want it to be me and the beach. Reid's been trying to reach out, but I can't talk to him yet. I need to clear my head.

The sun is fighting through the cloud cover, warming up pockets of the air. There's the softest breeze. I grab the sweater that I brought from the back seat and wrap myself in it. The clouds keep covering the sun, but each time, it pushes through again, warming my skin as I make my way to the trail that heads to the beach.

Little did I know that there'd be a half-mile hike through sloping sand dunes until I reached the beach. I expected to see the ocean open up from the parking lot, just like the beaches back home, but the blue waters are hidden. So I make the trek through the hills. After a little bit, I take off my sandals when the sand gets too soft, and I'm sweating by the time I reach the beach, regretting putting on this extra layer.

As soon as I get to the top of the last dune, I'm finally reunited with the Pacific Ocean. The sand stretches out so far, and the water just skims on top of it. I slide down the soft sand until I'm met with the beach. I trek through, trying to avoid any seaweed or driftwood, and leave my sandals about halfway as I wander over to the water. It's early morning, so there aren't too many people here. I see a man playing fetch with his Labrador down a far way, but it's mostly just me and the beach, just the way I wanted. I walk out, and the sand squishes under my feet as the tide gently rolls in and out. The sand is a bit rockier, and the water is freezing but feels nice after the hike from the parking lot. I walk out for what feels like a full minute until my legs are ankle-deep in the water. I close my eyes and breathe.

At first, I don't think about anything. I just breathe and listen to the sounds of the sea. I hear some birds fluttering around behind me. The soft tide flows in, tickling my legs. I hear the grass on the dunes swaying in the breeze. There's a lone bark from the Labrador in the distance. I take a deep breath as the tide flows back to the ocean and finally feel relaxed and at peace. I let the calmness wash over me, trying to empty my brain. But something keeps trying to push its way in. A dark cloud forms inside my head, and I'm sick to my stomach with shame again.

It can't be a coincidence that I've made my way up here, up to Reid again. I don't really believe in coincidences, anyway. I think this is how our paths link up. We keep winding around each other throughout our lives. I can't help but feel like we are at a crossroads. Either stay in each other's lives or part completely forever. I know, deep in my gut, I believe I did the right thing by making a move again. So why does it hurt so bad?

Maybe we were destined to just be friends. Though, I don't know if we can. But I can't keep running away. I love my life here. Everything about it makes my soul sing. I ran away from my life in San Diego. It feels easy to want to run away from here. I don't want to face him again, not when I know I won't be able to be his friend. I can't do it. I can't keep pretending to live a life that isn't mine. I want to be more than his friend.

I'm just not meant to find love. I keep messing things up.

IT'S BEEN A FEW MINUTES, and I've just been swaying gently with the breeze, ruminating these thoughts around my head. I think I'll go back to Ojai for a little bit. I miss my little brothers and my parents. The distance might help Reid and me cool off a bit. Then, maybe, we can try to be friends again, after some time apart. Although I don't think it's possible, I don't know what will happen to us. I have Chloe. I have my family. That's all I need. I'll figure out how to fill the emptiness later.

My feet are blue. The water in Oregon is much colder than the water in SoCal. I turn and start my walk back to my sandals in the middle of the beach. There are some sand dollars scattered about, and I think about collecting one for Chloe, except something catches my eye. A runner is jogging up the dune and starts to slide down the hill.

FORTY

REID

THAT DRIVE WAS TOO LONG, and my truck couldn't go fast enough. I ran every worst-case scenario through my head. She got in an accident, or she decided to go to a different beach instead. I tried to push all those thoughts away and drive. It wasn't until I saw her little red car that I threw my truck into the park and took off toward the beach. She is here. I still have time.

I run faster than I've ever run in my whole life. I've only come to the beach up here a handful of times, but I get winded every time I make my way through the dunes. I don't even care today. I need to reach her. I need to catch her before she slips away again. I run until I reach the top of the second to last dune and see her standing out in the middle of the beach with her feet in the water. She's standing with her arms at her sides, occasionally wrapping them around her shoulders. I can't stop running. I kept thinking over and over what I was going to say to her. Now that I see her, I don't know. I just need to get to her.

I slide down the dune to the beach and make my way over to her. I wait until she sees me before jogging.

The moment she looks up and registers it's me, she collapses.

FORTY-ONE

ANNIKA

HE WASN'T SUPPOSED to come here. I was supposed to run away again. I collapse to my knees as soon as I realize it's him. I am imagining everything. This is a daydream.

I flinch as I hear "Anni," and Reid runs over to me. *Is this real? Is he here?* I look up and see him standing over me. He reaches down and tries to wrap his arms around mine and pull me up to him. But I can't. I can't leave the spot where I'm crouched on the sand. It's safe down here.

He gives up quickly and joins me on the sand, pulling me against his chest and draping my legs over his left leg. He's holding me so tightly as I collapse against his chest. His hands are running through my hair and down my back while he rocks back and forth. I think I hear him saying in a whisper, "Don't go, please don't go."

Against my better judgment, I pull back and look him in those green-marbled eyes. I should've learned my lesson these past several years and even since my failed attempt last night. But if he's here, if this isn't a dream, then I need to be honest with him, honest with myself.

I look up at him, tears falling on both of our faces. I reach up and cup the side of his face.

I take a deep breath and say, "I'm sorry to tell you this, but no one will ever compare to the way you make me feel. I love who I am when I am with you. You make me want to savor every moment. I'm not capable of being just friends."

He grabs both sides of my face, using his thumbs to wipe away the wetness under my eyes. One hand trails behind my head, and he leans in. We rest our foreheads together for a moment and share an exhale. Just like the first time we kissed, I feel a rush of relief. The butterflies in my gut flutter up through my chest and finally release around me. It's as if I can feel them swirling around us as we embrace. Every spot he's touching me tingles, and I melt into his touch. We close the distance and melt into each other. He presses his lips against mine, saying a million words with one kiss. He pulls away and pecks the corners of my eyes softly before grazing the edge of my jaw and my shoulder with his mouth. We lean into each other, giving into all our pent up desires and cradling each other in the sand. I don't want this dream to end. This is how it's supposed to be. This is how it's supposed to end.

I open my eyes and realize it's real. We are tangled around each other, sand in all the wrong places. He's here. He came to me.

"You found me," I say to him.

"Please don't go, don't leave anymore. I love you, Annika I-still-don't-know-your-middle-name Gomes. It will always be you." I don't know whether to laugh or cry.

"How long has that been bothering you?"

"Too long. I felt like if I didn't know it, I can't love you."

"Well, I don't even have a middle name, so that's a silly rule," I say back to him. I feel the tears emerging again as we laugh. "What's your middle name?" I ask.

"Taylor, after my mom." I give him another soft kiss, running my fingers through his hair. He helps us stand up while I keep my arms wrapped around his torso. We shake the sand off each other.

He takes my hands and starts to sway us around the beach,

dancing to the sound of the waves. He starts humming a song I don't recognize, softly twirling me in the sand.

"I have something for you." He fades our dance and reaches into his pocket, pulling out a small black velvet bag. "I got this for you after our second date. I honestly don't know why I kept it after all these years. We have a lot to catch up on." He kisses my forehead as we keep swaying. "But I'm happy I held on to it. It feels like this is the moment I was meant to give it to you."

He hands the pouch to me, and I untie the top knot pulling it gently open. I tip the pouch over, and a gold necklace spills into the palm of my hand. The pendant is a small rectangle, and I realize what it is before I flip it around. A stamp. Like the tattoo on my back, but this one has a heart embossed inside. I don't know how many times I can fall in love with Reid Taylor Parker.

"Can you help me put it on?"

He gently sweeps my hair from my neck, kissing my skin as he does, and links the necklace. It falls to my chest, and I grab it.

"You've had this the whole time?"

"Honestly, I forgot about it for a while. There were a lot of times I was angry and frustrated about our relationship. About how I wished things had played out differently. The necklace was a reminder of all that. Everything that didn't work out. I guess maybe I was hoping one day it would."

"I wish we had done this earlier. I wish I wasn't so clueless before."

"Hey, hey, hey." He pulls me back to him and sways with me again. "We can't punish our past selves, but we can learn from them. We start now, right now. We do it right this time."

"Reid?" I say while I tug at his arm.

"Yeah, Anni?" He turns to look at me, softly stroking the side of my face.

"I'm starving."

Everything on his face brightens, and we laugh together. "Let's get some food. Maybe we can find a hotel instead of driving back home," he says while giving me a little wink. I still can't believe this is real.

"Sounds good to me," I say, pinching his butt.

He jumps at the reaction and turns to me. "Oh, you are going to surprise me a lot now, huh?"

"This is just the beginning, Parker."

FORTY-TWO

REID

IT FEELS UNREAL. I have my arm draped over Anni's shoulder as if we do this all the time. As if we've always been this close. We quietly make our way from the beach through the sand dunes back to the parking lot. I can't help but stop at every dip in the path to spin her around and hear her giggle into my chest. Kiss every inch of her face. I've been waiting too long for this. Nothing has ever felt so perfect. I know it will be harder for us in the beginning. We really should unpack our history so we can move past it, but right now, I just want her in my arms. I'm never going to let her go again.

We make it back to the parking lot, and the realization that we drove here separately hits me like a meteor.

"Have you been to this town before?" She looks up at me without separating yet.

"Only once before. I think there's a small main drag, I'm sure, that has food spots." My stomach growls aggressively at the thought of food. It's nearly four, and I doubt she's eaten anything either. "I'll text you a place, and I'll follow behind your car."

"See you soon, Parker," she says as she gives me a fist bump before heading to her car. I miss her already.

• • •

THE DRIVE only takes about ten minutes until we get to the center of the tiny town, which is a few blocks with a post office, a couple of restaurants, a coffee shop, and a couple of small stores. I thought Auburn Hills was a small town, but this is like its own different planet. The street overlooks the small harbor that connects to the Pacific Ocean, and the folks of the town are milling around, finishing up their day and, like Annika and I, looking for some food. We park next to each other on a side street and wander for a few minutes before our noses lead us to a little Italian restaurant on one of the street corners. It's decorated as if you are in a seaside town in Italy rather than Oregon. They have lattice and little grape vines hanging from them, covering the outdoor patio. Inside the walls are warm tones of oranges and greens with soft instrumental music playing. We get seated in a cozy corner spot on the outdoor patio.

We are silent as we scan the menu and order, and it's only until we take our first bites of complimentary bread and olive oil that we acknowledge each other's company.

"This bread is healing my soul," says Annika as she chews slowly like each bite is her last.

"I love the little crackle of spices in the olive oil. It's really tasty." We chew and look at each other, smiling. "What are you smiling about?"

"I can't believe we are here, that this is happening between us," she says as she tears another chunk of bread off, smooshing it in the olive oil spice mixture.

"I know what you mean, but I'm ready for this. All of this. I'm ready to go all in with you, Annika."

"Whoa, French bread makes you talk really seriously."

I crack a smile at her hint to lighten up. "Well, you mean a lot to me. I—"

"I don't want to lose you again, either. But you just came out of a relationship. And not even a short one, you guys dated for like a year."

"It's been several months since it ended."

"What happens if we start a relationship and you start comparing us, or you realize you haven't had enough time to heal?"

"Let me make this clear to you." I look her square in the eyes and grab her hand. "You are the one I compared everyone else to. You are my number one."

Her eyes start to get glassy. "Damn, Parker. You're making me cry over breadsticks."

"I just want us to be open with each other. I don't want us to hide our feelings. I think that's what went wrong before."

"There were so many other things that went wrong. I wasn't ready for any of it. I was in denial."

"Sometimes I wonder if things could have worked out differently."

She starts to shake her head as soon as I say that. "No, I don't."

"What do you mean? All that heartache and all those tears and frustration, I'd send it all away in an instant if I could start a relationship with you without having three extra bags to unpack." I look around the restaurant, realizing I'm getting riled up about our discussion of the past. Thankfully, the rest of the patrons are too busy with their evenings to realize two people are finally checking into reality.

"My mom always tells me, 'Everything happens for a reason.' I don't think there are coincidences. I think we were supposed to go through all that shit. Reid, I was lost for so long. I was pretending to be someone I thought I should be. It wasn't until I stopped caring what other people thought of me that I realized it's *my* life to live and that I was ready to love you."

"You love me?" I say with a goofy smile. Goosebumps rise at the four-letter word.

"Is that all you heard?" She laughs.

"I wish this was a booth so I could smother you right now."

Instead, I reach over and rest my hand on her thigh and kiss the side of her head.

"Speaking of that, you asked the hostess about hotels around here, right?" She wiggles her eyebrows again at me.

I return a devious smirk and say, "Yes, I already called. It's an inn that overlooks the ocean. They have a room available for us. That way, you know, we don't have to drive back tonight."

"Yes, of course, just because we don't have to drive." She hides her blushing cheeks behind her water glass as she takes a sip.

The waiter interrupts our flirtations by bringing us our entrees which we promptly scarf down. Our conversation flows between the town we are in, our jobs, Chloe and Tyler, and how Annika wants to take a trip back home soon. We occasionally bring up our past, and I know it won't be something we can resolve immediately. We both still have scars reminding us of the past. I know we can help each other heal.

The inn is a few blocks away, so we bring our cars over to the lot that connects to the building. I am both so incredibly nervous and excited. I'm also incredibly exhausted from the rollercoaster of emotions we've gone through.

Our room is simple and quaint. There is one king bed in the center with a sea foam green comforter and two nightstands. A small balcony sits just outside that opens up to a beautiful view of the ocean. Maybe we should stay here a couple of nights. I could prolong returning home for a bit longer to continue living in this fantasy with her.

We set our few belongings in the closet, and I see Annika realize we have no spare change of clothes.

"Oh, maybe we should stop at one of those little shops and get a change of clothes?"

"That's a great idea." I pull her nearer, wrapping my hands around her low back and giving her another deep kiss. I could get used to this. I love feeling her body fuse against mine. Two magnets finally drawn together.

We head down to the street, looking for any stores open. Luckily, a convenience store is open, and we are able to get some toiletries and some basic underwear. Not sexy at all, but this will at least be better than the sandy briefs I have on now.

A few doors down, a souvenir shop is still open. It's your typical small-town gift shop with magnets, postcards, mugs, and name key chains. We make a beeline for the back that has sweatshirts, T-shirts, and sweatpants folded along the wall. We decide on matching gray and green sweatsuits that have the town name across the chest and along the right leg. Annika swipes a postcard from the spinning display just before we check out, turning to give me a smile. She reaches up and touches her pendant again like it's always been there.

We walk along the street hand in hand, slowly making our way back to the inn with our loot.

"You inspired me to move out of San Diego, you know," she says, looking up at me.

I narrow my gaze. "How so?"

"When we matched on Flame, you told me to *figure it out*. And not to be dramatic, it has haunted me ever since. I realized I never knew what I actually wanted."

I wince. "Honestly, that whole interaction makes me feel like shit. I was so mean." She frowns at this.

"It didn't feel good, that's for sure, but it also was the truth. I kind of deserved it for how I ended things with us."

We find a bench outside the inn that overlooks the harbor and sit, continuing our conversation.

"Why did you end things? I thought, I mean, I know we had a connection. Clearly," I say, motioning between us, scooting closer to her.

She shrugs and shakes her head. "I was afraid, I guess. I was stressed about school and this idea of how I should be spending my college experience. I was so overwhelmed by my feelings toward you I chickened out. I was a coward. I'm sorry, Reid."

I exhale, pulling her into me. "I forgive you. We were so young, and I felt the same insecurities."

"But you went along anyway."

"I didn't care if you distracted me. I was enjoying being around you too much."

"I'm happy this is our moment. It feels right, even though it's thirteen years after I saw you in that stinky lunchroom."

She mindlessly drags her fingers along my arm, raising goose-bumps in their wake. I nuzzle my face in her head, yearning to get closer to her, to feel her skin against mine.

"Are you ready to go back to the room?" I look at her, discovering she has two flecks of light brown in her eyes.

She lights up with a mischievous smile. "Race ya!" Darting up off the bench, she flees through the inn entrance.

WE ARE FUMBLING around each other, giggling and kissing as we make our way up the stairs and to our room. I pull out my key and try to unlock the door, but Annika keeps trying to slide in front of me to kiss my neck.

I laugh. "Hold your horses. Let me get the door open."

"I can't wait."

I get the door open and push us through, closing it and pushing her back against the door. She flings the bags in the closet and wraps her arms around my back, and I lean down to press my mouth against her neck. I pull away and realize we are both still covered in bits of sand.

"Shower. Me and you," I say to her.

Her eyes bug out a bit, and I almost backtrack until she relaxes and reaches up to me, pulling my shirt over my head.

I let her take my shirt off, and she runs her hands across my chest and my abdomen as she goes down to unbutton my shorts.

She slides down my shorts, leaving my boxers on but it leaves no mystery to how aroused I am by her. She can undress me anytime.

I slip my hands under her cardigan and tug the fabric gently down her arms, kissing her left shoulder along the way, trailing over to her waist and unbuttoning her high waist shorts, pulling them down to reveal her navy blue underwear with little white flowers. I look up at her, and she's blushing. This is the most exposed she and I have ever been in front of each other. She goes to take her tank top off, but I move her hands away.

I grab the hem and slowly pull it up and over her head. She has a dark orange stretchy bra that cradles her breasts. I fight the sudden urge to smother my face in her cleavage.

"If I knew this was how my day would go, I would've at least put on a matching set," she says.

"It's not going to be on much longer, anyway," I say as I roll one of the straps off her shoulder, then the other. I remove her bra and underwear while she does the same to my boxers. Completely naked, we magnetize again, kissing and nipping each other's skin. We wander over to the bathroom, and I turn the shower on.

I step in first, then guide her in with me, the warm water cascading down our bodies. It feels warm and comforting. I can see the sand leaving our bodies and flowing down the drain.

"Turn around," I order her, and she obliges.

My erection is nearly horizontal and rests between her cheeks with her back toward me. I reach for the shampoo and start gently washing her hair. Her soft moans and the way her body sways heighten my arousal.

I finish washing and conditioning her hair before moving to the rest of her body. Lathering soap and cleaning her arms and chest, cupping her breasts softly and caressing her behind. I kneel and clean each of her legs, softly rubbing the center of her, which makes her flinch, then relax to my touch. I stand up and bring her back to my chest, reaching around her torso to rub her as the water hits the back of my head, keeping us warm.

She moans and reaches her arms behind her to grab my thigh as she tenses. Her sounds increase in speed as I pick up the pace, circling her heat until she lets out a gasp and grabs my hand, pushing me deeper. Each sound out of her mouth, adds to the tension I feel outside of her. We both let out an exhale, and I wash the remnants I've left off her backside.

She flips around and looks into my eyes, coating me in warm desire. She returns the shampooing favor and massages the lavender suds through my hair, tilting my head back gently to wash it out, leaving a trail of kisses from my chin and down my neck. She lathers soap around my body, making sure I'm nice and clean. Then she shoots me a devilish grin and gives my butt a little squeeze.

I think she's going to put her hands on me, but instead, she goes down on her knees. That view alone almost sets me off. She grabs my erection by the base and aims it toward her mouth. She licks the length of it and then sucks on the tip. I want to watch, but I can't concentrate. I tip my head back and close my eyes so the water washes down my face. I can feel her lips circling me, taking me in and out of her mouth while the water pours over both of us. The sensation is amazing, but knowing it's Anni is pure bliss. I'm so close to the edge, and I look back down and run my hand through her hair. She releases me from her mouth with a pop.

We exit the shower, drying each other off with towels. A giggle releases from her, and she scurries off to the bed, jumping in the center. I join her, and we bounce on our knees in silly glee before collapsing on the bed. She has a towel wrapped around her, and she lifts it so I join her inside her towel.

"I thought I'd mention again it's been a long time since I've had sex with anyone. Last time was with, well, you know." I don't want to hear her say any other guy's name right now. Especially anyone who's been inside her before me. I'll make sure to be her best. I'm never letting her go.

"It's okay. We can take it as slow or as fast as you want."

"Do you have a condom?" she asks, and I nod, separating from the bed and grabbing one from a box I bought at the convenience store earlier.

"Let's get under the covers."

We get bundled up under the comforter and continue where we left off from the shower, except it's me on my knees below her. This view, this feeling, I'm adding it to the collection of memories I'm bottling up to remember forever.

FORTY-THREE

ANNIKA

I QUICKLY REALIZE I've been having sex wrong this whole time. To be fair, I've only had sex with two and a half guys before this moment with Reid. And yes, I'm only counting Trey as half because it was not a mutual transaction. I feel nervous and silly. I am so at ease. I don't feel self-conscious about my body around him or that he saw my flower underwear. I'm not even wearing one of my lacy thongs. I'm wearing full-coverage boy shorts! I should be embarrassed, but the way he looked at me melted away all my insecurities. This guy is as obsessed with me as I am with him.

And frankly, no other showers will ever compare. He is required to wash my hair from now on.

We are curled around each other under the comforters now. I'm on my back as Reid trails kisses from my temple to my lips, down my neck, along my breasts. He detours to my nipples, where he gives each a lick and a suck, then continues to kiss my soft belly and my inner thighs. *Is he going to do what I think he's going to do?* I've never had a guy go down on me before, but I always wondered what it would feel like. A part of me feels embarrassed to be twenty-four years old and never received oral sex, but Reid's comfort dissolves my self-consciousness.

He rubs the sides of my thighs as he lowers his head to my center, parting me as he licks a long line from the base to the top, sucking hard.

Holy shit

The warm and wet feeling of his mouth against me is out of this world. I keep my gaze on him and run my fingers through his tousled wet hair. He is nuzzling his face in me, making grunts like it's the life force keeping him alive. I feel every sensation ripple through me. The heat in my core spreads to my entire body. My toes curl, and my back buckles. He places one hand on my hip, holding me in place, then slides two fingers inside me as he sucks.

I can't hold it any longer. The pleasure ripples through me like a wave crashing on a beach.

He kneels up slowly, and I look down at his erection, full and throbbing, the tip glistening. He grabs the condom on the bed and slides it over himself. I can see him wince as he puts it on.

"I don't know if I'm going to last very long," he says as he lowers himself over me, aiming himself at me.

He's warmed me up enough that he slides in like the final puzzle piece. We both share a moan and a gasp while I hook my legs around his back, curving my hips up to meet his. He rocks gently in me at first, and we kiss each other longingly. I feel the butterflies and heat building up again, and I angle my hips up to him, taking him in deeper as he increases his speed, letting another orgasm ripple out of me.

"My heart is yours," he whispers in my ear.

I kiss him deeply and look into his green eyes, eyes I'll look at forever, "Always yours," I reply softly.

"Flip around," I say, grabbing his shoulders and pushing him so I'm on top of him now.

He has this wicked look on his face, and a burst of courage runs through me. I straddle his hips and lower down onto him again. His head dips back toward the pillow, but I reach up and grab his head so he's looking at me.

I start rocking on him, circling my hips around his while my hands cradle his head. This position makes me feel like a bad bitch. And yet, I'm fully exposed to him and bucking my hips to increase our desire. I don't let myself overthink any move. I'm not getting in my own way any longer.

Reid starts to curl up off the bed toward me so we are facing each other, and I'm grinding in his lap. He cups the back of my ass, easing into him deeper. We both fire into each other, building up and up until we release. I grab his shoulders and pull him close... I can feel his release, and then he relaxes inside of me.

We collapse on the bed and savor a few moments longer in each other's arms. I'm at peace with him tucked under my arms, my big spoon to his little. He brings my hands up to his mouth, giving little kisses.

"I love you, Reid Taylor Parker," I say to his warm back.

He reaches his arm around to caress my thigh. "I love you too, Annika Gomes, I always will."

FORTY-FOUR

REID

I SPRING UP AWAKE, sweaty, my heart racing. I panic and close my eyes. *Please, please don't let that be a cruel sex dream. Please let her be next to me. Please, please, please.* I plead to the dream gods, and the hand on my back jolts me out of my chant.

"Hey, are you okay? Did you have a bad dream?" I turn to see Annika curled up under the sheets, her hair sticking in a hundred different directions and her eyes looking like she could use another hour of sleep. She's radiant, a perfect angel in bed next to me. She's better than any dream I've ever had.

"No, not a bad dream. It wasn't a dream at all." I curl back next to her and pull her to my chest. *This is real.* She still has the necklace draped around her neck. The necklace that's haunted me for years is finally where it's meant to be.

We turn to face the window, watching the waves crash on the sea from our bed. I recognize how the beach has brought us closer together once again. Maybe one day we'll move closer to the ocean. So we can walk to the beach every morning. Or get coffee and share a breakfast sandwich while watching the waves. I see our entire future, and instead of pushing it away, I let it flow through, squeezing her tighter. This is real.

Everything happens for a reason. I replay the words Anni told me yesterday. I've struggled for so long about how I could have changed the path of my life. I wanted to prevent ever being heart-broken. I wanted to grow up with a mom. I wanted to not move so much as a kid. I wanted to not fall so hard for her over and over. But with her in my arms, watching the ocean, I realize it's all meant to be. Every bump and pain. Every belly laugh and every tear-drenched pillow. It was all worth it, and I wouldn't have it any other way.

THE END

EPILOGUE

Anni,
will you go to the dance with me?
love, Reid

(p.s. do you want to be my girlfriend?)

4 People

ANNIKA

We are going to leave in like twenty minutes to pick you up Chloe. Then we'll get Tyler.

Reid is driving my car, don't worry i'm not driving.

REID

Hey Tyler, if you're picking up coffee, can you get me a cold brew?

ANNIKA

Oh, get me an iced chai while you're at it.

TYLER

Aren't you two together? Why are you texting separately?

ANNIKA

It's faster

REID

Oh, a splash of oat milk too please

ANNIKA

@Chloe Do you want Tyler to get you anything

CHLOE

Uh no, i'm good

ANNIKA

Are you sure? We are supposed to leave for the airport soon and it's like an hour and a half drive.

CHLOE

Yeah I already got something

REID

And you didn't ask us if we wanted anything?!

TYLER

I already got her coffee

ANNIKA

When?

TYLER

This morning

ANNIKA

It's 7am

TYLER

and?

ANNIKA

Chloe...where are you at right now?

REID

it's happening

CHLOE

I just came over Tyler's yesterday to check out the guest house.

And see the animals. I fell asleep here.

nothing is happening!

It's no big deal!!

TYLER

Came for the animals, stayed for me

CHLOE

Tyler!!!

ANNIKA

oh my god

REID

IT'S HAPPENING

ANNIKA

Please be ready...in 15 minutes! We'll be at Tyler's to get both of you so we can catch our flight to LAX on time.

TYLER

We are like 5 hours ahead of schedule, we'll make it

REID

Unless they get distracted...

ANNIKA

Oh my god, please, we will discuss this later. Chloe, you good to be ready?

TYLER

I ran in the bathroom, Chloe is upset I told you guys and started chasing me.

REID

Well, i'm not upset! This is great news.

ANNIKA

eye-roll emoji

CHLOE

We'll be ready. See you soon!!

ALSO BY ANJELICA ROSE

Title Coming Soon

Auburn Hills #2 (Chloe's Book)

Coming 2024

ACKNOWLEDGMENTS

To Adam, my life partner. My person I'd split a sandwich with while sitting on the beach any day. You encourage me to grow and chase my fears. Thank you for being my support and my biggest fan. I love you with my whole heart and soul.

To my parents that always support every crazy idea I've thought of over the years. I love you both so much. You are my rocks and I cannot thank you enough for everything you've provided me. Thank you for encouraging my wild creativity. However, you are both forbidden from reading this book. Love you.

To Tiffer and Crusty, my siblings. I love you both so much I could start crying just thinking about it. Thank you for always being there for me. I am so grateful to have you in my life.

To Courtney. My BFFL! I can't believe this whole thing started from a weird dream I had and little stories I'd write in our emails. Did you ever imagine I'd smush it all together and make a whole dang book out of it? I definitely didn't but I'm so happy I did. You are the Chloe to my Annika.

To my entire family. Alex, Aunt Gina and everyone else in the excessively long group chat who texts asking when they can order a book. I am delighted to have each of you in my life.

To Tavia, who always sends me updates about how excited she is to read the book. Your messages always come in at times where I would feel such self doubt. I love you my soul sister.

To Fern and Paul, my wonderful in-laws, always asking inquisitive questions about the progress. Fern, Thank you for being my book buddy. Having another person to nerd out about books is the most fun feeling.

To Karie, who revived my love for reading and books. Without you, kickstarting my reading renaissance, I'm not sure if this book would even exist. And I'm sorry I named the bitchy character after you.

To the best bitches, wow you all are such a group of gals I never imagined to meet and have the pleasure of getting to know these past few years. Thank you for being the best hype crew a girl could need. Whenever I had an idea or I needed feedback, you were there for me. I love you all so much.

To my discord friends, you incredible people! I cannot believe we've gathered together out of the love for books and games. Our conversations are my favorite and having you all on my side is the best feeling ever.

To my beta readers, I love you like family. I am so *immensely* grateful for you all. I still am baffled that five of you agreed to read such a rough draft of this story and provide feedback. Without you, some scenes and chapters wouldn't have existed. Tyler was born because of the beta readers, we all thank you for that.

To my work family. We are a bunch of jokesters constantly poking fun at each other but the end of the day, I can feel the care. I'm laughing writing this because I know none of you will take this seriously if you even read up to this part. Thanks Jacquelyn and Michael for listening to all my book updates and for being as excited as I am.

To the ARC readers, thank you for being so excited to read my book before it releases! I still am so baffled by the love and support of the book community.

To the book lovers on the internet!! I am so glad to find such a rad group of people, sharing their love for books. It's the best feeling ever.

To the coffee shop, The Story, and the baristas Rachel and Kirsten who asked me what I was doing every week typing on my laptop. I finally finished the book! Thanks for all the dirty chai lattes.

To you, reading this book. I can't believe you actually read it. I hope you liked it. If you didn't, don't tell me. I'm way to sensitive and won't take negative reviews well. In any case, I'm glad Annika and Reid's story made it to you. They are so special to me and I will keep them with me forever.

And to me. I cannot put into words how proud I am of myself. This was something I truly never imagined I'd do but I'm so happy I did. If you ever just get the feeling to try something different, even if every other path you went on in life is points a different way, just go for it. It might turn out to be amazing. And you won't know, until you try.

xo
Anjelica

ABOUT THE AUTHOR

Anjelica Rose is an emerging author who enjoys writing stories that follow the joys and struggles of everyday life. When she's not hunched over her laptop writing, she works full-time in the fashion industry. She lives in the Philly area with her Fiancé and spends her free time cooking, reading, tending to her greenhouse and enjoying a plethora of other hobbies. Anjelica Rose is delighted by this new passion in writing and hopes to one day have an expansive back log of books and stories. You can get in touch with her and join her newsletter at www.anjelicarosebooks.com or connect with her via social media, *@anjelicaroses* on all platforms.

 instagram.com/anjelicaroses